THE ORCHARD OF TEARS

THE ORCHARD OF TEARS

SAX ROHMER

WILDSIDE PRESS: MMIII

TO
THE SLAVES OF THE POMEGRANATE
SONS OF ADAM AND DAUGHTERS OF EVE
WHO DRINK AT THE FOUNTAIN OF LIFE
THIS CHALICE IS OFFERED AS
A LOVING-CUP

THE ORCHARD OF TEARS

For more information, contact:
Wildside Press
P.O. Box 301
Holicong, PA 18928-0301 USA

CONTENTS

PART FIRST

AT LOWER CHARLESWOOD

I

It was high noon of a perfect summer's day. Beneath green sun blinds, upon the terrace overlooking the lawns, Paul Mario, having finished his lunch, lay back against the cushions of a white deck-chair and studied the prospect. Sloping turf, rose-gay paths, and lichened brick steps, hollowed with age, zigzagging leisurely down to the fir avenue, carried the eye onward again to where the river wound its way through verdant banks toward the distant town.

A lark wooed the day with sweet music. Higher and ever higher rose the little sun-worshipper, pouring out his rapturous hymn to Apollo. Swallows, who but lately had crossed the battlefields of southern Europe, glided around Hatton Towers, describing mystic figures in the air, whilst the high feeble chirping of the younger generation sounded from the nest beneath the eaves. Amid the climbing roses bees were busy, their communal labours an object lesson for self-seeking man; and almost at Mario's feet a company of ants swarmed over the yet writhing body of an unfortunate caterpillar, who had dropped from an apple-tree to fall a prey to that savage natural law of death to the weak. The harsh voice of a sentinel crow spoke from a neighbouring cornfield, and a cloud of dusky marauders took the air instantly, and before the sharp crack of the farmer's fowling-piece came to confirm the warning. In the hush of noon the tones of some haymakers at their patriarchal labours in a meadow beyond the stream were clearly audible—and the atmosphere constantly vibrated with remote booming of guns on the Western front.

Paul Mario was sufficiently distinguished in appearance to have been a person of no importance. His virile, curling black hair had the raven's-wing sheen betraying remote Italian forebears, and for that matter there was in his entire cast of countenance and the poise of his fine head something statuesquely Roman, Southern, exotic. His large but deep-set eyes were of so dark a blue as very generally to pass for 'black'; and whilst in some moods they were soft and dreamy, in others, notably in moments of enthusiasm, they burnt darkly fierce in his pale olive face. In profile there was a certain resemblance to the Vatican head of Julius Caesar, save for the mouth, which had more gentle curves, and which was not unlike that of Dante; but seen fullface, and allowing for the fact that Paul Mario was cleanshaven, the likeness of feature to the traditional Christ was startling. The resemblance is equally

notable in the face of Shakespeare.

Rather above medium height, well but slightly proportioned, the uneasy spirit of the man ever looking out of those arresting eyes so wholly dominated him as to create a false impression of fragility, of a casket too frail to confine the burning, eager soul within. His emotions were dynamic, and in his every mannerism there was distinction. The vein of femininity, which is found in all creative artists, betrayed itself in one item of Mario's attire: a white French knot, which slightly overlay the lapels of his well-worn Norfolk jacket.

To the world's caricaturists, when Paul Mario, at the age of twenty-six, had swept across the literary terrain, storming line after line, the white knot had proved a boon. *Delilah,* a lyrical drama, written in French, and first published in Paris, achieved for this darling of Minerva a reputation which no man is entitled to expect during his lifetime. Within twelve months of the date of publication it had appeared in almost every civilized language, and had been staged in New York, where it created a furore. Of *Madame Caligula,* a novel, which followed it, thirty-one editions were subscribed in six days!

The miracle of Paul Mario's success was perhaps to be explained by the neutrality of his genius. A passionate, elemental sympathy with all nature, a seeming capacity to hear the language of the flowers, the voices of the stars and to love and understand the lowliest things that God has made, bore him straight to the heart of England as surely as it swept his name into the holy of holies of artistic France, spoke to Russia's sombre soul and temporarily revolutionized the literature of the United States. His work belonged to no 'school,' and its charm was not due to 'style'; therefore his books lost little in translation, for true genius speaks to every man in his tongue.

Sympathetic atmosphere was as necessary to Paul Mario as pure air to the general. Deliberate ugliness hurt him, and the ugliness which is the handiwork of God aroused within him a yearning sorrow for poor humanity who might be of the White Company, were it not for avarice, hate and lust. The war, even in its earlier phases, stirred the ultimate deeps of his nature, and knowing himself, since genius cannot be blind, for what he was, a world power, a spiritual sword, he chafed and fretted in enforced inactivity, striving valiantly to reconcile himself to the ugliness of military life. Courted as only poets and actors are courted, he was offered posts and commissions in bewildering variety; but all of them he scornfully rejected. The insane injustice of such selection enraged him.

A severe nervous lesion freed him from the galley-bench of a training-camp, and sent him on a weary pilgrimage through the military hospitals to discharge—and freedom; freedom, which to that ardent nature proved to be irksome. For whilst the very springs of his genius were dammed by the agony of a world in travail, he found himself outside the mighty theatre, a mere bystander having no part in the rebirth of humanity.

II

Someone was approaching along the path consecrated by a million weary feet and still known as the Pilgrim's Way, someone who wore the ugly uniform of a Guards officer (which is a sort of du Maurier survival demanding Dundreary whiskers). He seemed to hesitate ere he turned aside, opened the gate and began to mount those hundred and twenty mossy steps which led up to the terrace.

The newcomer, whose tunic had seen much service, was a man perhaps two or three years Paul Mario's senior, and already the bleaching hand of Time had brushed his temples with furtive fingers. He was dark but of sanguine colouring, now overlaid with a deep tan, wore a short military moustache and possessed those humorous grey eyes which seemed to detect in all creation hues roseate and pleasing; eyes made for laughter and which no man other than a good fellow ever owned.

Gaining the terrace and raising his hand to his cap in salute, the officer smiled, and his smile fulfilled all the promise of the grey eyes and would have brought a ray of sunshine into the deepest and darkest cell of the Bastille itself.

'I believe I am trespassing,' he began—then, as Paul Mario rose: 'By all that's gracious and wonderful, it's Paul!'

'Don!' exclaimed the other, and sprang forward in his own impetuous fashion, grasping the newcomer by both shoulders and staring eagerly into the sun-tanned face. 'Dear old Don! A thousand welcomes, boy!' And releasing his grip on the shoulders, he seized both hands and shook them with a vigour that was not assumed but was merely an outlet for his brimming emotions.

'Some kindly coy dryad of the woods has guided my footsteps to this blessed spot,' declared Don. 'The last inn which I passed—observe my selection of the word, passed—known, I believe, as the "Pig and Something-or-other," is fully three sunny miles behind me. From the arid and dusty path below I observed the siphon on your table—'

'And you determined to become a trespasser?' cried Paul Mario joyously, pushing his friend into the cane rest-chair and preparing a drink for him. 'I will build an altar to your dryad, Don; for there is certainly something miraculous in your appearance at Hatton Towers.'

'When I have suitably reduced my temperature I will explain. But I have yet to learn what *you* are doing here. I had always understood that Hatton Towers—'

'My dear fellow, it's mine!' cried Paul excitedly. 'My Uncle Jacques dramatically bequeathed this wonderful place to me, altering his will on the day that I renounced the pen and entered an officer's training corps. He was a remarkable old bachelor, Don—'

Don raised his hand, checking Paul's speech. 'My dear Paul, you cannot possibly amplify your own description of Sir Jacques, with which you entertained us one evening in a certain top set at Oxford. Do you remember those rooms, Paul?'

'Do I remember them!'

'I do, and I remember your account of the saintly Uncle, for your acquaintance had begun and terminated during a week of the previous long vacation which you had spent here at Hatton. "Uncle Jacques," you informed us, "is a delightful survival, bearing a really remarkable resemblance to a camel. Excepting his weakness for classic statuary and studies in the nude, his life is of *Mayflower* purity. He made his fortune on the Baltic Exchange, was knighted owing to a clerical error, and built the appalling church at Mid Hatton."'

Paul laughed boyishly. 'At least we were sincere in our youthful cynicism, Don. You may add the note to your very accurate recollections of Sir Jacques that on the publication of *Delilah* he instructed his butler to say that he was abroad whenever I might call!'

Fascinated as of old by his whimsical language, the cap-and-bells which he loved to assume, Paul watched affectionately the smiling face of Donald Courtier. Momentarily a faint tinge of melancholy had clouded the gaiety of Don's grey eyes; for this chance meeting had conjured up memories of a youth already slipping from his grasp, devoured by the all-consuming war; memories of many a careless hour treasured now as exquisite relics are treasured, of many a good fellow who would never again load his pipe from Paul

Mario's capacious, celebrated and hospitable tobacco jar, as he, Don, was doing; of days of sheer indolent joy, of nights of wild and carefree gladness.

'Good old Paul,' he murmured, raising his glass. 'Here's to the late Sir Jacques. So you are out of it?'

Paul Mario nodded and took from the pocket of his threadbare golf jacket the very twin of Don's curved and blackened briar, drawing towards him the tobacco jar upon the table—a Mycenaean vase from the tomb of Rameses III. A short silence fell between them.

'Frankly, I envy you,' said Don suddenly, breaking the spell, 'although I realize that actually you have suffered as deeply as many a man who has spent two years in the trenches. One cannot imagine the lyre of Apollo attuned to What's-the-name's marches.'

'Two years,' echoed Paul; 'is it really two years since we met?'

'Two years on June the twenty-second. On June the twenty-second, nineteen hundred and fifteen, you saw me off from Victoria of hateful memory. I have been home six or seven times in the interval, but somehow or other have always missed you. I was appalled when I heard you had joined. God knows we need such brains as yours, but they would be wasted on the Somme; and genius is too rare to be exposed to the sniper's bullet. What are you doing?'

The sympathy between the two was so perfect that Paul Mario knew the question to refer not to his private plans but to his part in the world drama.

'Beyond daily descending lower in my own esteem—nothing.'

'Yet you might do so much.'

'I know,' said Paul Mario. 'But—it awes me.'

If his work had not already proved him, the genius of the man must have been rendered apparent by his entire lack of false modesty. Praise and censure alike left him uninfluenced—although few artists can exist without a modicum of the former: he knew himself born to sway the minds of millions and was half fearful of his self-knowledge. 'I know,' he said, and pipe in hand he gazed wistfully across the valley.

A faint breeze crept through the fir avenue, bearing with it a muffled booming sound which was sufficient to raise the curtain of distance—never truly opaque for such as he—and to display to that acute inner vision a reeking battlefield. Before his shuddering soul defiled men maimed, blind, bleeding from ghastly hurts; men long dead. Women he saw in lowly hovels, weeping over cots fashioned from rough boxes; women, dry-eyed, mutely tragic, surrounded by softness, luxury and servitude, wearing love gifts of a hand for ever stilled, dreaming of lover-words whispered in a voice for ever mute. He seemed to float spiritually over the whole world upon that wave of sound and to find the whole world stricken, desolate, its fairness mockery and its music a sob.

'At the moment, no doubt,' said Don, 'you feel as though you had been knocked out of the ring in the first round. But this phase will pass. The point is, that you never had any business in the ring at all. No quarrel ever actually begins with a blow, and no quarrel was ever terminated by one. Genius—perverted, I'll grant you, but nevertheless genius—started this war; and we are English enough to think that we can end it by brute force. Pass the matches.'

'You are really of opinion,' asked Paul dreamily, 'that I should be doing my utmost if I stuck to my last?'

'Unquestionably. There are a thousand and one things of vital interest to all humanity which have not been said yet, which only you can say, a thousand and one aspects of the Deluge not yet presented to the world. Above all, Paul, there are millions of poor bereaved souls who suffer dumbly and vaguely wonder for what crime they are being punished.'

'Would you have me tell them that their faith, their churches, are to blame?'

'Not necessarily. The churches will receive many a hard knock without you adding your quota. Merry England has always nourished the "Down-wither"; we breed the "Down-withers"; and they will raise their slogan of "Down with everything" soon enough. I see your part, Paul, as that of a reconstructor rather than a "Down-wither." Any fool can smash a Ming pot, but no man living today can make one. You think that the churches have failed?'

'On the whole, yes. If we here in England are firm in our spiritual faith, why are the churches empty at such an hour as this and the salons of the crystal-gazers full?'

'Because we are *not* firm in our spiritual faith. But many of us know and admit that. The point is, can you tell us why, and indicate a remedy?'

Paul Mario's expression grew wrapt, and he stared out over the valley into a land which it is given to few ever to explore. 'I believe I can,' he answered softly; 'but I dare not attempt such a task without the unshakable conviction that mine is the chosen hand.'

'I am glad to hear you say it; those doubts prove to me that you recognize the power of your pen. They are fools who hold that a ton of high-explosive is worth all the rhetoric of Cicero. It was not Krupps who plunged the

Central Empires into the pit, Paul, but Bernhardi, Nietzsche and What's-his-name. Wagner's music has done more to form the German character than Bismarck's diplomacy. Shakespeare's *Henry the Fifth* means more to England than Magna Charta.'

'I agree.'

'When the last of our marshals has stuck the last of his pins in the last war map, all the belligerents will still be of the same opinion as before the war began. The statesman of today is perhaps past praying for, but your book will help to form the statesman of tomorrow.'

'You dazzle me. You would make me the spiritual father of a new Europe.'

'And a new America. Why not? You have heard the call, and you are not the man to shirk it. Lesser men than you have tried—all honour to them if they were sincere—to voice the yearnings, the questions, the doubts, of a generation that has out-grown its spiritual garments. All the world feels, knows, that a new voice *must* come soon. The world is waiting for you, Paul.'

III

Flamby Duveen was flat amid the bluebells, one hand outstretched before her and resting lightly upon a little mound of moss. It was a small brown hand, and she held it in such a manner, knuckles upward, and imparted to it so cunning and peculiar a movement that it assumed quite an uncanny resemblance to a tiny and shrinking hare.

Some four feet in front of her, at the edge of a small clearing in the bluebell forest, from a clump of ferns two long silky ears upstood, motionless, like twin sentries, and from between the thick stalks of the flowers which intermingled with the ferns one round bright eye regarded the moving hand fascinatedly.

Flamby's lips were pursed up and a soft low whistle quite peculiar in tone caused the silky ears of the watching hare to twitch sharply. But the little animal remained otherwise motionless, and continued to study the odd billowy motions of the brown hand with that eager wonder-bright eye. The whistling continued, and the hare ventured forth from cover, coming fully twelve inches nearer to Flamby. Flamby constrained her breathing as much as was consistent with maintaining the magical whistle. Her hand wriggled insinuatingly forward, revealing a round, bare arm, brown as a nut upon its outer curves and creamy on the inner.

The hypnotized subject ventured a foot nearer. Flamby's siren song grew almost inaudible above the bird-calls of the surrounding wood, but it held its sway over the fascinated hare, for the animal suddenly sprang across the space intervening between himself and the mysterious hand and sat studying that phenomenon at close quarters.

A little finger softly caressed one furry forepaw. Up went the hare's ears again, and his whole body grew rigid. The caress was continued, however, and the animal grew to like it. Two gentle fingers passed lightly along his back, and he was thrilled ecstatically. Now, his silky ears were grasped, firmly, confidently; and unresisting, he allowed himself to be couched in the crook of a soft arm. His heart was beating rapidly, but with a kind of joyous fear hitherto unknown and to which he resigned himself without a struggle.

Flamby wriggled up on to her knees, and holding the hare in her lap petted the wild thing as though it had been some docile kitten. 'Sweet little Silk Ears,' she whispered endearingly. 'What a funny, tiny tail!'

Quite contentedly now, the hare crouched, rubbing its blunt nose against her hands and peering furtively up into her face and quickly down again. Flamby studied the little creature with an oddly critical eye.

'Your funny ears go this way and that way,' she murmured, raising one hand and drawing imaginary lines in the air to illustrate her words; 'so and so. I never noticed before those little specks in your fur, Silk Ears. They only show in some lights, but they are there right enough. Now I am going to study your tiny toes, Silky, and you don't have to be afraid . . .'

Raising one of the hare's feet, Flamby peered at it closely, at the same time continuing to caress the perfectly happy animal. She was so engaged when suddenly up went the long ears, and uttering a faint cry resembling an infant's whimper the hare sprang from her lap into the sea of bluebells and instantly disappeared. A harsh grip fastened upon Flamby's shoulder.

Lithely as one of the wild things with whom she was half kin and who seemed to recognize the kinship, Flamby came to her feet, shaking off the restraining hand, turned and confronted the man who had crept up behind her.

He was an undersized, foxy fellow, dressed as a gamekeeper and carrying a fowling-piece under one arm. His small eyes regarded her through narrowed lids.

'So I've caught you at last, have I,' he said; 'caught you red-handed.'

He suddenly seized her wrist and dragged her towards him. The bright colour fled from Flamby's cheeks, leaving her evenly dusky; but her grey eyes flashed dangerously.

'Poachin', eh?' sneered the gamekeeper. 'Same as your father.'

Deliberately, and with calculated intent, Flamby raised her right foot, shod in a clumsy, thick-soled shoe, and kicked the speaker on the knee. He uttered a half-stifled cry of pain, releasing her wrist and clenching his fist. But she leapt back from him with all the easy agility of a young antelope.

'You're a blasted liar!' she screamed, her oval face now flushing darkly so that her eyes seemed supernormally bright. 'I wasn't poaching. My father may have poached, but *you* hadn't the pluck to try and stop him. Guy Fawkes! Why don't you go and fight like he did?'

Fawkes—for this was indeed the keeper's name—sprang at her clumsily; his knee was badly bruised. But Flamby eluded him with ease, gliding behind the trunk of a friendly oak and peering out at the enraged man elfishly.

'When are they going to burn you?' she inquired.

Fawkes laid his gun upon the ground, without removing his gaze from the flushed, mocking face, and began cautiously to advance. He was a man for whom Flamby in the ordinary way entertained a profound contempt, but there was that in his slinking foxy manner which vaguely disturbed her. For long enough there had been wordy warfare between them, but today Flamby realised that she had aroused something within the man which had never hitherto shown upon the surface; and into his eyes had come a light which since she had passed her thirteenth year she had sometimes seen and hated in the eyes of men, but had never thought to see and fear in the eyes of Fawkes. For the first time within her memory she realized that Bluebell Hollow was a very lonely spot.

'You daren't hit me,' she said, rather breathlessly. 'I'd play hell.'

'I don't want to hit you,' replied Fawkes, still advancing; 'but you're goin' to pay for that kick.'

'I'll pay with another,' snapped Flamby, her fiery nature reasserting itself momentarily.

But despite the bravado, she was half fearful, and therefore some of her inherent woodcraft deserted her, so much so that not noting a tuft of ferns which uprose almost at her heels, she stepped quickly back, stumbled, and Fawkes had his arms about her, holding her close.

'Now what can you do?' he sneered, his crafty face very close to hers.

'This,' breathed Flamby, her colour departing again.

She seized his ear in her teeth and bit him savagely. Fawkes uttered a hoarse scream of pain, and a second time released her, clapping his hand to the wounded member.

'You damned witch cat,' he said. 'I could kill you.'

Flamby leapt from him, panting. 'You couldn't!' she taunted. 'All you can kill is rabbits!'

Through an opening in the dense greenwood a ray of sunlight spilled its gold upon the carpet of Bluebell Hollow, and Flamby stood, defiant, head thrown back, where the edge of the ray touched her wonderful, disordered hair and magically turned it to sombre fire. Venomous yet, but doubtful, Fawkes confronted her, now, holding his handkerchief to his ear. And so the pair were posed when Paul Mario and Donald Courtier came down the steep path skirting the dell. Don grasped Paul by the arm.

'As I live,' he said, 'there surely is my kindly coy nymph of the woods— now divinely visible—who led me to your doors!'

Together they stood, enchanted by the girl's wild beauty, which that wonderful setting enhanced. But Flamby had heard their approach, and, flinging one rapid glance in their direction, she ran off up a sloping aisle of greenwood and was lost to view.

At the same moment Fawkes, hitherto invisible from the path, stooped to recover his fowling-piece and turned, looking up at the intruders. Recognising Paul Mario, he raised the peak of his cap and began to climb the dell-side, head lowered shamefacedly.

'It's Fawkes,' said Paul—'Uncle Jacques' gamekeeper. Presumably this wood belonged to him.'

'Lucky man,' replied Don. 'Did he also own the wood-nymphs?'

Paul laughed suddenly and boyishly, as was his wont, and nodded to Fawkes when the latter climbed up on to the path beside them. 'You are Luke Fawkes, are you not?' he asked. 'I recall seeing you yesterday with the others.'

'Yes, sir,' answered Fawkes, again raising the peak of his cap.

Having so spoken Fawkes become like a man of stone, standing before them, gaze averted, as a detected criminal. One might have supposed that a bloody secret gnawed at the bosom of Fawkes; but his private life was blameless and his past above reproach. His wife acted as charwoman at the church built by Sir Jacques.

'Did you not observe a certain nymph among the bluebells, Fawkes?' asked Don whimsically.

At the first syllable Fawkes sprang to an attitude of alert and fearful attention, listened as to the pronouncement of a foreman juror, and replied,

'No, sir,' with the relieved air of a man surprised to find himself still living. 'I see Flamby Duveen, I did,' he continued in his reedy voice—'poachin', same as her father . . .'

'Poachin'—same as her father,' came a weird echo from the woods.

Paul and Don stared at one another questioningly, but Fawkes' sandy countenance assumed a deeper hue.

'She's the worst character in these parts,' he went on hastily. 'Bad as her father, she is.'

'Father, she is,' mocked the echo.

'She'll come to a bad end,' declared the now scarlet Fawkes.

'A bad end,' concurred the magical echo, its accent and intonation eerily reproducing those of the gamekeeper. Then: 'Whose wife stole the key of the poor-box?' inquired the spirit voice, and finally: 'When are they going to burn you?'

At that Don succumbed to uncontrollable laughter, and Paul had much ado to preserve his gravity.

'She appears to be very young, Fawkes,' he said gently; 'little more than a child. High spirits are proper and natural after all; but, of course, I appreciate the difficulties of your position. Good day.'

'Good day, sir,' said Fawkes, again momentarily relieved apparently from the sense of impending harm. 'Good day, sir.' He raised the peak of his cap, turned and resumed his slinking progress.

'A strange coincidence,' commented Don, taking Paul's arm.

'You are pursuing your fancy about the nymph visible and invisible?'

'Not entirely, Paul. But you may remember, if the incident has not banished the fact from your mind, that you are at present conducting me, at my request, to Something-or-other Cottage, which I had failed to find unassisted.'

'Quite so. We are almost there. Yonder is Babylon Lane, which I understand is part of my legacy. Dovelands Cottage, I believe, is situated about half-way along it.'

'Babylon Lane,' mused Don. 'Why so named?'

'That I cannot tell you. The name of Babylon invariably conjures up strange pictures of pagan feasts, don't you find? The mere sound of the word is sufficient to transport us to the great temple of Ishtar, and to dazzle our imagination with processions of flower-crowned priestesses. Heaven alone knows by what odd freak this peaceful lane was named after the city of Semiramis. But you were speaking of a coincidence?'

'Yes, it is the mother of the nymph, Flamby, that I am going to visit; the Widow Duveen.'

'Then this girl of the siren hair is she of whom you spoke?'

'Evidently none other. I told you, Paul, that I bore a message from her father, given to me under pledge of secrecy as he lay dying, to her mother. Paul, the man's life was a romance—a tragic romance. I cannot divulge his secrets, but his name was not Duveen; he was a cadet of one of the oldest families in Ireland.'

'You interest me intensely. He seems to have been a wild fellow.'

'Wild, indeed; and drink was his ruin. But he was a man, and by birth a gentleman. I am anxious to meet his widow.'

'Of course she knows of his death?'

'Oh, you need fear no distressing scenes, Paul. I remember how the grief of others affects you. He died six months ago.'

'It affects me, Don, when I can do nothing to lessen it. Before helpless grief I find myself abashed, afraid, as before a great mystery—which it is. Only one day last week, passing through a poor quarter of south London, my cab was delayed almost beside a solitary funeral coach which followed a hearse. The coffin bore one poor humble little wreath. In the coach sat a woman, a young woman, alone—and hers was the wreath upon the coffin, her husband's coffin. He had died after discharge from a military hospital; so much I learned from the cabman, who had known the couple. She sat there dry-eyed and staring straight before her. No one took the slightest notice of the hearse, or of the lonely mourner. Don, that woman's face still haunts me. Perhaps he had been a blackguard—I gathered that he had; but he was her man, and she had lost him, and the world was empty for her. No pompous state funeral could have embodied such tragedy as that solitary figure following the spectre of her vanished joy.'

Don turned impulsively to the speaker. 'You dear old sentimentalist,' he said; 'do you really continue to believe in the faith of woman?'

Paul glanced aside at him. 'Had I ever doubted it, Yvonne would have reassured me. Wait until you meet Yvonne, old man; then *I* shall ask *you* if you really continue to believe in the faith of woman. Here we are.'

IV

A trellis-covered path canopied with roses led up to the door of Dovelands Cottage. On the left was a low lichened wall, and on the right a bed of flowers bordering a trimly kept lawn, which faced the rustic porch. Dovelands cottage was entirely screened from the view of anyone passing along Babylon Lane by a high and dense privet hedge, which carried on its unbroken barrier to the end of the tiny orchard and kitchen-garden flanking the bungalow building on the left.

As Paul opened the white gate a cattle-bell attached to it jangled warningly, and out into the porch Mrs. Duveen came to meet them. She was a tiny woman, having a complexion like a shrivelled pippin, and the general appearance of a Zingari, for she wore huge ear-rings and possessed shrewd eyes of Oriental shape and colour. There was a bluish tinge about her lips, and she had a trick of pressing one labour-gnarled hand to her breast. She curtsied quaintly.

Paul greeted her with the charming courtesy which he observed towards everyone.

'Mrs. Duveen, I believe? I am Paul Mario, and this is Captain Courtier, who has a message to give to you. I fear we may have come at an awkward hour, but Captain Courtier's time is unfortunately limited.'

Mrs. Duveen repeated the curtsey. 'Will it please you to step in, sirs,' she said, her eyes fixed upon Don's face in a sort of eager scrutiny. 'It is surely kind of you to come, sir'—to Don.

They entered a small living room, stuffy because of the characteristically closed windows, but marked by a neatness of its appointments for which the gipsy appearance of Mrs. Duveen had not prepared them. There were several unframed drawings in pastel and water-colour, of birds and animals, upon the walls, and above the little mantelshelf hung a gleaming German helmet, surmounted by a golden eagle. On the mantelshelf itself were fuses, bombs and shell-cases, a china clock under a glass dome, and a cabinet photograph of a handsome man in the uniform of a sergeant of Irish Guards. Before the clock, and resting against it so as to occupy the place of honour, was a silver cigarette case.

Don's eyes, as his gaze fell on this last ornament, grew unaccountably misty, and he turned aside, staring out of the low window. Mrs. Duveen, who throughout the time that she had been placing chairs for her visitors (first dusting the seats with her apron) had watched the captain constantly, at the same moment burst into tears.

'God bless you for coming, sir,' she sobbed. 'Michael loved the ground you walked on, and he'd have been a happy man today to have seen you here in his own house.'

Don made no reply, continuing to stare out of the window, and Mrs. Duveen cried, silently now. Presently Paul caught his friend's eye and mutely conveying warning of his intention, rose.

'Your grief does you honour, Mrs. Duveen,' he said. 'Your husband was one I should have been proud to call my friend, and I envy Captain Courtier the memory of such a comrade. There are confidences upon which it is not proper that I should intrude; therefore, with your permission, I am going to admire your charming garden until you wish me to rejoin you.'

Bareheaded, he stepped out through the porch and on to the trim lawn, noting in passing that the home-made bookshelf beside the door bore copies of Shakespeare, Homer, Horace and other volumes rarely found in a work-man's abode. Lémpriére's *Classical Dictionary* was there, and Kipling's *Jungle Book*, Darwin's *Origin of Species*, and Selous *Romance of Insect Life*. Assuredly, Sergeant Duveen had been a strange man.

Some twenty minutes later the widow came out followed by Don. Mrs. Duveen's eyes were red, but she had recovered her composure, and now held in her hand the silver cigarette case from the mantelpiece.

'May I show you this, sir,' she said, repeating her quaint curtsey to Paul. 'Michael valued it more than anything he possessed.'

Paul took the case from her hand and examined the inscription:

To Sergeant Michael Duveen,
—Company, Irish Guards,
from Captain Donald Courtier,
in memory of February 9th, 1916.

Opening the case, he found it to contain a photograph of Don. The lat-ter, who was watching him, spoke:

'My affairs would have terminated on February the ninth, Paul, if Duveen had not been there. He was pipped twice.'

'His honour doesn't tell you, sir,' added Mrs. Duveen, 'that he brought

Michael in on his back with the bullets thick around him.'

'Oh! oh!' cried Don gaily. 'So that's the story, is it! Well, never mind, Mrs. Duveen; it was all in the day's work. What the Sergeant did deserved the V.C., and he'd have had it if I could have got it for him. What I did was no more than the duty of a stretcher-bearer.'

Mrs. Duveen shook her head, smiling wanly, the thin hand pressed to her breast. 'I'm sorry you couldn't meet Flamby, sir,' she said. 'She should have been home before this.'

'No matter,' replied Don. 'I shall look forward to meeting her on my next visit.'

They took their departure, Mrs. Duveen accompanying them to the gate and watching Don as long as he remained in sight.

'Did you observe the drawings on the wall?' he asked Paul, as they pursued their way along Babylon Lane.

'I did. They were original and seemed to be interesting.'

'Remarkably so; and they are the work of our wood nymph.'

'Really! Where can she have acquired her art?'

'From her father, I gather. Paul, I am keenly disappointed to have missed Flamby. The child of such singularly ill-assorted parents could not well fail to be unusual. I wonder if the girl suspects that her father was not what he seemed? Mrs. Duveen has always taken the fact for granted that her husband was a nobleman in disguise! It may account for her adoration of a man who seems to have led her a hell of a life. I have placed in her hands a certain locket which Duveen wore attached to a chain about his neck; I believe that it contains evidence of his real identity, but he clearly intended his wife to remain in perpetual ignorance of this, for the locket is never to be opened except by Flamby, and only by Flamby on the day of her wedding. I fear this popular-novel theme will offend your aesthetic sensibilities, Paul!'

'My dear fellow, I am rapidly approaching the conclusion that life is made up more of melodrama than of psychological hair-splitting and that the penmen dear to the servants' hall more truly portray it than Henry James ever hoped to do or Meredith attempted. The art of today is the art of deliberate avoidance of the violent, and many critics persist in confusing it with truth. There is nothing precious about selfish, covetous, lustful humanity; therefore, good literature creates a refined humanity of its own, which converses in polished periods and never comes to blows.'

'What of *Madame Caligula*? And what of the critics who hailed *Francesca of the Lilies* as a tragedy worthy to name with *Othello!*

'Primitive passions are acceptable if clothed in doublet and hose, Don. My quarrel with today is that it pretends to have lived them down.'

'Let us give credit where credit is due. Prussia has not hesitated to proclaim her sympathy with the primitive. Did you observe an eagle-crowned helmet above Mrs. Duveen's fireplace?'

'Yes; you know its history?'

'Some part of its history. It was worn by a huge Prussian officer, who, together with his staff, was surprised and captured during the operations of March 1st, 1916; a delightful little coup. I believe I told you that Sergeant Duveen had been degraded, but had afterwards recovered his stripes?'

'You did, yes.'

'It was this incident which led to his losing them. He was taking particulars of rank and so forth of the prisoners, and this imposing fellow with the golden helmet stood in front of all the others, arms folded, head aloft, disdainfully surveying his surroundings. He spoke perfect English and when Duveen asked him his name and rank and requested him to hand over the sword he was wearing, he bluntly refused to have any dealings whatever with a 'damned common sergeant.' Those were his own words.

'Duveen very patiently pointed out that he was merely performing a duty for which he had been detailed and added that he resented the Prussian's language and should have resented it from one of his own officers. He then repeated the request. The Prussian replied that if he had him in his own lines he would tie him to a gun and flog him to death.

'Duveen stood up and walked around the empty case which was doing service as a table. He stepped up to take the sword which the other had refused to surrender; whereupon the Prussian very promptly and skilfully knocked him down. Immediately some of the boys made a rush, but Duveen, staggering to his feet, waved them back. He deliberately unbuttoned his tunic, took off his cap and unhitching his braces, fastened his belt around his waist. To everybody's surprise the lordly Prussian did likewise. A ring was formed and a fight began that would have brought in the roof of the National Sporting Club!

'Feeling ran high against the Prussian, but he was a bigger man than Duveen and a magnificent boxer. Excited betting was in full swing when I appeared on the scene. Of course my duty was plain. But I had young Conroy with me and he pulled me aside before the men saw us.

'"Five to one in fivers on the sergeant!" he said.

'I declined the bet, for I knew something of Duveen's form; but I did not interrupt the fight! And, by gad! it was a splendid fight! It lasted for seventeen minutes without an interval, and Duveen could never have stayed another two, I'll swear, when the Prussian made the mistake of closing with him. I knew it was finished then. Duveen got in his pet hook with the right and fairly lifted his opponent out of the sentient world.

'I felt like cheering; but before I could retire Duveen turned, a bloody sight, and looked at me, out of puffy eyes. He sprang to attention, and "I am your prisoner, sir," said he.

'That left me no way out, and I had to put him under arrest. Just as he was staggering off between his guards the Prussian recovered consciousness and managed to get upon his feet. His gaze falling on Duveen, he held out one huge hand to him—'

'Good! he was a sportsman after all!'

'Duveen took it—and the Prussian, grasping that dangerous right of the sergeant's in his iron grip, struck him under the ear with his left and knocked him insensible across the improvised table!'

Paul pulled up in the roadway, his dark eyes flashing: 'The swine!' he exclaimed—'the—ee swine!'

'I had all my work cut out then to keep the men off the fellow. But finally a car came for him—he was the Grand Duke of Something or other—and he was driven back to the base. He had resumed his golden helmet, and he sat, in spite of his bloody face, scornfully glancing at the hostile group about the car, like a conquering pagan emperor. Then the car moved off out of the heap of rubbish, once a village, amid which the incident had taken place. At the same moment, a brick, accurately thrown, sent the golden helmet spinning into the road!

'Search was made for it, but the helmet was never found. I don't *know* who threw the brick, Paul (Duveen was under arrest at the time), but that is the helmet above his widow's mantelpiece! The men who have witnessed incidents of this kind will no longer continue to believe in the veneer of modern life, for they will know that the true savage lies hidden somewhere underneath.'

They were come to the end of Babylon Lane and stood now upon the London road. Above the cornfield on the right hovered a sweet-voiced lark and the wild hedges were astir with active bird life. Velvet bees droned on their way and the air was laden with the fragrance of an English summer.

Along the road flashed a motor bicycle, bearing a khaki-clad messenger and above the distant town flew a Farman biplane gleaming in the sunlight. The remote strains of a military band were audible.

'The Roman road,' mused Don, 'constructed in the misty unimaginable past, for war, and used by us today—for war. Oh, lud, in a week I shall be in the thick of it again. Babylon Hall? Who resides at that imposing mansion, Paul?'

They stood before the open gates of a fine Georgian building, lying far back from the road amid neatly striped lawns and well-kept gardens.

'The celebrated Jules Thessaly, I believe,' replied Paul; 'but I have never met him.'

'Jules Thessaly! Really? I met him only three months ago near Bethune (a neighbourhood which I always associate with Milady and the headsman in *The Three Musketeers).*'

'What was he doing in Bethune?'

'What does he do anywhere? He was visiting the French and British fronts, accompanied by an imposing array of "Staffs." He has tremendous influence of some kind—financial probably.'

'An interesting character. I hope we may meet. By the way, do you manage to do much work nowadays? I rarely see your name.'

'It is impossible to do anything but war stuff, Paul, when one is in the middle of it. You saw the set of drawings I did for *The Courier?*'

'Yes; I thought them fine. I have them in album form. They were excellently noticed throughout the press.'

Don's face assumed an expression of whimsical disgust. 'There is a certain type of critic,' he said, 'who properly ought to have been a wardrobe dealer: he is eternally reaching down the "mantle" of somebody or other and assuring the victim of his kindness that it fits him like a glove. Now no man can make a show in a second-hand outfit, and an artist is lost when folks begin to talk about the "mantle" of somebody or other having "fallen upon him." A critic can do nothing so unkind as to brand a poor poet "The Australian Kipling," a painter "The Welsh Whistler," or a comedian "The George Robey of South Africa." The man is doomed.'

'And what particular offender has inspired this outburst?'

'Some silly ass who has dubbed me "the Dana Gibson of the trenches"! It's a miserable outrage; my work isn't scrap like Gibson's; it's not so well drawn, for one thing, and it doesn't even remotely resemble his in form. But never mind. When I come back I'll show 'em! What I particularly want to ask you, Paul, is to get in touch with Duveen's girl; she has really remarkable talent. I have never seen such an insight into wild life as is exhibited in her rough drawings. I fear I shall be unable to come down here again. There are hosts of sisters, cousins and aunts, all of whom expect to be taken to the latest musical play or for a week-end to Brighton: that's how we victimized bachelors spend our hard-earned leave! But I promised Duveen I would do all in my power for his daughter. It would be intolerable for a girl of that kind to be left to run wild here, and I am fortunately well placed to help her as she chances to be a fellow-painter. Will you find out all about her, Paul, and let me know if we can arrange for her to study properly?'

'You really consider that she has talent?'

'My dear fellow! go and inspect her work for yourself. Considering her limited opportunities, it is wonderful.'

'Rely upon me, Don. She shall have her chance.'

Don grasped his arm. 'Tell Mrs. Duveen that she will receive a special allowance on account of her husband's services,' he said, bending towards Paul. 'Don't worry about expenses. You understand?'

'My dear Don, of course I understand. But I insist upon sharing this protégée with you. Oh, I shall take no refusal. My gratitude to the man who saved my best pal *must* find an outlet! So say no more. Do you return to London tonight?'

'Unfortunately, yes. But you must arrange to spend a day, or at any rate an evening, with me in town before my leave expires. Are you thinking of taking up your residence at Hatton Towers?'

Paul made a gesture of indecision. 'It is a lovely old place,' he said; 'but I feel that I need to be in touch with the pulse of life, if I am to diagnose its ailments. Latterly London has become distasteful to me; it seems like a huge mirror reflecting all the horrors, the shams, the vices of the poor scarred world. To retire to Hatton in the companionship of Yvonne would be delightful, but would also be desertion. No idle chance brought us together today, Don; it was that Kismet to which the Arab ascribes every act of life. I was hesitating on a brink; you pushed me over; and at this very hour I am falling into the arms of Fate. I believe it is my appointed task to sow the seed of truth; a mighty task, but because at last I realise its dimensions I begin to have confidence that I may succeed.'

Don stood still in the road, facing Paul. 'Choose your seed with care, Paul, for generations yet unborn will eat of its fruit.'

V

Paul Mario dined alone in the small breakfast-room overlooking the sloping lawns, waited upon by Davison, the late Sir Jacques' butler, a useful but melancholy servant, having the demeanour of a churchwarden and a habit of glancing rapidly under tables and chairs as though he had mislaid a cassock or a Book of Common Prayer. The huge, gloomy dining-room oppressed the new owner of Hatton Towers, being laden with the atmosphere of a Primitive Methodist Sunday School.

Sir Jacques had been Paul's maternal uncle, and Paul had often wondered if there could have been anything in common between his mother—whom he had never known—and this smug Pharisee. His father, who had died whilst Paul was at Oxford, had rarely spoken of Paul's mother; but Paul had chanced to overhear an old clubman refer to her as having possessed 'the most fascinating ankles in London.' The remark had confirmed his earlier impression that his mother had been a joyous butterfly. For his father, a profound but somber scholar, he cherished a reverence which was almost Roman in its character. His portrait in oils occupied the place of honour in Paul's study, and figuratively it was a shrine before which there ever burned the fires of a deathless love and admiration.

Paul's acute response to environment rendered him ill at ease in Hatton Towers. The legacy embarrassed him. He hated to be so deeply indebted to a man he could never repay and from whom he would not willingly have accepted the slightest favour. It has been truly said that the concupiscence of the eye outlives desire. Tiberius succumbed to premature senility (and was strangled by Macro) in a bedchamber decorated with figures from the works of Elephantis; and Sir Jacques' secret library, which he had omitted to destroy or disperse, bore evidence to the whited sepulchre of his intellectual life.

This atmosphere was disturbing. Paul could have worked at Hatton Towers, but not upon the mighty human theme with which at that hour his mind was pregnant. For his intellect was like a sensitive plate upon which the thoughts of those who had lived and longed and died in whatever spot he might find himself, were reproduced eerily, almost clairvoyantly. It was necessary that he should work amid sympathetic colour—that he should appropriately set the stage for the play; and Fame having come to him, not empty-handed but laden with gold, he made those settings opulent.

He did spontaneously the things that lesser men do at behest of their press-agents. The passionate mediFval tragedy *Francesco of the Lilies,* destined to enshrine his name in the temple of the masters, he wrote at the haunted Palazzo Concini in Tuscany, where, behind tomb-like doors, iron-studded and ominous, he worked in a low-beamed windowless room at a table which had belonged to Gilles de Rais, and by light of three bronze lamps found in the ruins of the Mamertine dungeons.

For company he had undying memories of sins so black that only the silent Vatican archives held record of them; memories of unholy loves, of deaths whose manner may not be written, of births whereat the angels shuddered. Torch-scarred walls and worm-tunnelled furniture whispered their secrets to him, rusty daggers confessed their bloody histories, and a vial still bearing ghastly frost of Borgian *contarella* spoke of a virgin martyr and of a princely cardinal whose deeds were forgotten by all save Mother Church. Paul's genius was absorbent, fructiferous, prolific of golden dreams.

But the atmosphere of Hatton Towers stifled inspiration, was definitely antagonistic. The portrait of the late Sir Jacques, in the dining-room, seemed to dominate the house, as St. Peter's dominates Rome, or even as the Pyramids dominate Lower Egypt. The scanty beard and small eyes; the flat, fleshy nose; the indeterminable, mask-like expression; all were faithfully reproduced by the celebrated academician—and humorist—who had executed the painting. Soft black hat, flat black tie, and ill-fitting frock coat might readily have been identified by the respectable but unfashionable tradesmen patronized by Sir Jacques.

Paul, pipe in mouth, confronting the likeness after dinner, recalled, and smiled at the recollection, a saying of Don's: 'Never trust a whiskered man who wears a soft black felt hat and a black frock coat. The hat conceals the horns; the coat hides the tail!'

From room to room he rambled, and even up into the octagonal turret chambers in the tower. Here he seemed to be rid of the aura of the dining-room portrait and in a rarefied atmosphere of Tudor turbulence. In one of the turret chambers, that overlooking the orchard, he found himself surveying the distant parkland with the eyes of a captive and longing for the coming of one who ever tarried yet was ever expected. The long narrow gallery over the main entrance, with its six mullioned windows and fine collection of paintings, retained, as a jar that has held musk retains its scent, a faint perfume of Jacobean gallantry. But the pictures, many of them undraped studies collected by Sir Jacques, which now held the place once sacred to ancestors, cast upon the gallery a vague shadow of the soft black hat.

From a tiny cabinet at one end of the gallery a stair led down to my lady's garden where bushes masqueraded as birds, a sundial questioned the smiling moon and a gathering of young frogs leapt hastily from the stone fountain at sound of Paul's footsteps. Monkish herbs and sweet-smelling old-world flowers grew modestly in this domain once sacred to the chatelaine of Hatton; and Paul kept ghostly tryst with a white-shouldered lady whose hair was dressed high upon her head, and powdered withal, and to whose bewitching red lips the amorous glance was drawn by a patch cunningly placed beside a dimple. My lady's garden was a reliquary of soft whispers, and Paul by the magic of his genius reclaimed them all and was at once the lover and the mistress.

In the depths of the house he found a delightful dungeon. More modern occupiers of Hatton had used the dungeon as a wine-cellar and Sir Jacques had converted it to the purposes of a dark-room, for he had been a skilful and enthusiastic amateur of photography; but that it had at some period of its history served other ends, Paul's uncanny instinct told him. A sense of chill, not physical, indeed almost impersonal, attacked him as he entered, hurricane-lantern aloft. For the poet that informed his lightest action dictated that the ray of a lantern and not the glare of a modern electric appliance should illuminate that memory-haunted spot.

Gyves fastened up his limbs and dread of some cruel doom struck at his heart as he stooped to enter the place. Here again the powerful influence of Sir Jacques was imperceptible; the dungeon lay under the spell of a stronger and darker personality; and as he curiously examined its structure and form, to learn that it was older than the oldest part of the house above, he knew himself to be in a survival of some forgotten stronghold upon whose ashes a Tudor mansion had been reared. Searing irons glared before his eyes; in a dim, arched corner a brazier glowed dully; ropes creaked.

Returning to the library, he found himself again within the aura of his departed uncle. It was in this book-lined apartment that Sir Jacques had transacted the affairs of the ugly little church at Mid Hatton and the volumes burdening the leather-edged shelves were of a character meet for the eye of an elder. The smaller erotic collection in the locked bureau in the study presumably had companioned Sir Jacques' more leisured hours.

Paul sank into a deep, padded arm-chair. The library of Hatton Towers was in the south-east wing, and now because of the night's stillness dim booming of distant guns was audible. A mood of reflection claimed him, and from it he sank into sleep, to dream of the portrait of Sir Jacques which seemed to have become transparent, so that the camel-like head now appeared, as in those monstrous postcard caricatures which at one time flooded the Paris shops, to be composed of writhing nudities cunningly intertwined, of wanton arms and floating locks and leering woman-faces.

VI

Through the sun-gay gardens, wet with dew, Paul made his way on the following morning. The songs of the birds delighted him, and the homely voices of cattle in the meadows were musical because the skies were blue. A beetle crawled laboriously across the gravel path before him, and he stepped aside to avoid crushing it; a ladybird discovered on the brim of his had to be safely deposited on a rose bush, nor in performing this act of charity did he disturb the web of a small spider who resided hard by. Because the flame of life burnt high within him, he loved all life today.

The world grew blind in its old age, reverencing a man-hewn symbol, a fragment of wood, a sacerdotal ring, when the emblem of creation, of being, the very glory of God made manifest, hung resplendent in the heavens! Men scoffed at miracles, and the greatest miracle of all rose daily before their eyes; questioned the source of life, and every blade of grass pointed upward to it, every flower raised its face adoring it; doubted eternity whilst the eternal flames that ever were, are and ever shall be, burned above their heads! Those nameless priests of a vanished creed who made Stonehenge, drew nearer perhaps to the Divine mystery than modern dogma recognized.

So ran his thoughts, for on a sunny morning, although perhaps subconsciously, every man becomes a fire-worshipper. Then came the dim booming—and a new train of reflection. Beneath the joyous heavens men moiled and sweated at the task of slaying. Doubting souls, great companies of them, even now were being loosed upon their mystic journey. Man slew man, beast slew beast, and insect devoured insect. The tiny red beetle that he had placed upon the rose bush existed only by the death of the aphides which were its prey; the spider, too, preyed. But man was the master slayer. It was jungle law—the law of the wilderness miscalled life; which really was not life but a striving after life.

Realizing, anew, how wildly astray from simple truth the world had wandered, how ridiculous were the bickerings which passed for religious thought, how puerile, inadequate, the dogmas that men named creeds, he trembled spiritually before the magnitude of his task. He doubted his strength and the purity of his motives. 'Any fool can smash a Ming pot, but no man living today can make one.' Dear old Don had a way of saying quaint things that meant much. The world was very fair to look upon; but for some odd reason a mental picture of Damascus seen from the Lebanon Mountains arose before him. Perhaps that was how the world looked to the gods—until they sought to live in it.

Coming out into the narrow winding lane beyond the lodge gates, Paul saw ahead of him a shambling downcast figure, proceeding up the slope.

'Good morning, Fawkes,' he called.

Fawkes stopped as suddenly as Lot's wife, but unlike Lot's wife without looking around, and stood in the road as rigid as she. Paul came up to his side, and the gamekeeper guiltily raised the peak of his cap and remained standing there silent and downcast.

'A glorious morning, Fawkes,' said Paul, cheerily.

'Yes, sir,' agreed Fawkes, his breath bated.

'I want to tell you,' continued Paul, 'whilst I remember, that Mrs. Duveen's daughter, Flamby, is to be allowed to come and go as she likes anywhere about the place. She does no harm, Fawkes; she is a student of wild life, and should be encouraged.'

Fawkes' face assumed an expression of complete bewilderment. 'Yes, sir,' he said, his reedy voice unsteady; 'as you wish, sir. But I don't know about not doing no harm. She spoils all the shootin', alarms the birds and throws things at the beaters, she does; and this year she stopped the hounds, she did.'

'Stopped the hounds, Fawkes?'

'Yes, sir. The fox he ran to cover down Babylon Lane, and right into Dovelands Cottage. The hounds come through the hedge hard after him, they did, and all the pack jumped the gate and streamed into the garden. Colonel Wycherley and Lady James and old John Darbey, the huntsman, they was close on the pack, and they all three took the gate above Coates' Farm and come up in a bunch, you might say.'

Fawkes paused, glanced guiltily at Paul's face, and, reassured, lowered his head again and raced through the remainder of his story breathlessly.

'Flamby, she was peelin' potatoes in the porch, and she jumps up and runs down to the gate all on fire. The hounds was bayin' all round her as fierce as tigers, and she took no more notice of 'em than if they'd been flies. She see old John first, and she calls to him to get the pack out of the garden, in a way it isn't for me to say. . . .'

'On the contrary, Fawkes, I take an interest in Flamby Duveen, and I wish to hear exactly what she said.'

'Well, sir, if you please, sir, she hollers: 'Call your blasted dogs out of my garden, John Darbey!'

' "The fox is a-hiding somewhere here," says John.

' "To hell with the fox and you, too!" shouts Flamby, and pickin' up a big stick that's lyin' on the ground, she slips into them dogs like a mad thing. I'm told everybody was sure they'd attack her; but would you believe it, sir, she chased 'em out like a flock of sheep. She don't hit like a girl, Flamby don't; she means it.'

'She loves animals, Fawkes, and knows them; therefore she has great influence over them. I don't suppose one of them was hurt.'

'Anyway, sir, she got 'em all out in the lane and stood lookin' over the gate. John Darbey he was speechless in his saddle, like, but Lady James she told Flamby what she thought about her.'

Fawkes paused for breath and darted a second furtive glance at Paul.

'Proceed, Fawkes,' directed the latter. 'What was the end of the episode?'

'Well, sir, Flamby answered her back, but it's not for me to repeat what she said . . .'

'Since the story is evidently known to the whole countryside, you need have no scruples about the matter, Fawkes. What did Lady James say to Flamby?'

'She says, "You're a low, vulgar creature!" And Flamby says, "Perhaps I am," she says, "but I ain't afraid to tell anybody where I spend my week-ends!"'

'Ah,' interrupted Paul, hurriedly, 'you should not have repeated that, Fawkes; but I am to blame. See to it that you are more discreet in future.'

'Yes, sir,' said Fawkes, all downcast immediately. 'Shall I tell you what happened to the fox, sir?'

'Yes, you might tell me what happened to the fox.'

'Flamby had him locked in the tool-shed, sir!'

He uttered the words as a final, crushing indictment, and ventured a swift look at Paul in order to note its effect. Paul's face was expressionless, however, as a result of the effort to retain his composure.

'An awful character, Fawkes!' he said. 'Good morning.'

'Good morning, sir,' said Fawkes, raising the peak of his cap with that queer air of relief.

Paul set off along the lane, now smiling unrestrainedly, came to the stile where the footpath through the big apple orchard began, crossed it and stood for a moment watching a litter of tiny and alarmed pigs scampering wildly after their mother. One lost his way, and went racing along distant aisles of apple trees in quest of a roundabout route of his own. Paul, who symbolized everything, found food for reflection in the incident.

He lingered in the fragrant orchard looking at a flock of sheep who grazed there, and admiring the frolics of the lambs. In the beauty of nature he always found cause for sorrow, because every living thing is born to pain. Animals knew this law instinctively and received it as a condition of their being, but men shut their eyes to so harsh a truth, and cried out upon heaven when it came home to them. He thought of Yvonne, and his happiness frightened him. Gautama Buddha had left a lovely bride, to question the solitude and the sorrows of humanity respecting truth; he, Paul Mario, dared to believe that the light had come without the sacrifice. This mood bore him company to Babylon Lane, but the sight of the white gate of Dovelands Cottage terminated a train of thought. Here it was that the story related by Fawkes had had its setting.

No one responded to the ringing of the cattle-bell, and the door of the cottage was closed. In the absence of a knocker Paul rapped with his stick, and having satisfied himself that Mrs. Duveen and her daughter were not at home turned away disappointed. He had counted upon an intimate chat with Flamby, which should enable him to form some personal impression of her true character.

He returned slowly along Babylon Lane, and passing the path through the orchard, he chose that which would lead him through the fringe of the wood wherein he and Don had first seen Flamby. Evidently the wood was a favourite haunt of the girl's, for as he crossed the adjoining meadow he saw her in front of him, lying flat upon a carpet of wild flowers, now shadowed by the trees, her chin resting in one palm and her elbow upon the ground. In her right hand she held a brush, which now and again she applied with apparent carelessness to a drawing lying on the grass before her, but without perceptibly changing her pose.

The morning was steamy and still, giving promise of another tropically hot day, but Paul approached so quietly that he came within a few yards of Flamby without disturbing her. There he stopped, watching and admiring. She was making a water-colour drawing of a tiny lamb which lay quite contentedly within reach of her hand, sometimes looking up into her face confidently and sometimes glancing at the woolly mother who grazed near the fringe of the trees. Flamby was so absorbed in her work that she noted nothing of Paul's approach, but the mother sheep looked up, startled, and the lamb made a sudden move in her direction.

'Be good, Woolly,' said Flamby, and her voice had that rare vibrant note which belongs to the Celtic tongue; 'I have nearly finished now.'

But the lamb's courage had failed, and not even the siren voice could restore it. With the uncertain steps of extreme youth it sought its mother's side, and the two moved away towards the flock which grazed in a distant corner of the meadow.

'I fear I have disturbed you.'

The effect of Paul's words was singular. Flamby dropped her brush and seemed to shrink as from a threatened blow, drawing up her shoulders and slowly turning her head to see who had spoken. As her face came into view, Paul saw that it was blanched with fear.'

'Please forgive me,' he said with concern; 'but I did not mean to frighten you.'

'Oh,' moaned Flamby, 'but you did. I thought—' She rose to her knees and then to her feet, the quick colour returning in a hot blush.

'What did you think?' asked Paul gently.

'I thought you were Sir Jacques.'

She uttered the words impulsively and seemed to regret them as soon as spoken, standing before Paul with shyly lowered eyes. The attitude surprised him. From what he had seen and heard of Flamby he had not anticipated diffidence, and he regarded her silently for a moment, smiling in his charming way. She had evidently made some attempt this morning to arrange her rebellious hair, for it had been parted and brushed over to one side so that the rippling waves gleamed like minted copper where the sun kissed them. Flamby had remarkable hair, nut-brown in its shadows, and in the light glowing redly like embers or a newly extinguished torch.

Her face was a perfect oval, and she had the most beautifully chiselled straight little nose imaginable. Her face and as much of her neck as was exposed by a white jumper were tanned to gipsy hue; so that when, shyly raising her eyes, she responded to Paul's smile, the whiteness of her teeth was extraordinary. A harsh critic might have said that her mouth was too large; but no man of flesh and blood would have quarrelled with such lips as Flamby's. She was below medium height, but shaped like a sylph and had the airy grace of one. As Paul stood regarding her he found wonder to be growing in his mind, for such wild roses as Flamby are rare enough in the countryside, as every artist knows.

'Why,' he asked, 'should you be so afraid of Sir Jacques?'

'He's dead!' replied Flamby, an elfin light of mischief kindling in her eyes; yet she was by no means at her ease.

'And what made you mistake me for him?'

'Your voice.'

'Ah,' said Paul, to whom others had remarked on this resemblance; 'but you had no cause to fear him?—alive, I mean.'

'No,' replied Flamby, stooping to pick up her sketching materials.

Her monosyllabic reply was not satisfactory; but recognizing that if she did not wish to talk about the late Sir Jacques he must merely defeat his own purpose by endeavouring to make her do so, he abandoned the topic.

'My name is Paul Mario,' he said, 'and I came to see you this morning.'

Flamby stood up, paint-box, brushes and sketch in hand. 'To see *me?*'

'Yes! Why not?'

Flamby confronted him her natural self-confidence restored, and studied him with grave grey eyes. 'What did you want to see me about?' she asked; and in the tone of the question there was a restrained anxiety which Paul could not understand. Also there was a faint and fascinating suggestion of brogue in her accent.

'About yourself, of course,' he replied, and wondered more and more because of the knowledge—borne to him by that acute, almost feminine, intuition which was his—that the girl was fencing with him, and because of her strangeness and her beauty as she stood before him, hair flaming in the sunlight, and her eyes watching him observantly.

Now, her expression changed, and her pupils growing momentarily larger, he knew that her thoughts were in the past—and that they had brought relief from some secret anxiety which had been with her.

'Of course!' she said, and laughed with a sudden joyousness that was in harmony with the morning; 'you came yesterday with Captain Courtier. I understand, now.'

Swiftly as her laughter had come, it vanished, and her eyes grew dim with tears. Such tempestuous emotions must have nonplussed the average man, but to Paul Mario her moods read clearly as a printed page, so that almost as the image rose in Flamby's mind, it rose also in his; and he saw before him one who wore the uniform of a sergeant of Irish Guards. Hotly pursuing the tears came brave smiles. Flamby shook her curls back from her brow, gave Paul a glance which was half apologetic and wholly appealing, then laughed again and swept him a mocking curtsey.

'I am your honour's servant,' she said; 'what would you with me?'

The elfin light danced in her eyes again, and in this country damsel who used the language of an obsolete vassalage he saw one who mocked at his manorial rights and cared naught for king or commoner. Beyond doubt, Sergeant Duveen had been a strange man, and strangely had he trained his daughter.

'May I see your drawing?'

Flamby hesitated. 'Are you really interested?' she said wistfully, 'or are you just trying to be kind?'

Paul was tempted to laugh outright, but his delicate sensibilities told him that laughter would give offence. 'I am really interested,' he assured her earnestly, 'Captain Courtier is of opinion that you have a remarkable gift for portraying wild life.'

He selected his words deliberately with the design of reassuring her respecting the sincerity of his interest. He was aware of a vague fear that some ill-chosen remark would send Flamby flying from him, the coy wood-nymph to whom Don had likened her, and that she would disappear as she had done from Bluebell Hollow. But still she hesitated.

'You look as though you mean it,' she conceded, furtively glancing down at the sketching-board in her hand. 'But it's a rotter.'

'I'm afraid I am to blame. I spoiled it.'

'No you didn't. It was a mess before you came.' She glanced at him doubtfully, keeping the drawing turned away. 'You see,' she continued, 'the shadowy part of a lamb on a sunny morning is quite blue—*quite* blue. Did you know that?'

'Well,' replied Paul, musingly, shielding his eyes and looking toward the distant flock,' now that you have drawn my attention to the fact I perceive it to be so—yes.'

'But when you haven't got many colours,' explained Flamby, 'it's not so easy to paint. I've made my lamb too blue for anything!' She displayed the drawing, her eyes dancing with laughter. 'No man ever saw a blue lamb,' she said—'while he was sober!'

The words shed a sidelight upon the domestic habits of the late Sergeant Duveen, as Paul did not fail to note; and in the masculinity of Flamby's jesting he glimpsed something of the closeness of the intimacy which had existed between father and daughter. But, taking the drawing from her hands, he was astonished at the skill which it displayed and which surpassed that of any work he had seen outside the best exhibitions. It possessed none of the graceful insipidity of the water colours which young ladies are taught to produce at all good boarding-schools and convents, but was characterized by the same vigour which informed Flamby's conversation. Furthermore, it represented a living animal, soft of fleece and inviting a caress and was drawn with almost insolent ease. Paul looked into the girl's watching eyes.

'You are an artist, Flamby,' he said; 'and like all artists you are unduly critical of your work.'

A rich colour glowed through the tan upon Flamby's cheeks and she was aware of a delicious little nervous thrill. Paul Mario's fascinating voice had laid its thrall upon her and his eyes were far more beautiful even than she had supposed, when, confronting Fawkes in Bluebell Hollow, she had suddenly looked up to find Paul watching her. That easy self-possession which she had learned from her father and which deserted her rarely enough, threatened to desert her now; also, a poisonous doubt touched her joy. With its coming came a return of confidence and Flamby laid her hand confidingly upon Paul's arm.

'You really do mean what you say, don't you?' she asked wistfully.

'My dear little girl, why are you so doubtful of my honesty?'

Flamby lowered her fiery head. 'Except father,' she said, 'I never knew anybody who really thought I could paint. Some pretended to think so; and Miss Kingsbury at High Fielding, who ought to know, laughed at me—after she had asked me to go and see her—and told me to "try and find a nice domestic situation."'

The mimicry in the concluding words was delightfully funny, but Paul nodded sympathetically. A mental picture of Miss Kingsbury arose before him, and it was in vain that he sought to consider her and her kind without rancour. Beauty is a dangerous gift for any girl, making countless enemies amongst her own sex and often debarring her from harmless pleasures open to her plainer sisters. But the Miss Kingsburys of the smaller county towns are an especial menace to such as Flamby, although charity rarely assumes

THE ORCHARD OF TEARS

the dimensions of a vice among any of the natives of England's southern shires.

'And your father had intended that you should become a painter?'

Unconsciously he found himself speaking of the late Michael Duveen as of one belonging to his own station in life, nor did the wild appearance and sometimes uncouth language of Flamby serve wholly to disguise the blue streak in her blood.

'When he was sober,' she replied, and suddenly bursting into gay laughter, she snatched the drawing and turned away, waving her hand to Paul. 'Goodbye, Mr. Mario,' she cried. 'I like you heaps better than your uncle!'

Her impudence was delicious, and Paul detained her. 'You must not run away like that,' he said. 'Captain Courtier made me promise that I would arrange for you to pursue your art studies—'

Flamby shook her head. 'How can I do that?' she asked in a gust of scorn. Then, as suddenly, her gaze grew wrapt and her face flushed. 'But how I would love to!' she whispered.

'You shall. It is all arranged,' declared Paul earnestly. 'The—special pension which your mother will receive and which Captain Courtier is arranging will be sufficient to cover all costs.'

Flamby looked up at him, her eyes aglow with excitement. 'Oh, Mr. Mario,' she said, 'please don't think me ungrateful and a little beast; but—is it true?'

'Why should I mislead you in the matter, Flamby?'

'I don't know; but—if you knew how I've longed and longed to be able to go to London, among people who understand; to get away from these men and women who are really half vegetables!'

Paul laughed gaily. 'But you love the country?'

'I could not live long away from it. But the people! And I love the birds and the animals, and—oh!'—her voice rose excitedly—'don't kill it!'

A wasp was humming dangerously about Paul's head, and although his love of all things that had life was as strong as Flamby's, the self-protective instinct had lead him to endeavour to knock the wasp away. Now, Flamby extending one motionless hand, the gaudily striped insect alighted upon her finger and began busily to march from thence to the rosy tip of the next, and so on until it reached Flamby's little curved thumb. Holding the thumb upright, so that the wasp stood upon a miniature tower, she pursed her lips entrancingly and blew the insect upon its way as gently as if borne upon a summer zephyr.

'They only sting if you hurt them,' she explained; 'and so would you!'

'But,' said Paul, who had watched the incident wonderingly, 'if all insects were permitted to live unmolested and all animals for that matter, the world would become uninhabitable for man.'

'I know,' replied Flamby pensively—'and I cannot understand why nature is so cruel.'

Paul studied the piquant, sun-kissed face with a new interest. 'Flamby,' he said earnestly, 'one day you will be a great artist.'

She looked into his eyes, but only for a moment, turned and fled. There were a hundred things he had wanted to say to her, a hundred questions he had wanted to ask. But off she ran along the margin of the wood, and where a giant elm stood, a forest outpost at a salient, paused and waved her hand to him.

VII

For all the exquisite sympathy of his nature and intuitive understanding of others, there was a certain trait in the character of Paul Mario not infrequently found in men of genius. From vanity he was delightfully free, nor had adulation spoiled him; but his interest in the world was strangely abstract, and his outlook almost cosmic. He dreamed of building a ladder of stars for all earth-bound humanity, and thought not in units, but in multitudes. Picturesque distress excited his emotions keenly, and sometimes formed ineffaceable memories, but memories oddly impersonal, little more than appreciations of sorrow as a factor in that mystic equation to the solving of which he had bent all his intellect.

On the other hand he was fired by a passionate desire to aid; nor when occasion had arisen had he hesitated to sacrifice self for another's good. But such altruism was born of impulse and never considered. The spectacle of the universe absorbed him, and listening for the Pythagorean music of the spheres he sometimes became deaf to the voices of those puny lives about him. His attention being called to them, however, his solicitude was sweet and sincere, but once removed from his purview they were also dismissed from his mind; and because of his irresistible charm there were some who wept to be so soon forgotten. His intellect was patrician—almost deiform in the old Roman sense. Probably all great masters have been similarly endowed, for if in order that one shall successfully conduct a military campaign he must think in armies and not in squads, so, if another would aspire to guide Thought, presumably must he think in continents. It does not follow that he shall lack genius for love and friendship, but merely that he cannot distract his mind in seeking out individual sorrows. The physician tends the hurts of the body, the priest ministers to the ills of the spirit; Paul Mario yearned to heal the wounds of a stricken world.

But Flamby interested him keenly, and therefore he draped her in a mantle of poesy, obscuring those shades displeasing to his sensibilities; as, an occasional coarseness due to association with her father; and enhancing her charms and accomplishments. Her beauty and spirit delighted the Fsthete, and her mystery enthralled the poet. She had feared Sir Jacques. Why? Paul toyed with the question in his own fashion and made of Hatton Towers a feudal keep and of his deceased uncle a baron of unsavoury repute. The maid Flamby, so called because men had likened the glory of her hair to a waving flambeau, he caused to reside in a tiny cottage beneath the very shadow of Sir Jacques' frowning fortress; and the men at arms looking down from battlement and bartizan marvelled when the morning wove a halo around the head of the witch's daughter. (In the poem-picture which grew thus in his mind as he swung along towards Hatton, Mrs. Duveen had become even more shrivelled than nature had made her; her eyes had grown brighter and her earrings-longer.)

Word of the maid's marvellous comeliness reaching Sir Jacques, he won entrance to the cottage crouching against his outer walls, disguised as a woodman; for the mighty weald had reclaimed its own in the period visited by Paul's unfettered spirit and foresters roamed the greenwood. He wooed maid Flamby, employing many an evil wile, but she was obdurate and repulsed him shrewdly. Whereupon he caused Dame Duveen to be seized as a weaver of spells and one who had danced before Asmodeus at the Witches' Sabbath to music of the magic pipe. To serve his end Sir Jacques invoked inhuman papal witch-law; the stake was set, each faggot laid. But by stratagem of a humble cowherd who loved her with a fidelity staunch unto death, Flamby secured the Dame's escape and the two fled together covertly, through the forest and by night. . . .

VIII

A few paces beyond the giant elm, Flamby paused, breathless, looking down at the drawing which she held in her hand. Then turning, she retraced her steps until she could peep around the great trunk of the tree. Thus peeping she stood and watched Paul Mario until, coming to the stile at the end of the meadow, he climbed over and was hidden by the high hedgerow.

Flamby looked at the sketch again, seized it as if to tear the board across; then changed her mind, studied the drawing attentively, smiled, and looked straight before her, but not at anything really visible. She was dreaming, as many another had dreamed who had heard Paul Mario's voice and looked into Paul Mario's eyes. From these maiden dreams, which may not be set down because they are formless, like all spiritual things, her mind drifted into a channel of reflection.

The memory of Paul's voice came back again and thrilled her as though he had but just spoken. She grew angry because she had imagined his voice to resemble that of Sir Jacques. Poor little Flamby, the very name of Sir Jacques was sufficient to make her shudder, to cast black shadows upon the sunny fields of her dream-world. She dared not believe that Paul's interest was sincere and disinterested—yet her heart believed it.

Almost the earliest recollection to her young womanhood was of a man's interest in her welfare; that was at the big racing stables in Yorkshire where her father had trained for Lord Loamhurst. Flamby was thirteen, then, and already her beauty, later to develop into that elfin loveliness which had excited the wonder of Don, was unusual. The man in question was his lordship's nephew, and his interest had grown so marked that Michael Duveen had spoken to him, had received an insolent reply and had struck down the noble youth with one blow of his formidable fist. The episode had terminated Duveen's career as a trainer.

Thereafter had begun the nomadic life, with its recurrent phases of brawls, drunken debauches by her father, occasional brief intervals of prosperity and longer ones of abject poverty. Lower Charleswood had seemed as an oasis in the wilderness and the employment offered by Sir Jacques too bountiful to be real. Nevertheless, it was real enough, and all went well for a season. Michael Duveen gave the bottle a go-by, and the first real home that Flamby had known established its altars in Dovelands Cottage. The understanding between father and daughter was complete and was rendered more perfect by the necessity for companionship experienced by both. Poor Mrs. Duveen possessed the personality of a chameleon, readily toning with any background; but intellectually she was never present. Why Michael Duveen had selected such a mate was a mystery that Flamby, who loved her mother the more dearly for her helplessness, could never solve. It was a mystery to which Duveen, in his darker moods, devoted himself cruelly, and many were the nights that Flamby had sobbed herself to sleep, striving to deafen her ears to the hateful insults and merciless taunts which Duveen would hurl at his wife.

Following such an outburst, Michael Duveen would exhibit penitence which was almost as shocking as his brutality—but it was always to Flamby that he came for forgiveness, bringing some love-gift which he would proffer shamefacedly, tears trembling in his eyes.

'Ask your mother to come into town with me, Flamby asthore; I've seen a fine coat at Dale's that'll make her heart glad.'

It was invariably the same, and never was the olive branch rejected for a moment by his long-suffering wife. Hers was the dog-like fidelity which men of Duveen's pattern have the gift of inspiring in women, and had he been hailed to the felon's dock she would gladly and proudly have stood beside her man. So the years stole by, and Flamby crept nearer to womanhood and closer to her father's heart. The drinking-bouts grew less frequent and only once again did Duveen offer violence to his wife. It was on the occasion of a house-party at Hatton Towers, and a racy young French commercial man who was one of Sir Jacques' guests fell to the lure of Flamby's ever increasing charms.

Flamby, who now was wise with a wisdom possessed by few women, and who could confound a gallant with the wit of Propertius, or damn his eyes like any trooper, amused herself with the overdressed youth, and ate many expensive chocolates. Mistaking the situation, and used to the complaisance of the French peasant, M. le Petit-Maitre presented himself at Dovelands Cottage and made certain overtures of a financial nature to Mrs. Duveen. Between his imperfect English, his delicate mode of expressing the indelicate, and his great charm, poor Mrs. Duveen found confusion, brewed tea and reported the conversation to her husband.

Michael Duveen grew black with wrath, and, taking up a heavy dish from the table, he hurled it at the poor, foolish woman. As he did so the door opened and Flamby came in. The dish, crashing against the edge of the door, was shattered and a fragment struck Flamby's bare arm, inflicting a deep wound.

Like a cloak discarded, Duveen's wrath fell from him at sight of the blood on that soft round arm. He was a man suddenly sick with remorse; and, to the last, the faint scar which the wound left was as a crucifix before which he abased himself. He did not even thrash the Frenchman, but was content with sending to that astonished gallant an acknowledgment of his offer couched in such pure and scathing French prose that it stung more surely than any lash.

Duveen's was a strange nature, and to Flamby, as her powers of observation grew keener, he presented a study at once fascinating and mournful. He had deeper scholarship than many a man who holds a university chair; he knew the classics as lesser men know their party politics; and the woodlands, fields and brooks, with their countless inhabitants, held no mysteries for him. Yet he was content to be as Flamby had always known him—a manual labourer. The larder of Dovelands Cottage was well stocked, winter and summer alike, and Mrs. Duveen, who accepted what the gods offered unquestioningly, never troubled to inquire how folks so poor as they could procure game and fish at all proper seasons. Fawkes could have enlightened her; but there was no man in Lower Charleswood, or for that matter in the county, of a hardihood to cross Michael Duveen. Furthermore, Sir Jacques, who was a Justice of the Peace, would hear no ill of him. Finally, one bitter winter's morning in the first year of the war, Flamby learned why.

Sir Jacques, for the first time since the Duveens had resided there, crossed the threshold of Dovelands Cottage, bringing a letter which he had received from Duveen, then newly arrived in Flanders. That memorable visit was the first of many; and the diabolical patience with which Sir Jacques for over two years had awaited his opportunity was further exemplified in his conduct of the affair now that he was truly entered upon it.

At his first word of greeting, Flamby read his secret and her soul rose up in arms; by the time that he took his departure she doubted her woman's intuition—and wondered. Such was the magic of the silver voice, the Christian humility expressed in the bearing of that black figure. And when he had come again, and yet again, the first true image began to fade more and more, and she listened with less and less misgiving to the words of encouragement which he bestowed upon her drawings. Her father, although himself no draughtsman, understood art as he understood all that was beautiful, and had taught her the laws of perspective and the tricks of the pencil as he had taught her the ways of the woodland and of the creatures who dwelt there. On her sixteenth birthday he had presented Flamby with a complete water-colour outfit, together with a number of text books; and many a golden morning had they spent together in solving the problem of why, although all shadows look black, some are really purple and others blue, together with kindred mysteries of the painter's craft.

Now came Sir Jacques, a trained critic and collector, with helpful suggestion and inspiring praise. He made no mistakes; his suggestions held no covert significance, his praise was never extravagant. Miss Kingsbury, of High Fielding, the local Lady Butler, hearing of Sir Jacques' protégée, as she heard of everything else in the county, sent a message of honeyed sweetness to Flamby, desiring her to call and bring some of her work. Flamby had never forgotten the visit. The honey of Miss Kingsbury was honey of Trebizond, and it poisoned poor Flamby's happiness for many a day. Strange is the paradox of a woman's heart; for Flamby, well knowing that this spinster's venom was a product of jealousy—jealousy of talent, super-jealousy of youth and beauty—yet took hurt from it and hugged the sting of cruel criticism to her breast. In this, for all her engrafted wisdom, she showed herself a true limb of Eve.

It was Sir Jacques who restored her confidence, and Sir Jacques who seized the opportunity to invite her to study the works in his collection. The original image of the master of Hatton Towers (which had possessed pointed ears and the hoofs of a goat) was faded by this time, and was supplanted by that of a courtly and benevolent patron. Flamby went to Hatton Towers, and meeting with nothing but kindness at the hands of Sir Jacques, went again many times. With the art of a Due de Richelieu, Sir Jacques directed her studies, familiarising her mind with that 'broad' outlook which is essential to the artist. It was done so cleverly that even Flamby the wise failed to recognize whither the rose-strewn path was tending, and might have pursued it to the end but that Fate—or Pan, god of the greenwood, jealous of trespass—intervened and unmasked the presumptuous Silenus.

Like one of those nymphs to whom Don had detected her resemblance, Flamby, throughout the genial months, often betook herself at early morning to a certain woodland stream far from all beaten tracks and inaccessible from the highroads. Narcissi carpeted the sloping banks above a pool like a crystal mirror, into which the tiny rivulet purled through forest ways sacred to the wild things and rarely profaned by foot of man. In their shy, brief hour, violets lent their sweetness to the spot, and dusk came quiet creatures afoot and awing timidly to slake their thirst at the magic fountain. A verdant awning, fanlike, swayed above, and perhaps in some forgotten day an altar had stood in the shady groves which protected all approaches to this pool whereby Keats might have dreamed his wonder dreams.

One morning as she stepped out like Psyche from her bath, and stood for a moment where an ardent sunbeam entering slyly through the bower above wrapped her in golden embrace, upon that sylvan mystery intruded a sound which blanched the roses on Flamby's cheeks and seemed to turn her body to marble. It was a very slight sound, no more than a metallic click; but like the glance of Gyges it stilled her heart's beating. She had never known such helpless fear; for, without daring, or having power, to turn her head, she divined who hid beside the pool and the purpose of his coming.

In great leaps her heart resumed its throbbing, and Flamby, trembling and breathless, sprang into the undergrowth upon that side of the pool farthest from the high bank which masked the intruder and there crouched pitifully, watching. Another than she might have failed to discern him, so craftily did he crawl away; but Flamby, daughter of the woods, saw the wriggling figure, and knew it; moreover she knew, by the familiarity with the pathway which he displayed, that this was not the first time Sir Jacques had visited the spot.

She returned to the cottage, her courage restored and a cold anger in her breast, to find her mother alternately laughing and sobbing—because Michael Duveen would be home that day on leave. Whatever plan Flamby had cherished she now resigned, recognizing that only by silence could she avert a tragedy. But from that morning the invisible guardians of the pool lamented a nymph who came no more, and the old joy of the woods was gone for Flamby. At one moment she felt that she could never again suffer the presence of Sir Jacques, at another that if she must remain in Lower Charleswood and not die of shame she must pretend that she did not suspect him to have been the intruder. The subterfuge, ostrich-like, woman-like, finally was adopted; and meeting Sir Jacques in Babylon Lane she managed to greet him civilly, employing her mother's poor state of health as an excuse for discontinuing her visits to Hatton Towers. But if Flamby's passionate spirit had had its way Sir Jacques that day must have met the fate of Candaules at the hands of this modern Nyssia.

Standing there beneath the giant elm, Flamby lived again through the sunshine and the shadows of the past, her thoughts dwelling bitterly upon the memory of Sir Jacques and of his tireless persecution, which, from the time that she ceased her visits to Hatton Towers, became more overt and pursued her almost to the day of Sir Jacques' death. Finally, and inevitably, she thought again of Paul Mario, and still thinking of him returned to Dovelands Cottage.

Mrs. Duveen had gone into the town, an expedition which would detain her for the greater part of the day, since she walked slowly, and the road was hilly. Therefore Flamby proceeded to set the house in order. A little red-breasted robin hopped in at the porch, peeped around the sitting-room and up at the gleaming helmet above the mantelpiece, then finding the apartment empty hopped on into the kitchen to watch Flamby at work. Sunlight gladdened the garden and the orchard where blackbirds were pecking the cherries; a skylark rose from the meadow opposite the cottage, singing rapturously of love and youth—so that presently, the while she worked, Flamby began to sing, too.

IX

It was late on the following afternoon when the solicitors left Hatton Towers, and Paul, who detested business of every description, heaved a great sigh of relief as he watched the dust resettle in the fir avenue behind the car which was to bear the two legal gentlemen to the station. The adviser of the late Sir Jacques had urged him to keep up Hatton Towers, 'in the interests of the county,' even if he lived there only occasionally, and his own solicitor seemed to agree with his colleague that it would be a pity to sell so fine a property. A yearning for solitude and meditation was strong upon Paul, and taking a stout ash stick he went out on to the terrace at the rear of the house, crossed the lawns and made his way down to the winding path which always, now, he associated with Don.

An hour's walk brought him to the brink of the hilly crescent which holds the heathland of the county as a giant claw grasping a platter. Below him lay mile upon mile of England, the emerald meadows sharply outlined by their hedges, cornfields pale patches of gold, roofs of farms deep specks of grateful red, and the roads blending the whole into an intricate pattern like that of some vast Persian carpet. Upon its lighter tones the heat created a mirage of running water.

Human activity was represented by faint wisps of smoke, and by specks which one might only determine to be men by dint of close scrutiny, until a train crept out from the tunnel away to the left and crossed the prospect like a hurried caterpillar, leaving little balls of woolly vapour to float away idly upon the tideless air. A tang of the heather rose even to that height, and mingled its scent with the perfume of the many wildflowers cloaking the hillside. The humming of bees and odd chirping of grasshoppers spoke the language of summer and remotely below childish voices and laughter joined in the gladness.

Paul began to descend the slope. In the joyous beauty of English summer there was something at variance with his theme, and he found himself farther than ever from the task which he had taken up. Almost he was tempted to revise his estimate of the worth of things worldly and of the value of traditional beliefs. His imagination lingered delightedly over a tiny hamlet nestling about a Norman church as the brood about the mother. He pictured the knight of the Cross kneeling before the hidden altar and laying his sword and his life at the feet of the Man of Sorrows. He saw, as it is granted to poets to see, the plumed Cavalier leading his lady to that same altar and saw the priest bless them in the holy name. Almost he could read the inscriptions upon the tombs which told of generations of country gentlemen who had worshipped at the simple shrine, unquestioning, undoubting. The Roundheads dour, with their pitiless creed, had failed to destroy its fragrant sanctity, which lingered in those foot-worn aisles like the memory of incense, the echo of a monkish prayer. Was it all a great delusion?—or were our fathers wise in their simplicity? In the past men had died for every faith; today it would be hard to find men having any faith to die for.

A shadow crept over his mind, and although in his preoccupation he failed to observe the fact, it corresponded with the coming of an ominous cloud over the hill crest above and behind him; for we are but human lutes upon which nature plays at will, now softly and gently, now sounding chords of gladness, now touching to deep melancholy and the grandeur of despair. The promise of those days of tropical heat was about to be fulfilled, and already, three miles behind, black banks lowered over the countryside, turning its smile to a frown.

But even the remote booming of thunder failed to awaken Paul to the reality of the brewing tempest; it reached him in his daydream, but as a message not of the wrath of heaven but of the wrath of man. He mistook it for the ceaseless voice of the guns and weaved it into his brooding as Wagner wove the Valkyrie theme into the score of the *Nibelingen*. A faint breeze whispered through the tree-tops.

Paul came to the foot of the slope; and below him ran a continuous gully roofed over by stunted trees and conforming to the hillside as a brim conforms to a hat. Entrance might be made through any one of several gaps, and Paul, scrambling down, found himself in a dark tunnel, its brown, leafy floor patched at irregular intervals by grey light reflected from the creeping thunder cloud. Right and left it went, this silent gallery, and although he was unaware of the fact, it joined other like galleries which encircled the slopes and met and intercrossed so that one might wander for hours along these mystic aisles of the hills. Below again, beyond a sloping woody thicket, lay the meadows and farmlands sweeping smoothly onward to the heath. Now, the shadow of the storm had draped hillside and valley and was touching the bloom of the heather with the edge of its sable robe. Bird voices were still, and all life was hushed before the coming of the tempest. The ghostly trees bending low above the aisles whispered fearfully one to another, and about Paul was a darkness like that of a crypt. The earth and her children shrank as from an impending blow.

Several large raindrops, heralds of the torrent to come, fell through an opening above and pattered upon the dusty carpet at Paul's feet. He glanced upward at the darkening pall which seemed to rest upon the hill-top. Its oppressive blackness suggested weight, so that one trembled for the stability of the chalky scarp which must uphold that ebon canopy. Paul moved further along the aisle to a spot where the foliage was unbroken, as rain began a rapid tattoo upon the leafy roof. In the following instant the hillside was illuminated wildly as lightning wrote its message in angular characters across the curtain of darkness. Life cowered affrighted to the bosom of mother earth. The raindrops ceased, awaiting the crashing word of the thunder. It came, deafening, awesome; buffeting this bluff and that, rebounding, rebounding again and muttering down the valleys and the aisles of the hills. Then burst the rain, torrential, tropical.

In the emotional vision of Paul, horror rode the tempest. Man, discarding the emblem of the Cross and prostrating himself at the feet of strange idols, now was chained to a planet deserted by God, doomed and left to the mercy of monstrous earth spirits revitalized by homage and made potent again. To this gruesome fancy he resigned himself with the spiritual abandonment whereof he was capable and his capacity for which had made his work what it was: he grovelled before a nameless power which dwelt in primeval caverns of the underworld and spoke with the voice of the storm. Fear touched him, because the Divine face was turned from man. Awe wrapped him about, because the Word had failed to redeem, and a new message must be given. The Prince of Darkness became a real figure—and seemed to be very near him. As if the lightning had been a holy fire, with it enlightenment burst upon his mind, and he saw himself no longer unwanted, flotsam, a thing supine, but a buckler—a shield—one chosen and elected to a mighty task. The words of Don had first raised the curtain; now it was rent as the Temple veil and his eyes were dazzled. The Gate of Tophet had opened, and Something had crept out upon the world; it was for him to cast It back into the Pit!

He seemed to grow physically cold. Again the lightning blazed; and Paul, starting as one rudely awakened from sleep, saw that a man was standing close beside him.

X

That inclination to the marvellous which belongs to creative tempera-
ments led Paul to invest the stranger with the attributes of an apparition; he seemed to be a materialisation of the darkness which cloaked the modern world, a menace and a challenge; to stand for Lucifer. He was a man above average height, having a vast depth of chest and weight of limb, a strong, massive man. His suit of blue serge displayed his statuesque proportions to full advantage, and Paul's all-embracing glance did not fail to take note of the delicacy of hand and foot which redeemed the great frame from any suggestion of grossness. The stranger's head was bare, for he held in one gloved hand a hard black felt hat, flat topped and narrow of brim; and his small head, with close tight curls, set upon a neck like that of a gladiator, was markedly Neronian. The hue of this virile curling hair was a most uncompromising and fiery red, and equally red were the short moustaches and close-cut curling beard. It was a remarkable head, the head of a pagan emperor, rendered even more statuesque by an unusual ivory pallid skin and by large and somewhat prominent eyes of limpid golden brown.

He was staring at Paul, as Paul was staring at him; and, out of the darkness which instantly fell again, as the booming of thunder went rolling, demoniac, along the valleys, he spoke. His voice was rich and cultured. 'I fear I startled you—and you certainly startled me. I did not observe your approach.'

Paul laughed. 'Nor I yours. But I believe I was preoccupied, for I failed to notice the gathering storm until the rain attracted my attention.'

'I can guess at the nature of your preoccupation,' continued the deep voice. 'Unless the illustrated press has deceived me I have the pleasure of sharing this shelter with Mr. Paul Mario.'

'That is my name. May I ask if you are one of my neighbours?'

'I am called Jules Thessaly, and I have made Babylon Hall locally unpopular for some time past.'

'A stormy meeting, but none the less a welcome one, Mr. Thessaly. We have several mutual friends. Captain Courtier spoke of you to me only yesterday.'

'Captain "Don" Courtier?—a clever artist, and I believe a useful officer. I should have appreciated an opportunity of meeting him again. He has leave?' ·

'A few days; but the usual demands upon his time, poor fellow. You were also, I think, a friend of my late uncle?'

'I was acquainted with Sir Jacques—yes. Mr. Mario, our present meeting is more gratifying to me than I can hope to express. I may say that I had designed to call upon you had Fate not taken a hand.'

'Your visit would have been very welcome. I have been so busy with unavoidable affairs since my arrival, that I fear I have quite neglected social duties. With one or two exceptions, I know nothing of my neighbours. May I count upon the pleasure of your company at dinner tonight?'

'You forestall me, Mr. Mario. I was about to ask you to come over to me. Apart from my natural interest in yourself there is a matter which I particularly desire to discuss with you. I trust you will excuse my apparent rudeness, but indeed I know you will. Social dogma is the armour of the parvenu.'

Paul laughed again; Jules Thessaly was a welcome stimulant. 'Clearly we have many things in common,' he said. 'I shall be more than glad to join you. Fascinating rumours are afloat concerning your collection of Eastern wonders. May I hope that it is housed at Babylon Hall?'

A blaze of lightning came, illuminating the two figures, showing Paul Mario's fine face turned expectantly toward Jules Thessaly, and alive with an eagerness almost boyish; snowing the Neronian countenance of the other, softened by a smile which revealed small, strong teeth beneath the crisp red moustache.

'Rumour is a lying jade, Mr. Mario. My collection, I admit, is a good one, but there are at least three others in Europe and two in America which are better. It is unique in one particular: the section containing religious objects, totems, and gods of all ages is more complete than that of any other collector, or of any museum. The bulk of it unfortunately is at my house in London.'

'In these days of air raids would it not be safer at Babylon Hall?'

'If all the gods to whom man has offered prayer cannot protect their images in Park Lane, they cannot protect them in Lower Charleswood.'

'Diogenes speaks from his tub!'

'The truth is often cynical.'

'I fear that life has not a single illusion left for you.'

'All men work like rebels, Mr. Mario, to win freedom from youth's sweetest mistress—illusion, and spend the twilight of old age groping for what they have lost.'

'Yours must be a barren outlook. If I thought all the world a mere dream of some wanton god I should lay down my pen—for I should have nothing to say.'

'There can be nothing really new to say until man climbs up to another planet or until creatures of another planet climb down to this one.'

'A doctrine of despair.'

'Not at all—unless for the materialist.'

'How is that?'

'Would you trammel the soul with the shackles of the flesh?'

'You mean that literature and art persistently look in the gutter for subjects when they would be more worthily employed in questioning the stars?'

'I mean that if literature and art were not trades, inspiration might have a chance.'

'And you regard inspiration as a spiritual journey?'

'Certainly; and imagination as the memory of the soul. There is no such thing as intellectual creation. We are instruments only. John Newman did not invent *The Dream of Gerontius;* he remembered it. There is a strain in the music of *Samson et Dalila* which was sung in the temples of Nineveh, where it must have been heard by Saint Saens. The wooing of Tarone in your *Francesco of the Lilies* is a faithful account of a scene enacted in Florence during the feuds between the Amidei and Buondelmonti.'

Paul Mario fell silent. The storm was passing, and now ranged over the remote hills which looked out upon the sea; but the darkness prevailed, and he became aware of a vague disquiet which stirred within him. The conversation of Jules Thessaly impressed him strangely, not because of its hard brilliance, but because of a masterful certainty in that quiet voice. His words concerning Newman and Saint Saëns were spoken as though he meant them to be accepted literally—and there was something terrifying in the idea. For he averred that which many have suspected, but which few have claimed to know. Presently Paul found speech again.

'You believe, as I believe, that our "instincts" are the lessons of earlier incarnations. Perhaps you are a disciple of Pythagoras, Mr. Thessaly?'

'I am in one sense. I am a disciple of his Master.'

'Do you refer to Orpheus?'

Jules Thessaly hesitated, but the pause was scarcely perceptible. 'The Orphic traditions certainly embody at least one cosmic truth.'

'And it is?'

'That for every man there is a perfect maid, and for every maid a perfect lover; that their union be eternal, but that until it is accomplished each must remain incomplete—a work in two volumes of which one is missing.'

'Would you then revive the Eleusinian Mysteries?'

'Why not?'

'You would scandalize society!'

'In other words become the pet of the petty. You care as little for the institution called "Society" as I do, Mr. Mario. Moreover, there is no Society nowadays. Murray's has taken its place.'

Again the lightning flashed—less vividly; and in the glimpse thus afforded him of the speaker's face Paul derived the impression that Jules Thessaly was laughing, but of this he could not be sure. The thunder when it came spoke with a muted voice, for the storm was spreading coastward, and a light, cool breeze stole through the aisles of the hills. A grey eerie light began to spread ghostly along the gallery. The ebon cloud was breaking, but torrents of rain continued to descend. Paul's keen intuition told him that Jules Thessaly was indisposed to pursue the Orpic discussion further at the moment, but he realized that the owner of Babylon Hall was no ordinary man, but one who had delved deeply into lore which had engaged much of his own attention. He found himself looking forward with impatient curiosity to his visit to the home of this new acquaintance.

'You are comparatively a new-comer in Lower Charleswood, Mr. Thessaly?'

'Yes, Babylon Hall had been vacant for some years, having formerly belonged to a certain Major Rushin, a retired Anglo-Indian of sixty-five, with a nutmeg liver and a penchant for juvenile society. He was drowned one morning in the lake which lies beyond the house, whilst bathing with three young ladies who were guests of his at the time. He was one of the pillars of the late Sir Jacques' church.'

Paul laughed outright. 'Do you quarrel with the whole of humanity, Mr. Thessaly?'

'Not at all. I love every creature that has life; I share the very tremors of the sheep driven to the slaughter-house. Human sorrow affects me even more profoundly.'

'But you are hotly intolerant of human hypocrisy? So am I.'

'Yet it may be one of the principles of nature. Witness the leaf insect.'

'You don't believe it to be, though. You probably regard it as a hateful disguise imposed upon man by a moral code contrary to that of nature.'

'Mr. Mario, your words contain the germ of a law upon the acceptance of which I believe humanity's spiritual survival to depend.'

The elfin light was growing brighter by perceptible degrees; and Paul, looking toward the speaker, now was able to discern him as a shadowy bulk, without definite outline, but impressive, pagan—as a granite god, or one of those broken pillars of Medînet Habu. Either because Jules Thessaly had moved nearer to him, or by reason of an optical delusion produced by the half-fight, the space between them seemed to have grown less—not only phys- ically, but spiritually. The curves of their astral selves were sweeping inward to a point of contact which Paul knew subconsciously would be electric, odic, illuminating. He felt the driving force of Jules Thessaly's personality, and it struck from the lyre of his genius strange harmonious chords. He knew, as some of the ancients knew, that the very insect we crush beneath our feet is not crushed by accident, but in accordance with a design vast be- yond human conception; and he wondered what part in his life this strange, powerful man was cast to play. His thoughts found expression.

'There is no such thing as chance,' he said dreamily.

'No,' answered Jules Thessaly. 'There is no such thing in the universe. Our meeting today was an appointment.'

XI

Jules Thessaly, like the Indian rope trick, was a kind of phenomenon twice removed. In every capital throughout the world one heard of him; of his wealth, of his art collection, of his financial interests; but one rarely met a man who actually claimed to know him although every second man one met knew another who did.

When he acquired Babylon Hall, for so long vacant, the county was stirred from end to end. Lower Charleswood, which lacked a celebrity, felt assured at last of its place in history and ceased to cast envious glances towards that coy hamlet of the hills which enshrined the cottage of George Meredith. The Vicar of High Fielding, who contributed occasional 'Turn-overs' to the *Globe,* investigated the published genealogy of the great man, and caused it to be known that Jules Thessaly was a French Levantine who had studied at Oxford and Göttingen, a millionaire, an accomplished musician, and an amateur of art who had exhibited a picture in the Paris Salon. He was a member (according to this authority) of five clubs, had other country seats, as well as a house in Park Lane, was director of numberless companies—and was unmarried. Miss Kingsbury called upon the reverend gentleman for further particulars.

But when at last Jules Thessaly actually arrived, Lower Charleswood experienced a grievous disappointment. He brought no 'introductions,' he paid no courtesy calls, and those who sought him at Babylon Hall almost invariably were informed that Mr. Thessaly was abroad. When he entertained, his guests arrived from whence no one knew, but usually in opulent cars, and thereby departed no one knew whither. Lower Charleswood was patient, for great men are eccentric; but in the Lower Charleswood to its intense astonishment and mortification realized that Jules Thessaly was not interested in 'the county.' Lower Charleswood beheld itself snubbed, but preferred to hide its wounds from the world, and therefore sent Jules Thessaly ceremoniously to Coventry. He was voted a vulgar plutocrat and utterly impossible. When it leaked out that Lady James knew him well and that Sir Jacques frequently dined at Babylon Hall, Miss Kingsbury said, 'Lady *James?* Well, of course'— And Sir Jacques, as the only eligible substitute for a real notability, was permitted a certain license. He was 'peculiar,' no doubt, but he had built a charming church and was a bachelor.

Urged to the task by Miss Kingsbury, the vicar of High Fielding made further and exhaustive enquiries. He discovered that it was impossible to trace Jules Thessaly's year at Oxford for the same reason that it was impossible to trace anything else in history. One man knew another man whose brother was at Oriel with Thessaly; a second man had heard of a third man who distinctly remembered him at Magdalen. The vicar's cousin, a stockbroker, said that Thessaly's father had been a Greek adventurer. Miss Kingsbury's agent—who sometimes succeeded in disposing of her pictures—assured Miss Kingsbury that Jules Thessaly was a Jew. When war began all the county whispered that Jules Thessaly was a big shareholder in Krupps.

The constitution of his establishment at Babylon Hall was attacked in the local press. Babylon Hall was full of dangerous aliens. Strains of music had been heard proceeding from the Hall at most unseemly hours—by the village innkeeper. Orgies were held there. But Jules Thessaly remained silent, unmoved, invisible. So that at the time of Sir Jacques' death Lower Charleswood had passed through three phases: pique, wonder, apathy. One or two folks had met Thessaly—but always by accident; had acclaimed him a wonderful man possessing the reserve of true genius. Finally, Miss Kingsbury had met him—in Lower Charleswood post office, and by noon of the following day, all 'the county' knew that he was 'a charming recluse with the soul of a poet.'

And this was the man with whom Paul Mario paced along the green aisles toward the point where they crossed that Pilgrim's Way which linking town to village, village to hamlet, lies upon the hills like a rosary on a nun's bosom.

'My car is waiting below,' said Jules Thessaly. 'You will probably prefer to drive back?'

Paul assented. He was breathing deeply of the sweet humid air, pungent with a thousand fresh scents and the intoxicating fragrance of rain-kissed loam. The sound of greedily drinking plant things arose from the hillside. Beyond the purple heath hung the midnight curtain, embroidered fitfully with silver, and he removed his hat that the cool breeze might touch him. Hatless he was magnificently picturesque; Antinöus spared to maturity; the nature-worshipper within him stirred to quickness by magic perfumes arising from the breast of Mother Earth, he resembled that wonderful statue of the Bithynian which shows him as Dionysus the Twice-born, son of the rain-cloud, lover of verdure.

'The world,' said Jules Thessaly, 'is waiting for you.'

Through his abstract Orphic dreams the words reached Paul's mind; and they were oddly familiar. Who had spoken them—now, and once before? He awoke, and remembered. Don had said that the world awaited him. He turned and glanced at his companion. Jules Thessaly was regarding him fixedly.

'You spoke,' said Paul. 'Pardon my abstraction; but what did you say?'

'I said that when Nature endows a man at once with the genius of Dante and the appearance of a Greek god, that man holds the world in the hollow of his hand. He was born with a purpose. He *dare* not seek to evade his destiny.'

Paul met the glance of the golden, prominent eyes, and it held him enthralled. 'I do not seek to evade it,' he replied slowly. 'I accept it; but I am afraid.'

A low-pitched powerful French car stood at the foot of the slope, the chauffeur in his seat and a footman standing behind the open door. Poised ethereally betwixt solid earth and some sphere remote, peopled by Greek nature-myths, Paul found himself beside Jules Thessaly, and being borne swiftly, strongly upward to the hills. At the gap beyond the toll-gate, where one may view a prospect unique in all the county, the car stopped, perhaps in obedience to a summons of the master. From the open window Paul looked out over the valley; and a rainbow linked the crescent of the hills, point to point. Backed by the murk of the moving storm, Babylon Hall looked like a giant sarcophagus behind which Titan hands had draped a sable curtain; and it seemed to Paul as he looked, wondering, that the arc of heaven-born colours which no brush may reproduce, rested upon the hidden roof of Dovelands Cottage, crossed Babylon Hall, and swept down to the rain-mist of the horizon, down to the distant sea. The palette of the gods began to fade from view, and Paul turned impulsively to his companion.

Jules Thessaly, his elbows resting upon his knees, was staring down, apparently at the flat-crowned black hat which he held in his hands. The car had resumed its smooth progress.

'An omen!' cried Paul.' The world is *not* past redemption!'

He spoke wildly, emotionally, not choosing his words, scarce knowing what he desired to convey. Jules Thessaly glanced aside at him.

'The world *desires* redemption,' he said. ' It is for you to gratify the world's desire.'

XII

The mystery which steals out from the woods, creeps down from the hills, and lurks beneath the shadowed hedgerows at beckoning of dusk, was abroad and potent when Paul Mario that evening walked up Babylon Lane towards the Hall. Elemental forces, which the ancients clothed in semi-human shape and named and feared, moved beside him and breathed strange counsels in his ear. The storm had released uneasy spirits from their bondage in crannies of primeval hills, and it was on such a night as this that many a child has glimpsed the Folk tripping lightly around those fairy-rings which science would have us believe due to other causes than the mystic dance. The Pipes of Pan were calling, and up in the aisles of the hills moonbeams slyly sought and found bare-limbed dryads darting from the eagerness of wooing fauns. Progress has banished those Pandean spirits from the woodlands, but the moon is the mother of magic, and her children steal out, furtive, half fearful, when she raises her lamp as of old.

Between prescience and imagination the borderline is ill-defined. Although Dovelands Cottage was seemingly sleeping, or deserted, Paul pictured Flamby standing by the stile beyond, where the orchard path began. And when, nearing it, he paused, looking to the right, there was she, a figure belonging to the elfin world of which he dreamed, and seemingly on the point of climbing over the stile. 'Flamby!' he cried.

She turned, descended, and came forward slowly, a wild-haired nymph; and that odd shyness which sat so ill upon her was manifest in her manner. She had expected Paul; had really been waiting for him—and she felt that he knew it.

'Were you dreaming in the twilight?' he asked, merrily.

Flamby stood a little apart from him, staring down at the dusty road. 'No,' she replied. 'I was scared, so I came out.'

'Scared? Of what?'

'Don't know. Just scared. Mother is over at Mrs. Fawkes', and it's not likely I was going with her.'

'Why not?'

'She hates me,' explained Flamby, with brief simplicity.

'But why should she hate you?'

'Don't know,' said Flamby, busily burrowing a little hole in the road with the heel of her left shoe. Her shoes were new ones, and boasted impudently high heels. She had been proud of her arched instep when first she had worn the new shoes, and had been anxious that Paul, who hitherto had seen her shod in the clumsy boots which she called her 'Workers,' should learn that she possessed small feet and slim ankles. Now, perceiving his glance to be attracted to the burrowing operation, she flushed from brow to neck, convinced that he believed her to have worn the shoes for his particular admiration—which was true; and to have deliberately drawn his attention to them—which was untrue. She had been longing to hear Paul's voice again, and now that he stood before her she told herself that he must be comparing her with the hundreds of really pretty girls known to him, and thinking what an odd-looking, ignorant little fool she was. Gladly would Flamby have fled, but she lacked the courage to do so.

'So you were afraid,' said Paul, smiling; 'but not, on this occasion, of my late uncle, I hope?'

Flamby had half expected the question, but nevertheless it startled her. A Latin tag entered her mind immediately. 'O,' she began—and her strange shyness overwhelming her anew, said no more.

Paul assumed that he had misunderstood her. 'Pardon me,' he prompted, 'but I'm afraid I failed to catch what you said.'

'I said "*no*",' declared Flamby untruthfully, and silently blessed the dusk which veiled her flaming cheeks. Paul Mario abashed her. She delighted to be with him, and, with him, longed to run away. She had been conscious of her imperfections from the very moment that she had seen him in Blue-bell Hollow, had hesitated to speak, doubting her command of English, had ceased to joy in her beauty, and had wondered if she appeared to Paul as a weird little gnome. Now, she was resolved never to see him again—to hide away from him, to forget him—or to try.

'You are a true artist, Flamby,' he said; 'a creature of moods. Perhaps tonight the fairy gates have opened for you as they have opened for me. Titania has summoned you out into the woods, and you are half afraid. But the artist lives very near to Nature, and has nothing to fear from her. Surely you love these nights of the early moon?'

And as he spoke Flamby's resolution became as naught, and she knew that to hear him and to share his dreams was worth any sacrifice of self-esteem. Never since her father's death had she had a confidant to whom she might speak of her imaginings, from whom she might hope for sympathy and understanding. She forgot her shyness, forgot her new shoes.

"I have always loved the moon,' she confessed. 'Perhaps I thought of her as Isis once long ago.'

Now it was Paul who hesitated and wondered, his respect for Flamby and for the complex personality who had tutored her growing apace.

'But in London they must hate the moon,' she added, and the tone betokened one of her swift changes of mood.

"Yes,' said Paul, raising his eyes, 'the old goddess of the Nile seems to have transferred her allegiance to the Rhine.' He glanced at the luminous disc of his watch. 'I fear I am late. I shall call upon your mother to-morrow, if I may, and see if we can arrange something definite about your studies.'

'Oh!' cried Flamby—'what time will you come?'

'May I come in the morning?'

'Of course.'

'In the morning, then, about eleven o'clock. I must hurry, or Mr. Thessaly will be waiting. What do you think of your new and wonderful neighbour?'

'I have heard that he is a clever man and very rich; but I have never seen him.'

'Never seen him? And Babylon Hall is only a few hundred yards away.'

'I know. But I have never seen Mr. Thessaly.'

'How very queer,' said Paul. 'Well, good night, Flamby.'

He took off his soft grey hat and extended his hand. All Flamby's shyness descended upon her like the golden shower on Danae, and barely touching the outstretched hand she whispered, 'Good night, Mr. Mario,' turned and very resolutely walked away, never once looking back.

At the gate of the cottage she began to limp, and upon the instant of entering the sitting-room, where Mrs. Duveen, returned from her visit, was lighting a large brass table lamp, Flamby dropped cross-legged upon the floor and tenderly removed her left shoe. Having got it free of her foot, she hurled it violently into the kitchen.

'Hell!' she said, succinctly.

'Flamby!' cried her mother, in a tone of mild reproval. 'How can you swear like that!'

Flamby began to remove her stocking. '*You'd* swear if you had a damn great nail sticking in your heel!' she retorted.

XIII

Paul arrived at Babylon Hall exactly eight minutes late for his appointment. In the wonderful dusk unknown to the tropics, when sun contests with moon, disputing the reign of night, he walked up the long avenue past the silent lodge, and was shown into a small room adjoining the entrance hall. Of the latter he derived no very definite impression, except that it was queerly furnished. Wherein this queerness was manifested he found himself unable to decide on subsequent reflection. But the ante-room was markedly

THE ORCHARD OF TEARS

Eastern, having Arabesque mosaics, rugs and low tables of the Orient, and being lighted by a brass mosque-lamp. The footman who had opened the door for him was a foreigner of some kind, apparently a Greek.

He wondered at his reception; for the servant merely bowed and departed, without relieving him of hat and coat. Indeterminate, he stood, vaguely conscious of misgiving and questioning the stillness of the great house. But almost immediately a young man entered whose face expressed the utmost concern. He was clean-shaven, except for those frustrated whiskers once sacred to stage butlers, but latterly adopted as the sigil of the New Bohemia. He had pleasing dark brown hair, and if nature had not determined otherwise, might have been counted a handsome brunette. His morning-dress was worthy of Vesta Tilley's tailor. Paul detected the secretary even before the new arrival proclaimed his office.

'You have missed Mr. Thessaly by less than three minutes,' he said, glancing at his watch. 'I am his secretary, and upon me devolves the very delicate task of explaining his departure. In the absence of a hostess—this is a bachelor establishment—the position is peculiarly unfortunate—'

'Pray say no more, Mr.—'

'My name is Caspar.'

'I beg you to offer no apologies, Mr. Caspar. Believe me, I quite understand and sympathize. Mr. Thessaly has been called away at the last moment by affairs of urgent importance.'

'Exactly. I am indebted to you, Mr. Mario. The news—of a distressing nature—only reached us over the telephone five minutes ago. A groom was despatched immediately to Hatton Towers, but he seems to have missed you.'

'Nothing of a family nature, I trust.'

'Not exactly, Mr. Mario; but a matter of such urgency that there was no time for hesitation. Mr. Thessaly is already upon his way to London. He will write you a full explanation, and for that purpose took writing materials in the car. His letter should reach you by the first post in the morning. You will readily understand that the hospitality of Babylon Hall—'

Paul interrupted him. 'My dear Mr. Caspar, I could not think of intruding at a time of such distress and uncertainty. I can return to Hatton Towers in less than twenty minutes and the larder is quite capable of satisfying my modest requirements. Please say no more. Directly you are able to communicate with him express to Mr. Thessaly my sincere condolence.'

'A car is at your service, Mr. Mario.'

'I appreciate the kindness fully, but I should much prefer to walk. Please banish from your mind any idea that you have inconvenienced me. Good night, Mr. Caspar.'

The several extraordinary features of the incident he did not come to consider until later, but as he walked contemplative along Babylon Lane he detected sounds of distant gunfire, distinct from the more remote rumbling which was the voice of the battle front. He stood still—listening. An air raid on London was in progress.

'Thank God that Yvonne is out of it,' he said earnestly—'and may He be with every poor soul tonight who needs Him.'

Jules Thessaly and Babylon Hall were banished from his mind, although the raid on London might very well prove to be the explanation of Thessaly's sudden departure. From the stricken area his imagination recoiled, and in spirit he stood in a quaintly rambling village street of Devon before a rose-smothered cottage, looking up to an open casement window. It was there that Yvonne was, perhaps already sleeping—Yvonne, his wife. And all the old fear visited him as he contemplated their happiness, their immunity from the horrors, the sacrifices of an anguished world. Why was he spared when others, seemingly more worthy, suffered? True, he had suffered in spirit, which is the keenest torture of all; but he had emerged to a greater happiness, to a reunion with Yvonne which had been like a second and sweeter honeymoon. It could only be that he was spared for a great purpose, that he might perform a giant task. He was permitted, untrammelled, to view the conflict, the sorrow and the agony of mankind from an Olympic height, serene and personally untouched, only in order that he might heal the wounds laid bare before him. The world is waiting for you,' Don had said. Paul silently prayed that the world might not wait in vain.

'Master of destiny, inscrutable God, grant me light that I may see to perform the duty laid upon me. Use me, mould me, make of me an instrument. Millions have offered all and lost all. Guide my steps. If death lies upon the path I will not shrink, but suffer me to be of some little use to Thy scarred and bleeding world. Amen.'

The ominous gunfire had ceased when he retired to his room that night after a lonely dinner, and even the more distant booming to which he was growing accustomed was not audible. The lantern of the moon hung above such a serene countryside that thoughts of war were all but impossible, and Paul likened the heavens to the jewelled dome of some vast mosque wherein were gathered together all the clashing creeds of mankind, their differences forgotten in a universal love.

XIV

The summer days slipped by, each morning bringing a letter from Yvonne, each night a longing that it might be the last of their separation. But the affairs of the late Sir Jacques' estate were not easily dismissed, and Paul, eager with the ardent eagerness of a poet to set to work upon his task, yet found himself chained to Lower Charleswood. The place itself enchanted his imagination, and had his mind been free (and if Sir Jacques had never occupied Hatton Towers and impressed his individuality upon the house) Paul might have been content to stay—with Yvonne for a companion. But London called him urgently and inaction grew irksome.

Flamby Duveen he never tired of studying; she fascinated him like some rare palimpsest or Pythagorean problem. But Flamby was going to London as soon as arrangements could be made for her mother and herself to leave Dovelands Cottage. Mrs. Duveen had raised no objection to the proposed change; Mrs. Duveen had never raised an objection to anything throughout the whole of her docile career; and already Paul was weaving this oddly assorted pair into the scheme of that book which he projected as a challenge to the latent good in man.

Some of his neighbours he met, willynilly, but they took no place in his mental record of things, save perhaps the place of punctuation marks, commas and semicolons for the most part, rarely rising to the definite degree of a full point and never approaching the dramatic significance of an exclamation mark. Already he floated above the common world, looking down upon its tortured contours and half-defaced frontiers—for the true poet is a fakir who quits his physical body at the beck of inspiration, to return laden with strange secrets.

Jules Thessaly's letter explaining his extraordinary breach of good behaviour had been characteristic of the man. For whilst it was couched in more or less conventional terms of apology, the writer obviously regarded his action as justified and assumed in Paul an understanding which rendered pique impossible. Paul's theory regarding Thessaly's sudden departure had been correct.

'The gods are all dead,' ran one passage in the letter. 'A shell, one of our own, fortunately imperfect, entered the upper story of my house and rudely forced a passage through one floor and the outer wall. Some slight damage

SAX ROHMER

has been done to my collection'—etc.

The tangled details of Paul's legacy became disentangled at last, and he fixed a definite date for his departure. That same evening the weather broke and grey clouds veiled the stars. He was keenly susceptible to climatic changes, and this abrupt interruption of summer plunged him into a dark mood. Gone were the fairies from the meadows, gone the dryads from the woods. The birds grew mute and roses drooped their heads. He found himself alone facing a sorrowful world and sharing its sorrows. The shadow of the black hat in the dining-room portrait lay darkly on Hatton Towers.

When such a mood was upon him he would resign himself to it with all that spiritual and intellectual abandon of which he was capable, savagely goading himself to blacker despair and contemplating his own condition with the critical faculty of his mind, which at these times remained undisturbed. Whilst the rain beat upon the windows and draperies billowed eerily in the draught, he passed from the library into the study and unlocked that high black oak bureau which concealed the private collection of works artistic and literary which had informed him of the true character of his late uncle. He had caused a huge fire to be made up in the old open hearth in the dining-room and he proposed to spend the evening in building a pyre which should consume the memory of the secret Sir Jacques.

The books, many of them in handsome bindings, he glanced at, in order that no one worthy of life should be destroyed. The verdict pronounced he either laid the book aside or broke it up and threw it on to the great fire in the adjoining room. He worked for an hour, eagerly, savagely, his coat stripped off and his shirt sleeves rolled above the elbow. The collection, though valuable, was small, and within the hour the bulk of it was ashes. Paul the iconoclast then turned his attention to the portfolios of watercolours, etchings and photographs which occupied the lower and deeper shelves of the bureau.

Here he found exquisite reproductions of Pompeiian frescoes, illustrations in line and colour to divers works, as Pierre Louys' *Aphrodite,* the *Satyricon* of Petronius, and Ovid's *Amours.* The crowning horror of the thing was the artistic skill which had been prostituted to such ends. Technically, many of the pictures were above criticism; morally all were beyond. He consigned the entire heap of them to the flames.

Only the photographs remained, and a glance at the first of these resulted in a journey to the dining-room with laden arms. By impish chance two large and tastefully mounted panels both representing a sun-kissed nymph posed beside a pool slipped from the bundle and fell at his feet. Kicking the ash-stifled fire into a blaze, he stooped to recover them. So stooping he remained, staring down at the pictures on the floor. Then slowly, dazedly, he took them up, one in either hand. They were photographs of Flamby.

The fire roared up the brick chimney, the wind fought for entrance from above, rain beat dismally upon the high windows. The fire died down again, seeming to retire into the mound of grey ashes which it had created; and the photographs fell from Paul's grasp.

A wrought-iron poker hung from a rack in the hearth, and, his face set like a mask, Paul took the crude weapon in his hand, and slowly raised his head until he was looking up at the oil-painting above the mantelpiece. The sound of a dry and discreet cough close behind him drew his attention to the presence of Davison. He turned, a strange figure, something very menacing in his eyes. Davison glanced furtively under the gate-legged table.

'Mr. Thessaly has called, sir,' he said, and held out a salver upon which lay a visiting-card.

'Where is he?'

'He is in the library, sir.'

'Very good. I will join him there in a few moments.'

The portrait of Sir Jacques had been spared to posterity by that admirable tradition which denies an English gentleman any display of emotion in the presence of a servant.

XV

'I have seized the first opportunity,' said Thessaly, as Paul, composure restored, entered the library, 'of offering a personal explanation of my behaviour.'

Paul took his extended hand, waiving the proffered explanation. 'Except as regards the damage done to your property, I am not interested. Had your disappearance been dictated by nothing more than a sudden desire for solitude I should have understood. If I should ever be called upon to act as you did on that occasion I should know that a friend would understand. If he misunderstood he would not be a friend. I fear I am somewhat dusty. I have been destroying a portion of my legacy.'

Jules Thessaly, dropping back into the padded arm-chair in which he had been seated, stared hard at Paul.

'Not the illustrations to that portion of Scheherazade's narrative invariably expunged from all respectable editions of the *Thousand and One Nights?*"

Paul nodded, pushing a box of cigars across the table. 'You know them?'

'I know that Sir Jacques possessed such pictures.'

'I have destroyed them.'

'Why?'

Paul selected a cigar ere looking up to meet the faintly amused glance of Thessaly. 'They bore witness to a phase of his life which he chose to conceal from the world. I could do no less.'

'You speak with contempt.'

'The hypocrite is contemptible. A frank libertine may be an amusing fellow. If we do not think so, we can avoid him.'

'I agree with you up to a point. But in justice remember that every man has pages in his history which are never displayed to the world.'

'Very likely. But every man does not pose as a saint. Those who seek the company of a professed rake do so at their own peril. But the disguised satyr is a menace to the innocent.'

'I would suggest that some specific "innocent" occurs to your mind?'

'The adder does not bite itself. Were there no stories?'

'A few. But Sir Jacques was a model of discretion; as an under-secretary he would have glittered in the political firmament. There was a pretty village girl who promised at one time to provide the district with agreeable table-talk, but unfortunately for Miss Kingsbury and company the affair apparently fell through.'

'He was, as you say, a model of discretion.'

'Ah. There are records? Well, you were justified in destroying them.'

'It is hard to understand.'

'To understand whom—Sir Jacques or the girl? You cannot mean the girl. A man who reaches the age of thirty without understanding women is like a bluebottle who devotes a summer morning to an endeavour to fly through a pane of glass.'

'You speak like an early Roman.'

'What more admirable model? Consider the Roman institutions; perfect sanitation and slavery. We abolish one and adopt the other, with the result that a healthy democracy has swallowed us up. The early Romans were sages.'

'You have no sympathy for Sir Jacques' victims?'

'Except where the chivalrous warriors of Prussia are concerned, and with other rare exceptions, I never think of women as victims, Mr. Mario.'

'Not even in the case of an aged hypocrite who probably posed as the Platonic friend?'

'Platonic friendship is impossible up to sixty-five. The most ignorant girl knows it to be so, for every woman has hereditary memory.'

'Your creed is a harsh one. You take no count of snares and pitfalls.'

'Snares and pitfalls cannot be set upon the highroad.'

'And how should you define this highroad?'

'As the path selected by our unspoiled instincts. It is ignorance posing as education that first blunts those instincts, dogma disguised as religion and hypocrisy misnamed "good behaviour".'

'You would allow instinct to go unfettered?'

'Provided it remains unspoiled. But first I would sweep the world of lies.'

'Then you think the world ready for the truth?'

'I know that the world waits for it.'

'Do you think the world will recognize it?'

'In part the world has already recognized it. We lived in an age which was eternally demanding "proofs"—and which rejected them when they were offered. But the great catastrophe which has overwhelmed us has adjusted our perspective. Few of us today *dare* to doubt the immortality of the soul. We failed to recognize joy as a proof of our survival after death, but we cannot reject the teaching of sorrow.'

'Love and friendship, of course, are proofs not only of immortality, but of pre-existence and the survival of the individual.'

'And can you make the disciples of the clap-trap which passes for religion believe this, Mr. Mario?'

'I propose to try. But the task is hard. There are pieces difficult to fit into the scheme.'

'You agree with me that the war, which was born of ignorance, will bear the fruit of truth?'

'I agree that it will bear the fruit of truth, but I do not agree that it was born of ignorance. Men did not cause the war. It is a visitation from higher powers, and therefore has a grand purpose. There are no accidents in the scheme of the universe.'

'You think those higher powers are powers of good?'

'Wherever the powers of darkness walk the Powers of Light stand arrayed before them.'

There was a muffled crash in the adjoining room, which brought Paul, startled, to his feet. He crossed the library and entered the panelled dining-room. The portrait of Sir Jacques had fallen from its place above the mantelpiece, breaking a number of ornaments as it fell. Davison was already on the spot and stood surveying the wreckage.

'The 'eat of the extraordinary fire, no doubt, sir,' he said. 'The 'ook is loosened, as you observe.'

Paul stared at the man with unseeing eyes; he was striving to grasp the symbolic significance of the incident, but it eluded him, and presently he returned to the library, where Jules Thessaly was glancing at a book which he had taken from a shelf apparently at random.

'An accident?'

'Yes. A picture has fallen. Nothing serious.'

'Ah. Do you know this war-writer?' Thessaly held up the book in his hand—'Rudolf KjellPn.'

'By name,' replied Paul, absently. 'Does he understand?'

'Up to a point. His thesis is that a great and inevitable world-drama is being played and that he who seeks its cause in mere human plotting and diplomacy is a fool. States are superhuman but living biological personalities, dynamic, and moving toward inevitable ends beyond human control.'

'He is mad. All the German propagandists are mad. The insanity of Germany is part of the scheme of the world-change through which we are passing. He recognizes the superhuman forces at work and in the same breath babbles of "states." There is only one earthly State and to that State all humanity belongs.'

Jules Thessaly returned KjellPn's work to its place. 'If I do not misunderstand you,' he said, fixing his gaze upon Paul, 'you contemplate telling the world that the Churches have misinterpreted Revelation, and that Christ as well as the other Masters actually revealed reincarnation as the secret of heaven and hell?'

'That is my intention.'

'Your audience is a vast one, Mr. Mario. No man for many generations has been granted the power to sway thought, which nature has bestowed upon you. Your word may well prevail against all things—even in time against

Rome. You recognize that you are about to take up a mighty weapon?'

'I do. Publicity is the lever of which Archimedes dreamed; and I confess that I tremble. You think the Churches will oppose me?'

'Can you doubt it?'

'I fear you are right, yet they should be my allies, not my enemies. In the spectacle of a world in arms the Churches must surely recognize the evidence of failure. If they would survive they must open their doors to reform.'

'And what is the nature of the reform you would suggest?'

'Conversion from nineteen centuries of error to the simple creed of their Founder.'

'Impossible. Churches, like Russian securities, may be destroyed but never converted.'

'Yet in their secret hearts millions of professed churchmen believe as I believe—'

'—That heaven and hell are within every man's own soul and that the state in which he is born is the state for which he has fitted himself by the acts of his pre-existence?'

Paul inclined his head. 'No other belief is possible today.'

'There are higher planets than Earth, perhaps lower. The ultimate deep is Hell, the ultimate height Heaven. The universe is a ladder which every soul must climb.'

From a catechism Jules Thessaly's words had developed into a profession of faith, and Paul, who stood watching the speaker, grew suddenly aware—a phenomenon which all have experienced—that such a profession had been made to him before, that he had stood thus on some other occasion and had heard the same words spoken. He knew what Jules Thessaly was about to say.

'The knowledge which is yours is innate knowledge beyond human power to acquire in one short span of life; it is the result of many lives devoted to study. For the task you are about to take up you have been preparing since the world was young. All is ordained, even your presence in this room tonight—and mine. Where last did we meet—where first? Perhaps in Rome, perhaps Atlantis; but assuredly we met and we meet again to fulfil a compact made in the dawn of time. I, too, am a student of the recondite, and it may be that some of the fragments of truth which I have collected will help you to force recognition of the light from a world plunged in darkness.'

'In utter darkness,' murmured Paul. And clearly before him—so clearly as almost to constitute hallucination—arose a vision of Flamby Duveen as she appeared in the secret photographs.

'You have definitely set your hand to the plough?'

'Definitely.'

Jules Thessaly advanced, leaning forward across the table. He stared fixedly at Paul. 'Tonight,' he said, 'a new Star is born in the West and an hour will come when the eyes of all men must be raised to it.'

PART SECOND

FLAMBY IN LONDON

I

On a raw winter's morning some six months later Don Courtier walked briskly out of St. Pancras station, valise in hand, and surveyed a misty yellow London with friendly eyes. A taxi-driver, hitherto plunged in unfathomable gloom, met this genial glance and recovered courage. He volunteered almost cheerfully to drive Don to any spot which he might desire to visit, an offer which Don accepted in an equally cordial spirit.

Depositing his valise at the Services Club in Stratford Place, his modest abode when on leave in London, Don directed the cabman to drive him to Paul Mario's house in Chelsea.

'Go a long way round,' he said; 'through Piccadilly Circus, Trafalgar Square and up the Mall. I want to see the sights of London Town.'

Lying back in the cab he lighted a cigarette and resigned himself to those pleasant reflections which belong to the holiday mood. For the Capital of a threatened empire, London looked disappointingly ordinary, he thought. There seemed to be thousands of pretty women, exquisitely dressed, thronging the West End thoroughfares; but Don had learned from experience that this delusion was a symptom associated with leave. Long absence from feminine society blunts a man's critical faculties, and Robinson Crusoe must have thought all women beautiful.

There were not so many posters on the hoardings, which deprived the streets of a characteristic note of colour, but there were conspicuous encomiums of economy displayed at Oxford Circus which the shopping crowds along Oxford Street and Regent Street seemed nevertheless to have overlooked. A large majority of the male population appeared to be in khaki. The negligible minority not in khaki appeared to be in extremis or second childhood. Don had heard much of 'slackers' but the spectacle afforded by the street shops set him wondering where they were all hiding. With the exception of a number of octogenarians and cripples, the men in Regent Street wore uniform. They were all accompanied by lovely women; it was extraordinary, but Don knew that it would wear off. At Piccadilly Circus he found the usual congestion of traffic and more than the usual gala atmosphere for which this spot is peculiar.

People at Piccadilly Circus never appear to be there on business. They are either *au rendezvous* or bound for a restaurant or going shopping or booking theatre seats; and although Don had every reason for believing that a war was in progress, Piccadilly Circus brazenly refused to care. The doors of the London Pavilion were opened hospitably and even at that early hour the tables in Scott's windows were occupied by lobster fanciers. A newsboy armed with copies of an evening paper (which oddly enough came out in the morning) was shouting at the top of his voice that there had been a naval engagement in the Channel, but he did not succeed in attracting anything like the same attention as that freely bestowed upon a well known actress who was standing outside the Criterion and not shouting at all. It was very restful after the worry at the front. In Derbyshire, too, people had talked about nothing but the war.

There were attractive posters upon the plinth of Nelson's Monument, and the Square seemed to be full of Colonial troops. The reputation of Trafalgar Square ranks next to that of the Strand in the British Colonies. A party of Grenadier Guards, led by a band and accompanied by policemen and small boys, marched along the Mall. A phrase of the march haunted Don all the way to Chelsea.

Yvonne Mario in white décolleté blouse and simple blue skirt, made a very charming picture indeed. Her beauty was that of exquisite colouring and freshness; her hair seemed to have captured and retained the summer sunlight, and her eyes were of that violet hue which so rarely survives childhood. Patrician languor revealed itself in every movement of her slim figure. Don's smile betrayed his admiration.

'Do you know, Yvonne,' he said, 'I have been thinking coming along that there were thousands of pretty girls in London. I see now that I was wrong.'

'You are making me blush!' said Yvonne, which was not true, for her graceful composure seldom deserted her. 'I shall tell Paul that you have been paying me compliments.'

'I wish you would. I don't believe he thinks I appreciate you as highly as I do.'

'He does,' replied Yvonne naïvely; 'he regards you as a connoisseur of good looks!'

'Oh!' cried Don. 'Oh! listen to her! Yvonne, you are growing vain.'

'A woman without vanity is not appreciated.'

'A woman without vanity is not human.'

'If you are going to say cynical things I won't talk to you. You want a whiskey-and-soda.'

'I don't.'

'You do. The first thing to offer a man on leave is whisky-and-soda.'

'It is ritual, then?'

'It is the law. Sit down there and resign yourself to it. Do you really mean to tell me that you did not know Paul was in France?'

'It must be a dreadful blow to your self-esteem, Yvonne, but I really came here expecting to see him. When does he return?'

Yvonne rose as a maid entered with a tray bearing decanter and syphon. 'On Tuesday morning if the Channel is clear. Will you help yourself or shall I pour out until you say "When"?'

'Please help me. You cannot imagine how delightful it is to be waited upon by a nice girl after grubbing over there.'

'When do you have to go back, Don?'

'I have a clear week yet. When! How is Paul progressing with the book, Yvonne?'

'He has been collecting material for months, and of course his present visit to France is for material, too. I think he has practically completed the first part, but I have no idea what form it is finally to take.'

'His article in the *Review* made a stir.'

'Wasn't it extraordinary!' cried Yvonne, seating herself beside Don on the low window-seat and pressing the cushions with her hands. 'We were simply snowed under with letters from all sorts of people, and quite a number of them called in person, even after Paul had left London.'

'Did you let them in?'

'No; some of them quite frightened me. There was one old clergyman who seemed very suspicious when Eustace told him that Paul was abroad. He stood outside the house for quite a long time, banging his stick on the pavement and coughing in a nasty barking fashion. I was watching him through the curtains of an upstairs window. He left a tract behind called *The Path is Straight but Narrow.*'

'Did he wear whiskers?'

'Yes; long ones.'

'A soft black hat, a polo collar and a ready-for-use black tie?'

'I believe he did.'

'I am glad you did not let him in.'

Through the narrow-panelled windows of the charming morning-room Don could see the old sundial. He remembered that in the summer the miniature rock-garden endued a mantle of simple flowers, and that sweet scents were borne into the room by every passing breeze. A great Victorian painter had lived in this house, which now was destined to figure again in history as the home of the greater Paul Mario. He glanced around the cosy room, in which there were many bowls and vases holding tulips, those chalices of tears beloved of Hafiz, and he suppressed a little sigh.

'May I light a pipe before I go, Yvonne?' he asked. 'I am one of those depraved beings who promenade the streets smoking huge briars, to the delight of Continental comic artists.'

'I know you are. But you are not going to promenade the streets until you have had your lunch.'

'Really, Yvonne, thanks all the same, but I must go. Honestly, I have an appointment.'

Yvonne smiled in his face and her violet eyes held a query.

'No,' replied Don—'no such luck. The Pauls are the lucky dogs. All the nice girls are married. I am going to lunch with a solicitor!'

'Oh, how unromantic! And are you on leave!'

'Painful, I admit, but I am a stodgy old fogey. When the war is over I am going to buy a velvet coat and a little red pork-pie cap, with a green tassel. Is that old Odin I can hear barking?'

'Yes. He has heard your voice.'

'I must really say "How d'you do" to Odin. When I have lighted my pipe may I go out?'

'Of course. Odin would never forgive you if you didn't. Let me strike a match for you.'

'You are spoiling me, Yvonne.'

Don, his pipe well alight, stood up and went out into the garden where a wolf-hound was making an excited demonstration in the little yard before the door of his kennel.

'Hullo, Odin!' cried Don, as the great hound leapt at him joyfully, resting both paws upon his shoulders. 'How is old Odin? Not looking forward to compulsory rationing, I dare swear.'

He pulled the dog's ears affectionately and scratched his shapely head in that manner which is so gratifying to the canine species. Then from the pocket of his 'British-warm' he produced a large sweet biscuit, whereupon Odin immediately assumed a correct mendicant posture and sat with drooping forepaws and upraised eyes. Don balanced the big biscuit upon the dog's nose. 'When I say "Three," Odin. One!' Odin did not stir. 'Two!' Odin remained still as a dog of stone. '*Three!*' The biscuit disappeared, and Don laughed as loudly as though the familiar performance had been an entire novelty. 'Good morning, old fellow,' he said, and returned to the house.

Yvonne was awaiting him in the hall. 'What time shall you come on Tuesday?' she asked. 'Paul should be home to lunch.'

'You will want Paul all to yourself for awhile, Yvonne. I shall look in later in the afternoon.' He shook hands with his pretty hostess, put on his cap and set off for the offices of Messrs. Nevin and Nevin.

The offices of Messrs. Nevin and Nevin were of that dusty, gloomy and obsolete fashion which inspires such confidence in the would-be litigant. Large and raggedly bound volumes, which apparently had been acquired from the twopenny boxes outside secondhand bookshops, lined the shelves of the outer office, and the chairs were of an early-Victorian horsehair variety. Respectability had run to seed in those chambers. Mr. Jacob Nevin, the senior partner, to whose decorous sanctum Don presently penetrated, also had a second-hand appearance. Don had always suspected him of secret snuff-taking.

'Ah, Captain Courtier,' he said; 'very sad about Miss Duveen's second bereavement, very sad.'

'Yes. Fate has dealt unkindly with the poor girl. I understand that Mrs. Duveen died more than two months ago; but I only learned of her death quite recently. I wrote to Miss Duveen directly I knew that I was coming to England, and I was horrified to hear of her mother's death. You have got the affairs well in hand now?'

'Since receiving your instructions, Captain Courtier, I have pushed the matter on with every possible expedition—every expedition possible. The absence of Mr. Paul Mario in France had somewhat tied my hands, you see.'

'I will consult Mrs. Chumley, my aunt, and arrange, if possible, for Miss Duveen to live at the Hostel. I have already written to her upon the subject. If it can be managed I shall 'phone you later today, and perhaps you would be good enough to wire to Miss Duveen requesting her to come to London immediately. Don't mention my name, you understand? But let me know at the Club by what train she is arriving and I shall endeavour to meet her. We cannot expect Mario to attend to these details; he has a duty to the world, which only a man of his genius could perform.'

Mr. Nevin adjusted his pince-nez. 'Very remarkable, Captain Courtier,' he said gravely; 'a very strange and strong personality—Mr. Paul Mario. As my client his wishes are mine, but as a staunch churchman I find myself in disagreement with much of his paper, *Le Bateleur*—in disagreement but re-markable, very.'

Don laughed. 'You are not alone in this respect, Mr. Nevin. He is destined to divide the civilized world into two camps, and already I, who encouraged him to the task, begin to tremble for its outcome.'

II

Flamby arrived at London Bridge Station in a profoundly dejected condition. However happy one may be, London Bridge Station possesses the qualities of a sovereign joy-killer, and would have inclined the thoughts of Mark Tapley toward the darker things of life; but to Flamby, alone in a world which she did not expect to find sympathetic, it seemed a particularly hopeless place. She was dressed in black, and black did not suit her, and all the wisdom of your old philosophers must fail to solace a woman who knows that she is not looking her best.

Her worldly belongings were contained in a split-cane grip and the wraith of a cabin-trunk, whose substance had belonged to her father; her available capital was stuffed in a small leather purse. When the train with a final weary snort ceased its struggles and rested beside the platform, that murk so characteristic of London draped the grimy structure of the station, and a fine drizzle was falling. London had endued no holiday garments to greet Flamby, but, homely fashion, had elected to receive her in its everyday winter guise. A pathetic little figure, she stepped out of the carriage. Something in the contrast between this joyless gloom and the sun-gay hills she had known and loved brought a sudden mist before Flamby's eyes, so that she remained unaware of the presence of a certain genial officer until a voice which was vaguely familiar said: 'Your train was late, Miss Duveen.'

Flamby started, stared, and found Donald Courtier standing smiling at her. Although she had seen him only once before she knew him immediately because she had often studied the photograph which was inside the famous silver cigarette-case. The mistiness of vision troubled her anew as she held out her black-gloved hand. 'Oh,' she said huskily, 'how good of you.'

The last word was almost inaudible, and whilst Don grasped her hand between both his own and pressed it reassuringly, Flamby stared through the mist at three golden stars oil the left shoulder of his topcoat.

'Now,' cried Don cheerily, 'what about our baggage?'

'There's only one old trunk,' said Flamby, 'except this funny thing.'

'Give me the funny thing,' replied Don briskly, 'and here is a comic porter who will dig out the trunk. Porter!'

Linking his left arm in Flamby's right, Don, taking up the cane grip, moved along the platform in the direction of the guard's van, which was apparently laden with an incredible number of empty and resonant milk cans. The porter whom he had hailed, a morbid spirit who might suitably have posed for Coleridge's Ancient Mariner, approached regretfully.

' 'Ow many?' he inquired. 'Got the ticket?'

He did not disguise his hopes that it might prove to be lost, but they were shattered when the luggage ticket was produced from Flamby's black glove, and in due course the antique cabin-trunk made its appearance. That it was an authentic relic of Duveen's earlier days was testified by the faded labels, which still clung to it and which presented an illustrated itinerary of travels extending from Paris to New Orleans, Moscow to Shanghai. The new label, 'London Bridge,' offered a shocking anti-climax. Trundled by the regretful porter the grip and the trunk were borne out into the drizzle, Don and Flamby following; a taxi-cab was found, and Don gave the address of The Hostel. Then, allowing Flamby no time for comment, he began talking at once about the place for which they were bound.

'Mr Nevin selected The Hostel as an ideal spot,' he said, 'where you would be free from interference and able to live your own life. He was influenced, too, by the fact that I have an aunt living there, a Mrs. Chumley, one of the most delightful old souls you could wish to meet.'

Flamby was watching him all the time, and presently she spoke. 'Are you quite sure, Captain Courtier, that the money from the War Office will be enough to pay for all this?'

Don waved his hand carelessly. 'Ample,' he declared. 'The idea of The Hostel, which was founded by Lady Something-or-other, is to afford a residence for folks placed just as you are; not overburdened with means—you see? Of course, some of the tenants are queer fish, and as respectable as those dear old ladies who live amongst the ghosts at Hampton Court. But there are a number of women writers and students, and so forth: you will be quite at home in no time.'

Flamby glanced down at the black dress, which she had made, and had made tastefully and well, but which to its critical creator looked painfully unfinished. 'I feel a freak,' she said. 'Dad didn't believe in mourning, but they would have burned me alive at Lower Gharleswood if I hadn't gone into black. Do you believe in mourning?'

'Well,' replied Don, 'to me it seems essentially a concession to popular opinion. I must admit that it strikes me as an advertisement of grief and about on a par with the wailing of the East. I don't see why we should go about inviting the world to weep. Our sorrows are our own affairs, after all, like our joys. We might quite as reasonably dress in white when a son and heir is born to us.'

'Oh, I'm so glad you think so,' said Flamby, and her voice was rather tremulous. 'I loved mother more than anything in the world, but I hate to be reminded that she is dead by everybody who looks at me.'

Don grasped her hand and tucked it confidently under his arm. 'Your father was a wise man. Never be ashamed of following his advice, Flamby. May I call you Flamby? You seem so very grown-up, with your hair all tucked away under that black hat.'

'I'm nearly eighteen, but I should hate you to call me Miss Duveen. Nobody ever calls me Miss Duveen, except people who don't like me.'

'They must be very few.'

'Not so few,' said Flamby thoughtfully. 'I think it's my hair that does it.'

'That makes people dislike you?'

'Yes. Other women hate my hair.'

'That *is* a compliment, Flamby.'

'But isn't it horrible? Women are nasty. I wish I were a man.'

Don laughed loudly, squeezing Flamby's hand more firmly under his arm. 'You would have made a deuce of a boy,' he said. 'I wonder if we should have been friends.'

'I don't think so,' replied Flamby pensively.

'Eh!' cried Don, turning to her—'why not?'

'Well, you treat women so kindly, and if I were a man I should treat them so differently.'

'How do you know that I treat women kindly?'

'You are very kind to me.'

'Ha!' laughed Don. 'You call yourself a woman? Why you are only a kid!'

'But I'm a wise kid,' replied Flamby saucily, the old elfin light in her eyes. 'I know what beasts women are to one another, and I often hate myself because I'm a little beast, too.'

'I don't believe it.'

THE ORCHARD OF TEARS

'That's because you are one of those nice men who deserve to know better.'

Don leaned back in the cab and laughed until the tears came to his eyes. He had encouraged this conversation with the purpose of diverting Flamby's mind from her sorrow, and he was glad to have succeeded so well. 'Do men hate you, too,' he asked.

'No, I get on much better with men. There are some fearful rotters, of course, but most men are honest enough if you are honest with them.'

'*Honi soit qui mal y pense,*' murmured Don, slowly recovering from his fit of laughter.

'*Ipsissima verba,*' said Flamby.

Don, who was drying his eyes, turned slowly and regarded her. Flamby blushed rosily.

'What did you say?' asked Don.

'Nothing. I was thinking out loud.'

'Do you habitually think in Latin?'

'No. It was just a trick of dad's. I wish you could have heard him swear in Latin.'

Don's eyes began to sparkle again. 'No doubt I should have found the experience of great educational value,' he said; 'but did he often swear in Latin?'

'Not often; only when he was *very* drunk.'

'What was his favourite tongue when he was merely moderately so?'

Flamby's expression underwent a faint change, and looking down she bit her under-lip. Instantly Don saw that he had wounded her, and he cursed the clumsiness, of which Paul could never have been guilty, that had led him to touch this girl's acute sensibilities. She was bewildering, of course, and he realized that he must step warily in future. He reached across and grasped her other hand hard. 'Please forgive me,' he said. 'No man had better reason for loving your father than I.'

Flamby looked up at him doubtfully, read sincerity in the grey eyes, and smiled again at once. '*He* wouldn't have minded a bit,' she explained, 'but I'm only a woman after all, and women are daft.'

'I cannot allow you to be a woman yet, Flamby. You are only a girl, and I want you to think of me—'

Flamby's pretty lips assumed a mischievous curve and a tiny dimple appeared in her cheek. 'Don't say as a big brother,' she cried, 'or you will make

81

me feel like a penny novelette!'

'I cannot believe that you ever read a penny novelette.'

'No; I didn't. But mother read them, and dad used to tear pages out to light his pipe before mother had finished. Then she would explain the plot to me up to the torn pages, and we would try to work out what had happened to the girl in the missing parts.'

'A delightful literary exercise. And was the principal character always a girl?'

'Always a girl—yes; a poor girl cast upon the world; very often a poor governess.'

'And she had two suitors.'

'Yes. Sometimes three. She seemed inclined to marry the wrong one, but mother always read the end first to make sure it came out all right. I never knew one that didn't.'

'No; it would have been too daring for publication. So your mother read these stories? Romance is indeed a hardy shrub.'

The cab drew up before the door of The Hostel, a low, half-timbered building upon Jacobean lines which closely resembled an old coaching inn. The windows looking out upon the flower-bordered lawn had leaded panes, the gabled roof was red-tiled, and over the arched entrance admitting one to the rectangular courtyard around which The Hostel was constructed hung a wrought-iron lamp of delightfully mediFval appearance.

Don opened the gate and walked beside Flamby under the arch and into the courtyard. Here the resemblance to an inn grew even more marked. A gallery surrounded the courtyard and upon it opened the doors of numerous suites situated upon the upper floor. There was a tiny rock garden, too, and altogether the place had a charming old-world atmosphere that was attractive and homely. The brasswork of the many doors was brightly polished, and all the visible appointments of the miniature suites spoke of refined good taste.

'It's very quiet,' said Flamby.

'Yes. You see most of the people who live here are out during the day.'

'Please where do I live?'

'This way,' cried Don cheerily, conducting her up the tiled steps to the gallery. 'Number twenty-three.'

His good cheer was infectious, and Flamby found herself to be succumbing to a sort of pleasant excitement as she passed along by the rows of well-groomed doors, each of which bore a number and a neat name-plate. Some of the quaint leaded lattices were open, revealing vases of flowers upon the ledges within, and the tiny casement curtains afforded an index to the characters of the various occupants, which made quite fascinating study. There was Mrs. Lawrence Pooney, whose curtains were wedgwood blue with a cream border; Miss Hook, whose curtains were plain dark green; Miss Aldrington Beech, whose curtains were lemon coloured with a Chinese pattern; and Mrs. Marion de Lisle, whose curtains were of the hue of the passion flower.

The door of Number 23 proved to be open, and Flamby, passing in, stood looking around her and trying to realize that this was the stage upon which the next act of her life story should be played. She found herself in a rather small rectangular room, lighted by one large casement window and a smaller latticed one, both of them overlooking the courtyard. The woodwork was oaken and the walls were distempered a discreet and restful shade of blue. There were a central electric fitting and another for a reading-lamp, a fireplace of the latest slow-combustion pattern and a door communicating with an inner chamber.

'Oh!' cried Flamby. 'What a dear little place!'

Don, who had been watching her anxiously, saw that she was really delighted, and he entered into the spirit of the thing immediately. 'I think it is simply terrific,' he said. 'I have often envied the Aunt her abode and wished I were an eligible spinster or widow. You have not seen the inner sanctuary yet; it is delightfully like a state-room.'

Flamby passed through the doorway into the bedroom, which indeed was not much larger than a steamer cabin and was fitted with all those space-saving devices which one finds at sea; a bureau that was really a wash-basin, and a hidden wardrobe.

'There is a communal kitchen,' explained Don, 'with up-to-date appointments, also a general laundry, and there are bathrooms on both floors. I don't mean perpendicular bathrooms, so I should perhaps have said on either floor. In that cunning little alcove in the sitting-room is a small gas-stove, so that you will have no occasion to visit the kitchen unless you are preparing a banquet. You enjoy the use of the telephone, which is in the reading-room over the main entrance—and what more could one desire?'

'It's just great,' declared Flamby, 'and I can never hope to thank you for being so good to me. But I am wondering how I am going to afford it.'

'My dear Flamby, the rent of this retreat is astoundingly modest. You will use very little coal, electric and gas meters are of the penny-in-the-slot variety immortalized in song and story by Little Tich, and there you are.'

'I was thinking about the furniture,' said Flamby.

'Eh!' cried Don—'furniture? Yes, of course; upon more mature consideration I perceive distinctly that some few items of that kind will be indispensable. Furniture. Quite so.'

'You hadn't thought of that?'

'No—I admit it had slipped my memory. The question of furniture does not bulk largely in the mind of one used to billeting troops, but of course it must be attended to. Now, how about the furniture of What's-the-name Cottage?'

Flamby shook her head. 'We had hardly any. Dad used to make things out of orange boxes; he was very clever at it. He didn't like real furniture. As fast as poor mother saved up and bought some he broke it, so after a while she stopped. I've brought the clock.'

'Ah!' cried Don gaily—'the clock. Good. That's a start. You will at least know at what time to rise in the morning.'

'I shall,' agreed Flamby—'from the floor!'

The fascinating dimple reappeared hi her cheek, and she burst into peals of most musical laughter. Don laughed, too; so that presently they became quite breathless but perfectly happy.

III

'I vote,' said Don, 'that we consult the Aunt. She resides at Number Nineteen on this floor, and her guidance in such a matter as furnishing would be experienced and reliable.'

'Right-oh,' replied Flamby buoyantly. 'I have a little money saved up.'

'Don't worry about money. The pension has been finally settled between Mr. Nevin and the Government people, and it dates from the time—'

'Of dad's death? But mother used to draw that.'

'I am speaking of the special pension,' explained Don hurriedly, as they walked along the gallery, 'which Mr. Nevin has been trying to arrange. This ante-dates, and the first sum will be quite a substantial one; ample for the purpose of furnishing. Here is the Aunt's.'

Pausing before a door numbered 19, and bearing a brass plate inscribed 'Mrs. Chumley,' Don pressed the bell. Whilst they waited, Flamby studied the Aunt's curtains (which were snowy white) with critical eyes, and tried to make up her mind whether she liked or disliked the sound of 'Mrs. Chumley.'

'The Aunt is apparently not at home,' said Don, as no one responded to the ringing. 'Let us return to Number 23 and summon Reuben, who will possibly know where she has gone.'

Accordingly they returned to the empty suite and rang a bell which summoned the janitor. Following a brief interval came a sound resembling that of a drinking horse, and there entered a red-whiskered old man with a neatly pimpled nose, introducing an odour of rum. He was a small man, but he wore a large green apron, and he touched the brim of his bowler hat very respectfully.

'Excuse me breathin' 'eavy, sir,' he said, 'but it's the *hahsma*. The place is hall ready for the young madam, sir, to move 'er furniture in, and Mrs. Chumley she's in the readin'-room.'

'Ah, very good, Reuben,' replied Don. 'Will you get the trunk and basket in from the taxi, and you might pay the man. The fare was four and something-or-other. Here are two half-crowns and sixpence.'

'Yes, sir.' responded Reuben; 'and what time am I to expect the other things?'

'Miss Duveen is not quite sure, Reuben, when they will arrive. As a matter of fact, she has several purchases to make. But probably the bulk of it will arrive tomorrow afternoon.'

'Yes, sir,' said Reuben, and departed respiring noisily. As he made his exit Flamby carefully closed the door, and—'Oh,' she cried, 'what a funny old man! Whatever did he mean by *hahsma?*'

'I have been struggling with the same problem,' declared Don, 'and I have come to the conclusion that he referred to asthma.'

'Oh,' said Flamby breathlessly. 'I hope he won't mind me laughing at him.'

'I am sure he won't. He is a genial soul and generally liked in spite of his spirituous aroma. Now for the Aunt.'

They walked around two angles of the gallery and entered a large room, the windows of which overlooked the front lawn. It was furnished cosily as a library, and a cheerful fire burned in the big open grate. From the centre window an excellent view might be obtained of Reuben struggling with the cabin-trunk, which the placid taxi-driver had unstrapped and lowered on to the janitor's shoulders without vacating his seat.

'I hope he won't break the clock,' said Flamby, *sotto voce.* She turned as Don went up to a little table at which a round old lady, the only occupant of the room, was seated writing. This old lady had a very round red face and very round wide-open surprised blue eyes. Her figure was round, too; she was quite remarkably circular.

'Ha, the Aunt!' cried Don, placing his hands affectionately upon her plump shoulders. 'Here is our country squirrel come to town.'

Mrs. Chumley laid down her pen and turned the surprised eyes upon Don. Being met with a smile, she smiled in response—and her smile was oddly like that of her nephew. Flamby knew in a moment that Mrs. Chumley was a sweet old lady, and that hers was one of those rare natures whose possessors see ill in no one, but good in all.

'Dear me,' said Mrs. Chumley, in a surprised silvery voice, a voice peculiarly restful and soothing, 'it is Don.' She stood up. 'Yes, it is Don, and this is Flamby. Come here, dear, and let me look at you.'

Flamby advanced swiftly, holding out her hand, which Mrs. Chumley took, and the other as well, drawing her close and kissing her on the cheek in the simple, natural manner of a mother. Then Mrs. Chumley held her at arms' length, surveying her, and began to muse aloud.

'She is very pretty, Don,' she said. 'You told me she was pretty, I remember. She is a sweet little girl, but I don't think black suits her. Do you think black suits her?'

'Any old thing suits her,' replied Don, 'but she looks a picture in white.'

'Quite agree, Don, she would. Couldn't you dress in white, dear?'

'If nobody thought it too awful I would. Dad never believed in mourning.'

'Quite agree. Most peculiar that I should agree with him, but I do. Don does not believe in mourning, either. I should be most annoyed if he wore mourning. Was your mother pretty? Don't tell me if it makes you cry. What beautiful hair you have. Hasn't she beautiful hair, Don? May I take your hat off, dear?'

'Of course,' said Flamby, taking off her hat immediately, whereupon the mop of unruly hair all coppery waves and gold-flecked foam came tumbling about her face.

'Dear me,' continued Mrs. Chumley, whilst Don stood behind her watching the scene amusedly, 'it *is* remarkable hair.' Indeed the sight of

Flamby's hair seemed almost to have stupefied her. 'She is really very pretty. I like you awfully, dear. I am glad you are going to live near me. What did you call her, Don?'

'What did I call her, Aunt?'

'When you first came in. Oh, yes—a squirrel.'

She placed her arm around Flamby and gave her a little hug. 'Quite agree; she *is* a squirrel. You are a country squirrel, dear. Do you mind?'

'Of course not,' said Flamby, laughing. 'You couldn't pay me a nicer compliment.'

'No,' replied Mrs. Chumley, lapsing into thoughtful mood. 'I suppose I couldn't. Squirrels are very pretty. I am afraid I was never like a squirrel. How many inches are you round the waist?'

'I don't know. About twenty,' replied Flamby, suddenly stricken with shyness; but I'm only little.'

'Are you little, dear? I should not have called you little. You are taller than I am.'

Since Mrs. Chumley was far from tall, the criterion was peculiar, but Flamby accepted it without demur. 'I'm wearing high heels.' she said. 'I am no taller than you, really.'

'I should have thought you were, dear. I am glad you wear high heels. They are so smart. It's a mistake to wear low heels. Men hate them. Don't you think men hate them, Don?'

'The consensus of modern masculine opinion probably admits distaste for flat-heeled womanhood, in spite of classic tradition.'

'Dear me, that might be Paul Mario. Do you like Paul Mario, dear?'—turning again to Flamby and repeating the little hug.

Flamby lowered her head quickly. 'Yes.' she replied.

'I thought you would. He's so handsome. Don't you think him handsome?'

'Yes.'

'He is astonishingly clever, too. Everybody is talking about what they call his New Gospel. Do you believe in his New Gospel, dear?'

'I don't know what it is.'

'I'm not quite sure that I do. What is his New Gospel, Don?'

'That he alone can explain, Aunt. But it is going to stir up the world. Paul is a genius—the only true genius of the age.'

'Quite agree. I don't know that it isn't just as well. Don't you think it may be just as well, dear?'

'I don't know,' said Flamby, looking up slowly.

'I'm not quite sure that I do. Has your furniture arrived, dear?'

'Not yet, Aunt,' replied Don on Flamby's behalf. 'Most of it will have to be purchased, and I thought you might give Flamby some sort of a notion what to buy. Then we could trot off up town and get things.'

'How delightful. I should have loved to join you, but I have promised to lunch with Mrs. Pooney, and I couldn't disappoint her. She is downstairs now, cooking a chicken. Some one sent her a chicken. Wasn't that nice?'

'Very decent of some one. I hope it is a tender chicken. And now, Aunt, could Flamby take a peep at your place and perhaps make a sort of list. Some of the things we could get today, and perhaps tomorrow you could run along with her and complete the purchases.'

'I should love it. Dear me!' Into the round blue eyes came suddenly tears of laughter, and Mrs. Chumley became convulsed with silent merriment, glancing helplessly from Don to Flamby. This merriment was contagious; so that ere long all three were behaving quite ridiculously.

'Whatever is the Aunt laughing about?' inquired Don.

'Dear me!' gasped Mrs. Chumley, struggling to regain composure— 'poor child! Of course you have nowhere to sleep tonight. How ridiculous—a squirrel without a nest.' She hugged Flamby affectionately. 'You will stay with me, dear, won't you?'

'Oh, but really—may I? Have you room?'

'Certainly, dear. Friends often stay with me. I have a queer thing in my sitting-room that looks like a bookcase, but it is really a bed. You can stay with me just as long as you like. There is no hurry to get your own place ready, is there? There isn't any hurry, is there, Don?'

'No particular hurry, Aunt. But, naturally, Flamby will get things in order as soon as possible.'

'Thank you so much,' said Flamby, faint traces of mist disturbing her sight.

'Not at all, dear. I'm glad. The longer you stay the gladder I shall be. What an absurd word—gladder. There is something wrong about it, surely, Don?'

'More glad would perhaps be preferable, Aunt.'

Mrs. Chumley immediately succumbed to silent merriment for a time. 'How absurd!' she said presently. 'Gladder! I don't believe there is such a word in the dictionary. Do you believe there is such a word in the dictionary, dear?'

'I don't think there is,' replied Flamby.

'No, I expect there isn't. I don't know that it may not be just as well. Come along, dear. You can come, too, if you like, Don, or you might prefer to look at your own drawings in the *Courier*. If *I* drew I should love to look at my own drawings. You may smoke here, Don, of course. A number of the residents smoke. Do you smoke, Flamby?'

'No, but I think I should like it.'

'Quite agree. It *is* soothing. You will wait here, then, Don? Come along, dear.'

IV

An hour later when Flamby and Don came out of The Hostel, the rain clouds were breaking, and sunlight—somewhat feeble, but sunlight withal—was seeking bravely to disperse the gloom. Flamby was conscious of an altered outlook; the world after all was not utterly grey; such was the healing influence of a sympathetic soul.

'You know,' said Don, as they passed through the gateway, 'I am delighted with the way you have taken to the dear old Aunt. She is so often misunderstood and it makes me writhe to see people laugh at her—unkindly, I mean. Of course her method of conversation is ridiculously funny, I know; but a woman who can suffer the misfortunes which have befallen the Aunt and come out with the heart of a child is worth studying, I think. Personally, I always feel a lot better after a chat with her. She is a perfect well of sympathy.'

'I think she is the sweetest woman I have ever met,' declared Flamby earnestly. 'How could anyone help loving her?'

'People don't or won't understand her, you see, and misunderstanding is the mother of intolerance. Ah! there is a taxi on the rank.'

'Oh,' cried Flamby quickly— 'please don't get another cab for me.'

'Eh? No cab?'

'I cannot afford it and I could not think of allowing you to pay for everything.'

'Now, let us have a thorough understanding, Flamby,' said Don, standing facing her, that sunny rejuvenating smile making his tanned face look almost boyish. 'You remember what I said on the subject of misunderstanding?

Listen, then: I am on leave and my money is burning a hole in my pocket; money always does. If I had a sister—I have but she is married and lives at Harrogate—I should ask her to take pity upon me and spend a few days in my company. An exchange of views with some nice girl who understands things is imperative after one has been out of touch with everything feminine for months and months. It is a natural desire which must be satisfied, otherwise it leads a man to resort to desperate measures in the quest for sympathy. Because of your father you are more to me than a sister, Flamby, and if you will consent to my treating you as one you will be performing an act of charity above price. The Aunt quite understands and approves. Isn't that good enough?'

Flamby met his gaze honestly and was satisfied. 'Yes,' she replied. 'Myself and what is mine to you and yours is now converted.' The end of the quotation was almost inaudible, for it had leapt from Flamby's tongue unbidden. The idea that Don might suspect her of seeking to impress him with her learning was hateful to her. But Don on the contrary was quite frankly delighted.

'Hullo!' he cried—'is that Portia?'

'Yes, but please don't take any notice if I say funny things. I don't mean to. Dad loved *The Merchant of Venice*, and I know quite a lot of lines by heart.'

'How perfectly delightful to meet a girl who wears neither sensible boots nor spectacles but who appreciates Shakespeare! Lud! I thought such treasures were mythical. Flamby, I have a great idea. If you love Portia you will love Ellen Terry. I suppose her Portia is no more than a memory of the old Lyceum days, but it is a golden memory, Flamby. Ellen Terry is at the Coliseum. Shall we go tonight? Perhaps the Aunt would join us.'

'Oh!' said Flamby, her eyes alight with excitement; but the one word was sufficient.

'Right!' cried Don. 'Now for Liberty's.'

They entered the cab, and as it moved off, 'What is Liberty's?' asked Flamby.

'The place for rummy furniture,' explained Don.' Nobody else could possibly provide the tilings for your den. The Aunt once had a cottage in Devon furnished by Liberty and it was the most perfect gem of a cottage one could imagine.'

'Was she very well off once?'

'The Aunt? Why the dear old lady ought to be worth thousands. Her husband left her no end of money and property. She has travelled nearly all over the civilized world, Flamby, and now is tied to that one tiny room at The Hostel.'

'But how is it? Did she lose her money?'

'She gave it away and let everybody rob her. The world unfortunately is full of Dick Turpins and Jack Sheppards, not to mention their lady friends.'

'Ah,' said Flamby and sat silent for some time studying the panorama of the busy London streets. 'Is Liberty's dear?' she inquired presently.

'Not at all; most reasonable.'

'I'm glad,' replied Flamby. 'I have got seven pounds ten saved. Will that be enough?'

Don held his breath. Flamby's extraordinary erudition and inherent cleverness had not prepared him for this childish ignorance of the value of money. But he realized immediately that it was no more than natural after all and that he might have anticipated it; and secretly he was delighted because of the opportunity which it offered him of repaying in part, or of trying to repay, the debt which he owed to Michael Duveen. Moreover he had found that to give pleasure to Flamby was a gracious task.

'It may not cover everything,' he said casually, 'but the sum held by Mr. Nevin will more than do so. Think no more about it. I will see that your expenditures do not exceed your means.'

They alighted near that window of Messrs. Liberty's which is devoted to the display of velvet robes—of those simple, unadorned creations which Golders Green may view unmoved but which stir the aesthetic soul of Chelsea. In the centre of the window, cunningly draped before an oak-panelled background, hung a dress of grey velvet which was the apogee and culmination of Flamby's dreams. For not all the precepts of the Painted Portico can quench in the female bosom woman's innate love of adornment. Assuredly Eve wore flowers in her hair.

'Oh,' whispered Flamby, 'do you think it is very dear?'

Don having paid the cabman, had joined her where she stood. 'Which one?' he inquired with masculine innocence.

'The grey one. There is nothing on it at all. I have seen dresses in Dale's at home with yards of embroidery that were only four pounds.'

'I don't suppose so,' said Don cheerfully. 'Let us go in and try it on. *You* try it on, I mean.'

'Oh, I daren't! I didn't dream of *buying* it,' cried Flamby, flushing hotly.

'I was only admiring it.'

'And because you admire it you don't dream of buying it? That is odd. And surely grey is what is known as "half-mourning" too, is it not? Absolutely correct form.'

'But it may be frightfully dear. I will ask the price when Mrs. Chumley is with me.' Flamby was weakening.

Don grasped her firmly by the arm and led her vastly perturbed into the shop, where a smiling saleswoman accosted them. 'This lady wishes to see the grey gown you have in the window,' he said. He drew the woman aside and added, 'Don't tell her the price! You understand? If she insists upon knowing take your cue from me.' He could say no more as Flamby had drawn near.

'How much is it?' she inquired naïvely.

'I don't know yet,' replied Don. 'Won't you look at it first?'

'The dress is a model, madam,' said the puzzled modiste. 'Probably we should have to alter it to fit you.'

'Would that be extra?' asked Flamby.

'Only a trifle,' Don assured her, 'if you really like it.'

'How much is it, please?' Flamby asked.

Don, standing just behind her became troubled with a tickling in the throat, and the woman, hesitating, looked up and detected his urgent glance. He raised three fingers furtively. She could scarcely conceal her amazement, but an emphatic nod from Don left her in no doubt respecting his meaning.

'I believe it is—three guineas, madam,' she replied in a forced and unnatural voice. She was wondering what would become of her if this very eccentric officer played her false.

Flamby turned thoughtfully to Don. 'That's expensive, isn't it?' she said.

The saleswoman's amazement increased; words failed her entirely, and to cover her embarrassment she opened the screen at the back of the window and took out the grey gown. Flamby's eyes sparkled.

'But isn't it sweet,' she whispered. 'Where do I go to try it on?'

'This way, madam,' said the woman, darting an imploring glance at Don to which he was unable to respond as Flamby was looking in his direction.

Flamby disappeared into a fitting-room and Don sat down to consider the question of how far he could hope to pursue his plot without being unmasked.

THE ORCHARD OF TEARS

He lighted a cigarette and gave himself up to reflection on the point. When presently Flamby came out, radiant, followed by the troubled attendant carrying the grey gown, he was prepared for her.

'I'm going to have it!' she said. 'Am I frightfully extravagant?'

'Not at all,' Don assured her; and as she took out her purse. 'No,' he added, 'you must not pay cash, Flamby. It would confuse Nevin's books. I will write a cheque and charge it to your account together with the other purchases.'

He withdrew with the saleswoman, leaving Flamby seated looking at the velvet frock draped across a chair. Having proceeded to a discreet distance—'What is the price of the dress, please?' he asked.

'With the alterations which madam requires, eighteen guineas, sir.'

'I will give you a draft on Uncle Cox,' replied Don, taking out his cheque-book and fountain-pen. 'You must feel rather bewildered, but the fact of the matter is that the lady chances to be the orphan of a very dear friend, and coming from a country place she has no idea of the cost of things. I would not disillusion her for the world, just yet. Will you please make a note to send the gown to Miss Duveen at this address.' He laid one of his aunt's cards upon the table. 'But—an important point—enclose no receipt; nothing that would afford a clue to the price. Will you remember?'

'I shall remember,' said the saleswoman, greatly relieved and beginning to smile once more.

So the quaint comedy of deception began and so it proceeded right merrily; for passing on to the furniture department, Don took the man aside and succeeded, although not without difficulty in this case, in making him an accomplice. As a result of the conspiracy Flamby purchased an exquisite little dressing-table of silver-maple (for thirty-five shillings), a large Axminster carpet and a Persian rug (three pounds, fifteen shillings), a miniature Jacobean oak suite (six guineas), a quaint bureau and bookcase (fifty shillings), and a perfect stack of cushions (at prices varying from half-a-crown to three shillings and elevenpence-three-farthings, or, in technical terminology, 'three-and-eleven-three'). The man became infected with the quixotic spirit of the affair and revealed himself in his true colours as a hierophant of the higher mysteries. Producing secret keys, he exhibited those arcana of the inner rooms which apparently are not for sale but which are kept solely for the purpose of dazzling the imagination; jade Buddahs, contemplative and priceless, locked in wonderful Burmese cabinets, strange ornaments of brass and perfume-burners from India, mandarin robes of peacock-blue, and tiny caskets of that violet lacquering which is one of the lost arts of Japan.

With some few items of glassware, vases and pictures purchased else-where, Flamby's expenditure amounted to more than twenty-five pounds, at which staggering total she stared in dismay. 'Shall I really be able to pay it?' she asked.

'My dear Flamby, you have only just begun. The really essential things you will be able to buy when the Aunt is with you. I am instructing all the shops with which you may have occasion to do business to send accounts to Nevin. He will let you know quickly enough if you overstep the margin.'

'How much money, for goodness sake, is the Government paying?'

'I don't know exactly, but in addition to the regular allowance and ar-rears there is a gratuity of something over a hundred pounds to your account.'

They were crossing Regent Street, and Flamby narrowly escaped being run over—but the pavement gained in safety, '—A hundred pounds!' she ex-claimed—'*I* have a hundred pounds!'

'Roughly,' said Don, smiling and taking her arm. 'Then there are the weekly instalments, of course. Oh, you have nothing to worry about, Flamby. Furthermore it will not be very long before you find a market for your work and then you will be independent of State aid.'

In truth, now that he was hopelessly enmeshed in his own net, Don ex-perienced dire misgivings, wondering what Flamby would say, wondering what Flamby would do, when she learned of the conspiracy as she could not fail to learn of it sooner or later. But at the moment he was solely concerned with making her forget her sorrows, and in this he had succeeded. Flamby was radiantly happy and at last could think of the sweet countryside she had left behind without discovering a lump in her throat.

Luncheon in a popular Piccadilly grill-room provided an intensely thrilling experience. Flamby's acute sensibilities and inherent appreciation of the fitness of things rendered her ill at ease, but the gay music of the or-chestra did much to restore her to harmony with herself, and Don's unaf-fected delight in her company did the rest. So in time she forgot the home-made black dress and became fascinated by her novel surroundings and lost in the study of these men and women who belonged to a new, a partly preceived world, but a world into which she had longed to enter. Her per-sonal acquaintance with the ways of modern Babylon was limited to the crowded experiences of a day-visit with her father and mother, a visit eagerly anticipated and never forgotten. Michael Duveen had seemingly never regretted that place in the world which he had chosen to forfeit. He had lived and worked like a labouring man and had taken his pleasures like one. On that momentous day they had visited Westminster Abbey, the Tower Bridge, the Houses of Parliament and Nelson's Monument, had lunched at one of Messrs. Lockhart's establishments, had taken a ride in the Tube and performed a hasty tour of the Zoo, where they had consumed, variously, cups of tea, ginger beer, stale buns and ices. Hyde Park they had viewed from the top of a motor bus and descending from this chariot at London Bridge had caught the train home. In the train Flamby had fallen asleep, utterly exhausted with such a saturnalia, and her parents had eaten sandwiches and partaken of beer from a large bottle which Mrs. Duveen had brought in a sort of carpet-bag. Flamby remembered that she had been aroused from her slumbers by her father, who conceiving a sudden and violent antipathy against both bag and bottle (the latter being empty) had opened the carriage window and hurled them both out on to the line.

It was an odd memory but it brought a cloud of sadness, and Don, quick to detect the shadow, hurried Flamby off to the Coliseum and astounded her by booking a stage box. The Aunt was consulted over the telephone, the Aunt agreed to join the party in the evening, and during the remainder of that eventful afternoon there were all sorts of wonderful sights to be seen; delightful shops unlike any that Flamby had imagined, and an exhibition of watercolours in Bond Street which fired her ambition like a torch set to dry bracken, as Don had designed that it should do. They had tea at a fashionable tea-shop, and Don noted that even within the space of twenty-four hours the number of lovely women had perceptibly diminished. This historic day concluded, then, with dinner at the Carlton and Ellen Terry at the Coliseum. How otherwise an excellent programme was constituted mattered not, but when the red-robed Portia came finally before the curtain and bestowed one of her sweet smiles exclusively upon the enraptured girl, Flamby found that two big tears were trickling down her hot cheeks.

V

And now another figure in the pageant which Iamblichos called 'the indissoluble bonds of Necessity' was about to reappear in his appointed place in response to the call of the unseen Prompter. Hideous are the settings of that pageant today; for where in the glowing pages of Dumas we see D'Artagnan, the gallant Forty-five and many another good friend riding in through the romantic gates of Old Paris, the modern historian finds himself concerned with railway stations which have supplanted those gates of Paris and of London alike. Thus Don entered by the gate of St. Pancras, Flamby by the smoky portal of London Bridge; and, on the following morning, Yvonne Mario stood upon a platform at Victoria awaiting the arrival of the Folkestone boat-train. She attracted considerable attention and excited adverse criticism amongst the other ladies present not only because of her personal charm, but by reason of her dress. She wore a coat of black coney seal trimmed with white fox, and a little cap of the same, and her high-legged boots had white calf tops. Her complexion alone doomed her to the undying enmity of her sex, for the humid morning air had enhanced that clear freshness which quite naturally and properly annoyed every other woman who beheld it.

Several pressmen and photographers mingled with the groups for the party with which Paul had been touring the French and British fronts included at least two other notable personages; and Bassett, Paul's press agent, said to Yvonne: 'You will smile across a million breakfast tables tomorrow morning, Mrs. Mario, and from a thousand cinema screens later in the week.'

Yvonne smiled there and then, a charming little one-sided smile, for she was really a very pretty woman in spite of her reputation as a beauty. 'Modern journalism leaves nothing to the imagination,' she replied.

'And very wisely. So few people have any.'

They paced slowly along the platform. Excepting the porters who leaned against uptilted trucks and stared stolidly up the line, a spirit of furtive unrest had claimed everyone. People who meet trains always look so guilty, avoiding each other's glances and generally behaving as though their presence were a pure accident; periodically consulting the station clock as who should say, 'If this train is not signalled very shortly I must be off. My time is of value.' There is another type, of course, much more rare, who appears at the last moment from some subterranean stairway. He is always running and his glance is wild. As the passengers begin to descend from the train he races along the platform, now and again pausing in his career and standing on tiptoe in order to look over the heads of the people in front of him. To every official he meets he says: 'This train *is* the Folkestone train?' He rarely waits for a reply.

Indeed, at a modern railway station, as of old at the city gates, the fatuity of human aspirations may be studied advantageously. Soldiers were there, at Victoria, hundreds of them, lined up on a distant platform, and they symbolized the spirit of an age which exalts Mechanism to the pinnacle of a deity and which offers itself as a sacrifice upon his iron altars.

The train arrived in due course; cameras and note-books appeared; and people inquired 'Is it Sir Douglas Haig they are expecting?' But presently the initiated spread the news that it was Paul Mario who returned from the Western front, and because his reputation was greater than that of Gabrielle D'Annunzio or Charlie Chaplin, everyone sought to obtain a glimpse of him.

He wore a heavy fur-lined coat, and his eyes were dark with excitement. Surrounded by the other members of the party, like an emperor by his suite, Paul's was the outstanding personality among them all. There was a distinguished French general to bow, courtly, over Yvonne's hand, and a Labour Member to quote Cicero. But it was to Paul that the reporters sought to penetrate and upon Paul that the cameras were focussed. Bassett, who did not believe in thwarting the demands of popularity, induced him to say a few words.

'Gentlemen,' he said, 'I have no impressions to impart. My mind is numbed. I had never hitherto appreciated the genius of Philip Gibbs . . .'

In the car Paul talked exclusively to Jules Thessaly, who had accompanied him upon his tour. Yvonne was silent. When first he had seen her awaiting him upon the platform his eyes had lighted up in that ardent way which she loved, and he had pressed her hands very hard in greeting. But thereafter he had become absorbed again in his giant dreams, and now as they sped through the London streets homeward, he bent forward, one hand resting upon Thessaly's knee, wrapped up in the companionship of his memories.

'That château, Thessaly, holds a secret which if it could be divulged to the world would revolutionize theology.'

'Of what château do you speak?' asked Bassett.

'On my way to the French front I was entertained for a night at a wonderful old château. The devouring war had passed it by, and it stood like a dignified *grand seigneur* looking sorrowfully over the countryside. In order to understand how the sight of the place affected me you must know that as a boy I was several times visited by a certain dream. I last dreamed this dream during the time that I was at Oxford, but I have never forgotten it. I used to find myself in a spacious salon, its appointments and fashion those of Louis

Treize, with ghostly moonlight pouring in at lofty church-like windows and painting distorted shadowgraphs of heraldic devices upon the floor. My costume was that of a Cavalier, and I held a long sword in my hand. I was conscious of pain and great weakness. Creeping stealthily from recess to recess, window to window, I would approach the double doors at the end of the salon. There I would pause, my heart throbbing fiercely, and press my ear to the gaily painted panels. A murmur of conversation would seem to proceed from the room beyond, but forced onward by some urgent necessity, the nature of which I could never recall upon awakening, I would suddenly throw the doors widely open and hurl myself into a small ante-room. A fire of logs blazed in the open hearth, and some six or eight musketeers lounged about the place, hats, baldrics, swords and cloaks lying discarded upon tables, chairs and where not. All sprang to their feet as I entered, and one, a huge red fellow, snatched up his sword and stood before a low door on the right of the room which I sought to approach. We crossed blades . . . and with their metallic clash sounding in my ears I invariably awoke. I have spoken of this to you, Yvonne?'

Paul glanced rapidly at Yvonne, but proceeded immediately without waiting for a reply. 'As Thessaly and I were conducted to our rooms on the night of which I am speaking, I found myself traversing the salon of my dreams!'

'Most extraordinary,' muttered Bassett. 'Nothing about the aspect of the other rooms of the château had struck you as familiar?'

'Nothing; except that I was glad to be there. I cannot make clear to you the almost sorrowful veneration with which I entered the gate. It was like that of a wayward son who returns, broken, to the home upon which he has brought sorrow, to find himself welcomed by his first confessor, old, feeble, lonely, but filled with sweet compassion. I ascribed this emotion to the atmosphere of a stately home abandoned by its owners. But the salon revealed the truth to me. Heavy plush curtains were drawn across the windows, but the flames of three candles in a silver candelabra carried by the servant created just such a half-light as I remembered. I paused, questioning the accuracy of my recollections, but it was all real, unmistakable. We passed through the doorway at the end of the salon—and there was my guardroom! A modern stove had taken the place of the old open hearth, and the furniture was totally different, but I knew the room. The servant crossed before me to a door which I could not recall having noticed in my dream. As he opened it I looked to the right; and where the other door had been before which I had many times crossed swords with the red musketeer I saw a blank wall.'

'It was no more than a very remarkable coincidence after all?' said Bassett.

'On the contrary. I called to the man, a bent old fellow, his face furrowed with age and heavy with care. "Have you been long in the service of the family?" I asked him. His eyes glistened tearfully. "Forty-five years, monsieur," he answered. "Then perhaps you can tell me if there was ever a door opening on the right, yonder, beside that armchair?"

'He stared at me, Bassett, like a man dismayed, and his hand trembled so that spots of grease were shaken from the candles on to the floor. "How can you know of the Duc's door?" he whispered, watching me all the time as if fascinated. "How can *you* know of the Duc's door, monsieur?" His fear, his consternation, were so evident, that I recognized the necessity of reassuring him in order to learn more. Therefore, "I have heard of it, or seen it depicted, somewhere in England," I replied; "but the story associated with it escapes my memory."

'He began to look less frightened as I spoke, and finally, having several times moistened his dry lips, he replied. "It has been walled up for more than two hundred years. It opened upon a staircase leading to the State apartments." "And why was it closed, my friend?" I asked. The old man shrugged his angular shoulders and moved on out of the room. "That I cannot say, monsieur," he answered: "but in the reign of Louis XIII, Henri, second Duc de Montmorency, by whose father this château was built, escaped one night from the apartment in which he had been imprisoned under sentence of death, and attempted to force his way into the presence of the King, then lying in the château. At the foot of those stairs the Duc was mortally wounded by Guitry, Captain of the Bodyguard. . . ."'

During lunch the conversation rarely became general. Bassett talked to Yvonne, bestowing upon her an elderly admiration which was not lacking in a poetry of its own, and Paul exchanged memories with Thessaly. His mental excitement was tremendous, and contagious, but of the three who listened to him Thessaly alone seemed to respond sympathetically. Bassett had never pretended to understand his distinguished client. He was always covertly watching Paul, his fat face wrinkled with perplexity, as though one day he hoped for a revelation by light of which he might grasp the clue to a personality that eluded him entirely.

'That boasted civilization,' said Paul—'the German Kultur—has thrown us back to the earliest savagery of which we hold record. All that education has done for us is to hold the savage in check for a time. He is still there. Spiritually humanity's record is one of retrogression.'

Luncheon over, Paul accompanied Thessaly and Bassett to the latticed gate in the high monastic wall which concealed his house from the road. They walked away together and he stood for a time gazing after them, then returned and went to his study. Yvonne, who had watched him from the dining-room window, heard the study door close. She sat quite still looking across the table at a chair which Paul had occupied, her fair hair a crown about her brow as the wintry sunlight shone in upon it. Chelsea sometimes may seem as quiet as a lonely riverside village, and at the moment which followed the sound of the closing door it seemed to have become so to Yvonne. Only that muted droning which arises from the vast hive of London told of four millions of workers moving intimately about her. The house was perfectly still. Odin, Paul's wolf-hound, tugged at his chain in the garden and whined quayeringly. He had heard Paul arrive and was disappointed because his master had forgotten to pay him a visit. He was angry, too, because he had heard the deep voice of Jules Thessaly; and Odin did not like Jules Thessaly.

A quantity of personal correspondence had accumulated, and Paul proceeded to inspect it. A letter addressed in Don's familiar sprawling hand demanded precedence, and Paul noted with excitement that it bore a Derbyshire postmark. It was dated from the house of one of Don's innumerable cousins, a house of a type for which the Peak district is notable, a manner of ghostly repute. This cheerful homestead was apparently constructed in or adjoining an ancient burial ground, was in fact a converted monastery, and Don dealt in characteristically whimsical fashion with its unpleasant peculiarities.

'One can scarcely expect a house constructed in a graveyard,' he wrote, 'to be otherwise than a haunted house. It is a house especially built for a ghost; it is not a house to which a ghost has come; it is a ghost around whom a house has been built. Erratic manifestations are to be looked for from hitherto free and unfettered spectre who discovers himself to be confined in a residence possibly uncongenial to his taste and to have thrust upon him the society of a family with whose habits and ideals he has nothing in common. . . .'

Finally, Don inquired how the affairs of Flamby were proceeding, and something very like a pang of remorse troubled Paul. The open letter lying before him, he fell into a reverie, arraigning himself before the tribunal of his own conscience. Had his attitude toward Flamby changed? It had done so. What was the nature of the change? His keen personal interest had given place to one impersonal, although sincere in its way. What was the explanation of this? He had enshrined her, set her upon a fairy pedestal, only to learn that she was humanly frail. Had this discovery hurt him? Intensely. How and why? It had shattered him in his omniscience. Yes, that was the unpalatable truth, brought to light at last. Frailty in woman he looked for, and because he knew it to be an offshoot of that Eternal Feminine which is a root-principle of the universe, he condoned. But in Flamby he had seemed to recognize a rare spirit, one loftily above the common traits of her sex, a fit companion for Yvonne; and he had been in error. For long after the finding of those shameful photographs he had failed to recover confidence in himself, and had doubted his fitness to speak as a master who could be blinded by the guile of a girl.

It was, then, offended *amour propre* which had prompted him to hand over to Nevin, his solicitor, this sacred charge entrusted to him by Don? It was. Now he scourged himself remorsefully. If only because her fault was chargeable on one of his own kin he should have striven with might and main to help Flamby. The fact that she was daughter of the man who had saved Don's life at peril of his own redoubled the sanctity of the charge. And how had he acquitted himself of his stewardship? Pitifully. A hot flush rose to his brow, and he hesitated to open a letter from Nevin which also awaited his attention. But he forced himself to the task and read that which completed his humility. Mrs. Duveen had died of heart-failure two months before, whilst Paul had been abroad, and Flamby was an orphan.

'Captain Courtier, who is at present home on leave, has favoured us with direct instructions in the matter,' Nevin continued, 'and has placed a generous credit at our disposal for the purpose of securing suitable apartments for Miss Duveen, and for meeting the cost of her immediate maintenance and fees, together with other incidental disbursements. We have also secured authority to watch her interests in regard to any pension or gratuity to which she may be entitled as a minor and orphan of a non-commissioned officer killed in action. . . .'

In the drawing-room, Yvonne very softly was playing a setting of Edgar Allan Poe's exquisite verses, *To One in Paradise,* and such is the magic of music wedded to poetry that it opened a door in Paul's heart and afforded him a glimpse of his inner self. He had neglected poor little Flamby, and his sensitive mind refused to contemplate her loneliness now that her last friend had been taken from her.

> 'Thou wast all that to me, love,
> For which my soul did pine—
> A green isle in the sea, love,
> A fountain and a shrine,
> All wreathed with fairy fruits and flowers,
> And all the flowers were mine . . .'

Paul rose and quietly entered the drawing-room. Yvonne looked up as he opened the door, and he saw that her eyes were dim. He knelt on a corner of the music-chair and clasped his arms tightly about her shoulders, pressing her cheek against his. As she ceased playing and turned her head he kissed her ardently, holding her fast and watching her with those yearning eyes whose gaze can make a woman's heart beat faster. She leaned back against him, sighing.

'Do you know that that is the first time you have kissed me since you have returned?' she asked.

'Yvonne, forgive me. Don't misunderstand. You never doubt me, do you?'

'Sometimes—I don't seem to matter to you so much as I did.'

Never releasing her he moved around so that they were side by side upon the narrow seat. 'You matter more than anything in the world,' he said. 'You are so near to my heart day and night that I seem to have you always in my arms.' He spoke softly, his lips very close to Yvonne's; her golden hair brushed his forehead. 'You are the music to which I write the words. The memory of your lightest action since the very hour we met I treasure and revere. Without you I am nothing. All I dream and all I hope and dream and hope for you.'

Yvonne ran her white fingers through his hair and looked up into his face. Paul kissed her, laughing happily. 'My darling Yvonne,' he whispered. 'Do I sometimes forget to make love to you? It is only because I feel that you are so sure of me. Do you know that since I left you I have heard your voice like a prayer at twilight, seen your eyes watching me as I slept and found your hair gleaming in many a golden sunset.'

'Of course I don't,' cried Yvonne, with mock severity. 'How can I possibly know what you are thinking when you are hundreds of miles away! I only know that when you come back you forget to kiss me.'

'I don't forget, Yvonne. I think of you a thousand times a day, and every thought is a kiss.'

'Then you have only thought of me twice today,' said Yvonne, standing up and crossing to a Chesterfield. She seated herself, resting her head upon a black cushion and posing deliberately with the confidence of a pretty woman.

'That is a challenge,' replied Paul, 'and I accept it.'

He followed her, but she covered her face with her hands tauntingly, and only resigned her lips after a long struggle. Then they sat silently, very close together, the golden head leaning against the dark one, and ere long Paul's restless mind was at work again.

'Don is on leave, Yvonne,' he said. 'Isn't that fine?'

'Oh, yes,' replied Yvonne, stifling a sigh. 'He called yesterday.'

'He called!' cried Paul, sitting upright excitedly. 'You did not tell me.'

'How could I tell you, Paul? I have not seen you alone until now. Don did not know you were away. A letter came from him two days ago—'

'I know. That was how I learned of his being home.'

'He said he would come this afternoon. Oh—perhaps here he is.'

Yvonne smoothed her skirt and moved to a discreet distance from Paul as a parlourmaid came in. Paul leapt up eagerly.

'Captain Courtier?' he cried to the girl.

'Yes, sir.'

Paul ran out into the hall. Yvonne rose from the Chesterfield and slowly walked back to the piano. She stood for a while idly turning over the pages of music; then, as her husband did not return, she went up to her room. She could hear Paul talking excitedly as she passed the study door.

VI

Don gazed curiously around the large and lofty room. In early Victorian days this apartment had been a drawing-room or salon, wherein crinolined dames and whiskered knights had discoursed exclusively in sparkling epigrams according to certain memoirs in which this salon was frequently mentioned. It had been selected by Paul for a work-room because of its charming outlook upon the secluded little garden with its sundial and irregularly paved paths, and because it was the largest room in the house. Although in a lesser degree than Paul, Don also was responsive to environment, and he found himself endeavouring to analyse the impression made upon his mind by Paul's study.

He had last seen it during the time that Paul, newly returned from Florence, was passing the proofs of his great tragedy, *Francesca of the Lilies*. Then it had been the study of a Cardinal of the Middle Ages or of a mediFval noble devoted to the arts. In what respect did it differ now? The massive table of cedar of Lebanon, figured in ivory and mother o' pearl with the Rape of Proserpine, the work of a pupil of Benvenuto Cellini, remained, as also did the prie-dieu, enriched with silver daisies, which Michelangelo had designed for Margaret of Navarre. The jewelled crucifix was gone, together with the old chain bible and ebony lectern from the Cistercian Monastery at La Trappe. The curious chalice, too, of porphyry starred with beryl, taken at the sack of Panama, and recovered a century later from an inn at Saragossa, had disappeared from its place; and where illuminated missals and monkish books had formerly lain upon the long window seat were works dealing with the war, associated with its causes or arising out of it: Ambassador Gerard to *The Book of Artemas, God the Invisible King* and also *Sprach Zarathustra*. Even the magnificent *Book of Hours* bearing the monogram of Diana of Poictiers and bound by Aldo Manuzio, Byzantine fashion, in carved ivory wreathed about with gold filigree and studded with fourteen precious stones, was hidden.

Those tapestries for which Paul had paid so extravagant a price at the sale of the Mayence heirlooms were stripped from the wall, and gone were the Damascus sword, the lance-head and black armour of Godfrey de Bouillon. A definite note was lacking; the stage was in a state of transition, and not yet set for the new drama.

Paul came in, hands extended in cordial welcome. 'Good old Don!' he cried. 'On Friday I was within twenty miles of the part of the line where I imagined you to be, but was unable to get across.'

'How fortunate. You would have had a vain journey, Paul. I was in Derbyshire on Friday. I would have met you this morning, but I knew you would prefer to be *tLte-B-tLte* with Yvonne.'

'My dear fellow, Bassett ordained it otherwise. I found myself surrounded by pressmen and picture people. Of course, he disclaimed responsibility as usual, but I could read his guilt in his eyes. He persists in "booming"

me as though I were an operatic nightingale with a poor voice or a variety comedian who was not funny.'

'Yvonne told you I had called?'

'Yes. You did not know I was away?'

'My knowledge of your movements up to the time that I left France was
based upon those two or three brief communications, partially undecipher-
able, with which you have favoured me during the past six months. I read
your paper, *Le Bateleur,* in the *Review.* Everybody has read it. Paul, you have
created a bigger sensation with those five or six thousand words than
Hindenburg can create with an output of five or six thousand lives!'

'It was designed to pave the way, Don. You think it has succeeded?'

'Succeeded! You have stirred up the religious world from Little Bethel to
St. Peter's.' Don dropped into an arm-chair and began to load his pipe from
the MycenFan vase. 'Some of your facts are startlingly novel. For instance,
where on earth did you get hold of that idea about the initiation of Christ by
the Essenes at Lake Moeris in Egypt?'

Paul's expression grew wrapt and introspective. 'From material in the
possession of Jules Thessaly,' he replied. 'In a tomb near the Pyramid of
Hawara in the Egyptian Fayfm was found the sarcophagus of one Menahîm,
chief of the Order of the Essenes, who were established near Lake Moeris.
Menahîm's period of office dated from the year 18 B.C. to the year of his
death in the reign of Caligula, and amid the dust of his bones was found the
Golden Chalice of Initiation. I cannot hope to make clear to you without a
very lengthy explanation how the fact dawned upon my mind that
Jehoshoua of Nazareth, son of Joseph, became an initiate, but the significance of these dates must be evident. When you see the Chalice you will understand.'

'Had it been found in Renan's time what a different *Vie de Christ* we
should have had.'

'Possibly. Renan's *Vie de Christ* is an exquisite evasion, a jewelled confession of failure. But there are equally wonderful things at Thessaly's house,
Don. You must come there with me.'

'I shall do so without fail. It appears to me, Paul, that you have materi-
ally altered your original plan. You have abandoned the idea of casting your
book in the form of a romance?'

'I have—yes. The purely romantic appeal may be dispensed with, I think,
in this case. *Zarathustra* has entered the blood of the German people like a vi-

rus from a hypodermic needle. I do not hesitate to accept its lesson. Where I desire to cite instances of illustrative human lives they will be strictly biographical but anonymous.'

'You hope to succeed where Maeterlinck failed.'

'Maeterlinck thinks as a poet and only fails when he writes as a philosopher. Don, I wish I could have you beside me in my hours of doubt. Thessaly is inspiring, but his influence is sheerly intellectual. You have the trick of harmonizing all that was discordant within myself. I see my work as a moving pageant and every figure is in its appointed place. I realize that all the knowledge of the world means nothing beside one short human existence. Upon the Ogam tablets, the Assyrian cylinders, the Egyptian monuments is written a wisdom perhaps greater than ours, but it is cold, like the stone that bears it; within ourselves it lives—all that knowledge, that universe of truth. What do the Egyptologists know of the message of Egypt? I have stood upon the summit of the Great Pyramid and have watched its shadow steal out and out touching the distant lands with its sceptre, claiming Egypt for its own; I have listened in the profound darkness at its heart to the voice of the silence and have thought myself an initiate buried, awaiting the unfolding of the mystic Rose of Isis. And science would have us believe that that wondrous temple is a tomb! A tomb! when truly it is a birthplace!'

His dark eyes glowed almost fiercely. To Don alone did he thus reveal himself, mantled in a golden rhetoric.

'Mitrahîna, too, the village on the mounds which cloak with their memorable ashes the splendour that was Memphis; who has not experienced the mournful allurement of those palm-groves amid which lie the fallen colossi of Rameses? But how many have responded to it? They beckon me, Don, bidding me to the gates of royal Memphis, to the palace of the Pharaoh. A faint breeze steals over the desert, and they shudder and sigh because palace and temple are dust and the King of the Upper and Lower Land is but a half-remembered name strange upon the lips of men. Ah! who that has heard it can forget the call, soft and mournful, of the palm-groves of Mitrahîna?

'I would make such places sacred and no vulgar foot should ever profane them. Once, as I passed the entrance to the tomb of Seti in the Valley of the Kings, I met a fat German coming out. He was munching sandwiches, and I had to turn aside; I believe I clenched my fists. A picture of the shameful Clodius at the feast of Bona Dea arose before me. My very soul revolted against this profanation of the ancient royal dead. To left and right upon the slopes above and perhaps beneath the very path along which the gross Teuton was retiring lay those who ruled the world ere Rome bestrode the seven hills, whose body-slaves were princes when the proud states and empires of today slumbered unborn in the womb of Time. Seti I! what a name of power! His face, Don, is unforgettable and his image seems to haunt those subterranean halls in which at last he had thought to find rest. Today his tomb is a public resort, his alabaster sarcophagus an exhibit at the Sloane Museum, and his body, stripped of its regal raiment, is lying exposed to curious eyes in a glass case in Cairo!

'We honour the departed of our own times, and tread lightly in God's acre: why, because they passed from the world before Western civilization had raised its head above primeval jungles, should we fail in our respect for Egypt's mightier dead? I tell you, Don, there is not one man in a million who understands; who, having the eyes to see, the ears to hear, has the soul to comprehend. And this understanding is a lonely, sorrowful gift. I looked out from an observation-post on the Somme over a landscape like the blasted heath in *Macbeth*. No living thing moved, but the earth was pregnant with agony and the roar of the guns from hidden pits was like that of the grindstones of hell. There, upon the grave of an epoc, I listened to that deathly music and it beckoned to me like the palm frond of Mitrahîna and spoke the same message as the voice of the pyramid silence. Don! all that has ever been, is, and within us dwells the first and the last.'

VII

A silence fell between them which endured for a long time, such an understanding silence as is only possible in rare friendships. Paul began to fill his pipe, and Don almost regretfully broke the spell. 'My real mission,' he said, 'is to release you from a bargain into which you entered blindfolded, without realizing that you had to deal with an utterly unprincipled partner.'

'Whatever do you mean?'

'I owe a debt to the late Michael Duveen, Paul, which you generously offered to assist me in liquidating—'

Paul reached over and grasped Don's arm. 'Stop there!' he cried, 'and hear me. You are going to say that my enthusiasm has cooled—'

'I am going to say nothing of the kind.'

'Ah, but you think it is so. Yet you know me so well, Don, that you should understand me better. I handed the whole affair over to Nevin, and to you that seems like ennui, I know. But it does not mean that; it simply means that as a hopeless man of business I appoint another to do what I know myself incapable of doing. Once I am committed to the production of a book, Don, I cease to exist outside its pages. I live and move and have my being in it. But please don't misunderstand. Anything within my power to do for Flamby I will do gladly. I only learned today of her second bereavement. Don, we must protect her from the fate which so often befalls girls in such circumstances.'

'My dear Paul, in accusing me of misjudging *you*, you are misjudging *me*. If I don't understand you nobody does. My offer to release you from the bargain is not to be understood as a reproach; it is a confession. I am a man utterly devoid of common sense, one to whom reason is a stranger and moderation an enemy. I am a funny joke. I should be obliged if you would sell me to *Punch*.'

'You puzzle me.'

'I puzzle myself. Don Courtier is a conundrum with which I struggle night and morning. In brief, Paul, I have been shopping with Flamby.'

'With Flamby? Then she is in London?'

'She arrived yesterday morning, a most pathetic little picture in black. I wish you could have seen her, Paul; then you might understand and condone.'

The vertical wrinkle between Paul's brows grew darker. His mind was a playground of conflicting thoughts. When he spoke he did so almost automatically. 'She has never had a chance, Don. God knows I am eager to help her.'

'But I cannot permit it. To put the matter in a nutshell, I have already spent roughly a hundred and twenty pounds in this worthy cause!'

Paul laughed outright. 'My dear fellow, what are a hundred and twenty pounds in the scale against your life? You are worth more to me than sixty pounds!'

'This is only the beginning. Having beguiled her into an extravagant mode of expenditure, from motives of self-protection I have been forced to plunge deeper into the mire of deception. I have informed her that she is to refer all tradespeople to Nevin. Quite innocently she may let us in for any amount of money!'

Paul put his hands upon Don's shoulders, laughing more loudly than ever. 'I don't know to what extent your service has depleted your exchequer, and how far you can afford to pursue the Quixotic, but for my own part all I have is at your disposal—and at Flamby's.'

'I shall see that no such demand is made upon you. But you must come and visit her, Paul. She has few friends.'

'Poor little girl. I will come when you like, Don. Tonight I am going to Thessaly's, and I wish you could join the party. He would welcome you, I know.'

'Impossible, unfortunately. I am dining with a man who was attached to us for a time.'

'Don't fill up your entire programme, Don, and leave no room for me. Give me at least one whole day.'

'Tomorrow, then.'

'Splendid. Thessaly will be joining us in the evening, too, and I am anxious for you to renew your acquaintance. We had projected a ramble around London's Bohemian haunts. I must keep in touch with the ideas of contemporary writers, painters and composers, for these it is who make opinion. Then I propose to plumb the depths of our modern dissipations, Don. The physician's diagnosis is based upon symptoms of sickness.'

'Certainly. A nation is known not by its virtues, but by its vices. In the haversack of the fallen Frenchman it is true that we may find a silk stocking, or a dainty high-heeled shoe, but in that of the German we find a liver sausage. Most illuminating, I think. Tomorrow, then. Shall I call here for you? Yvonne might like to lunch with us. The wife of a genius must often be very lonely.'

VIII

Before the bookstall in the entrance to the Café Royal, Paul stood on the following night, with Jules Thessaly and Don.

'I shall never cease to regret Kirchner,' said Thessaly. 'He popularised thin legs, and so many women have them. Ha, Mario! here you are again on the front page of a perfectly respectable weekly journal, just alighting from the train. You look like an intelligent baboon, and your wife will doubtless instruct Nevin directly her attention is drawn to this picture. It creates an impression that she was not sober at the time. What a public benefactor was he who introduced popular illustrated journalism. He brought all the physical deformities of the great within reach of the most modest purse.'

'It is very curious,' said Don, 'but you do not appear in the photograph, Mr. Thessaly. You appear in none that I have seen.'

'Modesty is a cloak, Captain Courtier, which can even defy the camera. Let us inhale the gratifying odour, suggestive of truffles frying in oil, which is the hall-mark of your true café, and is as ambergris in the nostrils of the gourmand. Do you inhale it?'

'It is unavoidable,' replied Paul. 'The triumph of Continental cookery rests upon a basis of oil.'

'We will bathe in the unctuous fumes. Enter, my friends.'

Passing the swing-door they entered the café, which was full as usual, so that at first it seemed as though they would find no accommodation.

'Twenty-five per cent. of elbows are nudging fifty per cent. of ribs,' said Thessaly, 'and ninety per cent. of eyes are staring at Paul Mario. Personally, my extreme modesty would revolt. I once endeavoured to visualize Fame and the resultant picture was that of a huge room filled with pretty women, all of whom watched me with the fixed gaze of nascent love. It was exquisite but embarrassing. I think there is a table near the corner, on the right, a spot sanctified by the frequent presence of Jacob Epstein. Let us intrude.'

They made their way to the table indicated by Thessaly, and the curious sudden silence which notability imposes upon the ordinary marked their progress. Paul's handsome olive face became the focus of a hundred glances. Several people who were seated with their backs toward the entrance, half rose to look covertly at him as he walked in. They seated themselves at the marble-topped table, Don and Paul upon the plush lounge and Thessaly upon a chair facing them. 'I have a mirror before me,' said Thessaly, 'and can stare without fear of rebuke. Yonder is a group of Johnsons.'

'To whom do you refer?' asked Don.

'To those young men Wearing Soho whiskers and coloured collars. I call them Johnsons because they regard Augustus John as their spiritual father.'

'And what is your opinion of his school?' inquired Don.

'He has no school. His work is aspirative, if you will grant me the word; the striving of a soul which knew the art of an earlier civilization to seek expression in this. Such a man may have imitators, but he can never have disciples.'

'He is a master of paint.'

'Quite possibly. Henry James was a master of ink, but only by prayer and fasting can we hope to grasp his message. Both afford examples of very strange and experienced spirits trammelled by the limitations of imperfect humanity. Their dreams cannot be expressed in terms within the present human compass. Debussy's extraordinary music may be explained in the same way. Those who seek to follow such a lead follow a Jack-o'-lantern. The more I see of the work of the Johnsons the more fully I recognize it to embody all that we do not ask of art.'

'Those views do not apply to the Johnsons' spiritual father?' suggested Paul, laughingly.

'Not in the least. If we confounded the errors of the follower with the message of the Master must not the Messianic tradition have died with Judas?'

Paul gave an order to the waiter and Don began to load his pipe. Thessaly watched him, smiling whilst he packed the Latakia mixture into the bowl with meticulous care, rejecting fragments of stalk as Paphnutius rejected Thais; more in sorrow than in anger.

'Half the absinthe drinker's joy is derived from filtering the necessary drops of water through a lump of sugar,' he said as Don reclosed his pouch; 'and in the same way, to the lover of my lady Nicotine the filling of the pipe is a ritual, the lighting a burnt offering and the smoking a mere habit.'

'Quite agree,' replied Don, fumbling for matches in the pocket of his trench-coat, 'as the Aunt would say. Our own pipe never tastes so sweet as the other fellow's smells. There is Chauvin over there, and I want to speak to him. Perhaps he fails to recognize me in uniform. Ah! he has seen me.' He waved his hand to a fresh-coloured, middle-aged man seated with a lady dressed in green, whose cerise hair lent her an interesting likeness to a human geranium. Chauvin rose, having obtained the lady's permission, bowed to her, and coming across to the table, shook Don warmly by the hand.

'Paul,' said Don, 'This is Claude Chauvin. You have one of his pictures in your dining-room. Paul Mario—Mr. Jules Thessaly. Chauvin, I know you require another assistant in your studio. You cannot possibly turn out so much black and white stuff for the sporting journals and all those etchings as well as your big pictures.'

'It is hopeless to expect to find anyone to help me,' replied Chauvin. 'Nobody understands animals nowadays. I would pay a good assistant any amount as well as putting him in the way of doing well for himself later on.'

'I am bringing a girl around to you in the morning who knows nearly as much about animals as you know yourself.'

'A girl.'

'A girl—yes; a female Briton RiviPre.'

Chauvin's rather tired-looking eyes lighted up with professional interest, and he bent lower over the table upon which he was resting his hands. 'Really! Who is she?'

'Flamby Duveen. I would never trust her to anybody's care but yours, Chauvin. She is the daughter of a man who saved my life, and she is a born artist as well. She starts at Guilder's on Monday. Her style wants broadening of course. But look at this.'

Don dived into the capacious pocket of his trench-coat and brought forth a large envelope marked 'On His Majesty's Service. *Strictly confidential.*' From the envelope he took a water-colour drawing representing a pair of long-legged ungainly colts standing snuggled up to their mother under a wild briar hedge. He handed the drawing to Chauvin, and Chauvin, adjusting a pair of huge horn-rimmed spectacles upon his nose, examined it critically. All three watched him in silence. Presently he removed the spectacles and laid the drawing down on the table. He held out his hand to Don.

'Bring her along early,' he said. 'Good night.' He returned to the human geranium.

Don replaced the drawing in the official envelope, smiling happily. 'Old Chauvin is not exactly chatty,' he remarked; 'but he knows.'

'I should say that he was a man of very extraordinary talent,' said Thessaly, 'even if I were unacquainted with his work. His choice of a companion alone marks him as no ordinary mortal.'

Don laughed outright, fitting the envelope into his pocket again. 'The lady is a Parisienne,' he replied, 'and very entertaining company.'

'Parisiennes make delightful companions for any man,' declared Thessaly, 'and good wives for one who is fond of adventure. She is studying you with keen interest, Mario.'

'She probably regards me as an embodiment of mediFval turpitude. People persist in confusing novelists with their creations.'

'Quite so. Yet because De Quincey was an opium-fiend, Poe a drunkard and Oscar Wilde a pervert, it does not follow that every clever writer is unfit for decent society. Even if he were, his popularity would not suffer. Few things help a man's public reputation so much as his private vices. Don't you think you could cultivate *hashish*, Mario? Sherlock Holmes' weakness for cocaine has endeared him to the hearts of two generations.'

'I shall endeavour to dispense with it, Thessaly. Excepting a liking for honey which almost amounts to a passion, my private life is exemplary.'

'Honey? Most peculiar. Don't let Bassett know, or he will paragraph the fact. Honey to my way of thinking is a much overrated commodity which survives merely because of its Biblical reputation and its poetic life-history. It is only one's imagination which lends to it the fragrance of flowers. Personally I prefer treacle. Is Chauvin's attachment to the French lady of a Platonic nature, Captain Courtier?'

'I cannot say. He is quite capable of marrying her.'

'Probably he knows his own mind,' Paul murmured absently.

'Quite probably; but does he know hers?' asked Thessaly. 'I always think this so important in London, although it may not matter in Paris. Some infatuations are like rare orchids. A certain youth of Cnidus fell in love with a statue of Aphrodite, and my secretary, Caspar, has fallen in love with Gaby Deslys. Apollonius of Tyana cured the Cnidian youth, but what hope is there for Caspar? My nightly prayer is that he may find the courage to shave his side-whiskers and renounce the passionate life—a second Plato burning his poems.'

Paul became absorbed in contemplation of the unique turmoil about him. The excitement created by his entrance had somewhat subsided, and the various groups in the café had resumed their respective characteristics. The place was seething with potential things; the pressure of force might be felt. At a centre table a party of musicians talked excitedly, one of them, a pale young man with feline eyes, shouting hoarsely and continuously. Well-known painters were there, illustrating the fact that many a successful artist patronizes a cheap tailor. There was a large blonde woman who smoked incessantly as she walked from table to table. She seemed to have an extensive circle of acquaintances. And there was a small dark girl with eyes feverishly bright who watched her; and whenever the glances of the twain met, the big woman glared and the small one sneered and showed her white teeth. A little fat man with a large fat notebook sat near the door apparently engaged in compiling a history of some kind and paying no attention whatever to a tall thin man who persistently interrupted him by ordering refreshments. The little fat man absently emptied glass after glass; his powers of absorption were remarkable.

There were models with pale faces and short fabulous hair surrounding a celebrated figure-painter who was said to have seven wives named after the days of the week, and there were soldiers who looked like poets and artists who looked like soldiers. A sculptor who had discovered the secret of making ugliness out of beauty and selling it, was deep in conversation with an author of shocking mysteries whose fame rested largely upon his creation of the word 'beetlesque' and the appearance of a certain blue-faced ourang-outang in every story which he published.

Paul's immediate neighbours on the right-hand side were two earnest young brushmen, one wearing military uniform, and the other a rational check suit designed with much firmness. They shared a common pencil and drank black coffee, demonstrating their ideas in line upon the marble table-top. They evidently thought with Mr. Nevinson, that man invented circles but the Lord created cubes. Beyond them was a lady of title who aspired to the mantle of George Sand. In the absence of an Alfred de Musset she had fled from her husband with a handsome actor of romantic roles whom later she had left for an ugly violinist with a beautiful technique. She was sipping pomegranate juice in the company of her publisher and glancing under her lashes at a ferocious-looking ballad writer who had just seated himself behind the next table from whence he directed a malevolent glare upon no one in particular.

'His gentle work deserves a kinder master,' said Thessaly, observing Paul watching the melody-maker. 'I have noticed, Mario, that although there are few pressmen present, there are a number of publicists. Our progress is merely in terminology after all. The writers who matter may readily be recognized by their complacent air; the others, who have not yet succeeded in mattering, by their hungry look. They have missed a course in the banquet of life. They have failed to grasp the fact that our artificial civilization has made a mystery of marriage, which, veil by veil, it is the duty of the successful novelist to disclose. If I were a novelist I should seek my characters in the Divorce Court; if I were a painter I should study those superstitions which have grown up around human nudity so that the very word "naked" has become invested with a covert significance and must very shortly be obsolete. I contemplate opening a new Pythagorean Institute for instruction of the artistic young. Above the portal I shall cause to be inscribed the following profound thought: "Art does not pay; portrait and figure painting do."'

'Some portrait painters are artists,' said Don.

'I agree: Velasquez, for instance; and consider the treatment of the velvet draperies in Collier's *Pomps and Vanities* so widely popularized by its reproduction in the Telephone Directory.' He turned to Paul. 'I have noted no fewer than six novelists, Mario, engaged in outlining to admirers projected masterpieces dealing with the war from a psychological aspect. Think of the disappointments. Excepting the creators of omniscient detectives and exotic criminals (who form a class apart, self-contained, opulent and immune from the stress of life) every writer dies with his greatest work unwritten. We are beginning to bore one another. Let us proceed to Murray's and contemplate bare backs.'

IX

One evening early in the following week Flamby and Mrs. Chumley stood upon a platform of Victoria Station looking after a train from which protruded a forest of waving hands. Somewhere amongst them was the hand of Don, but because of that uncomfortable mistiness which troubled her sight at times, Flamby was quite unable to distinguish anything clearly. 'Damn the German pigs,' she said under her breath.

'Did I hear you swearing, dear?' asked Mrs. Chumley tearfully. 'So many girls seem to be able to swear nowadays. No doubt they find it a great relief.'

'I am so sorry,' said Flamby breathlessly. 'I had really made up my mind never to swear again and never to say things in Latin or quote Shakespeare; but it's very hard for me.'

'It must be, dear. Quite agree. I once tried to make up my mind never to give money to blind beggars again. It was in Cairo, and I found that so many of them were not really blind at all. Do you know, dear, it was not a bit of good. I found myself doing it when I wasn't thinking. I tried going out without money, and then all the blind men followed me about the streets. It was most awkward. The poor things couldn't understand why I had changed, of course.'

'You had not changed, Mrs. Chumley. You never could change,' said Flamby, squeezing the old lady's arm as they made their way out of the station. 'You will always be generous, but I hope I shall not always swear on the slightest provocation.'

'I hope you won't, dear, if you think it would be as well.'

Number twenty-three at The Hostel now was converted into a miniature suite de luxe. Flamby's instinctive good taste had enabled her to arrange her new possessions and her old to the best possible advantage. The cost of

those purely useful articles which had not been purchased under the guidance of Don, as compared with such delightful things as cushions and
gowns, surprised her very much indeed, but the ingenious Don had secured
a quantity of cutlery, linen and other household necessities from an acquaintance 'in the wholesale trade,' thus saving Flamby more than half the usual
cost. Once committed to an emprize, Don's resource was limitless.

Flamby switched on the centre light of her little domain, fitted with a
charming shade of Japanese silk, and removing her coat (purchased locally at
a price which she had considered preposterous) she stood gazing vacantly
into the little square mirror above the mantelpiece behind the china clock. It
reflected the figure of a slim girl wearing a blue serge skirt, a blue jersey coat
and a grey velour hat—a very pretty girl indeed, her colour heightened by the
humid night air.

How swiftly her life had moved in that one short week. She stared at her
reflection with a sudden interest, seeking for signs of age. Eight days ago she
had possessed no friend in all the world; now, friends seemed to have sprung
up around her miraculously, and all at the bidding of Don. From such
lonely despondence as she had never known he had lifted her into a new and
brighter world. She had seen the studio of the great Claude Chauvin; she was
actually going to work there on three days of every week. On the other three
she was to attend the art school. The crowning wonder of it all lay in the fact
that Chauvin proposed to pay her a salary. Her father had taught her to expect nothing but rebuffs, although he had assured her that some day she
would make a reputation as an animal painter. She recognized that Don was
the magician whose transmuting wand had surrounded her with the gold of
good fellowship. He had forgotten nothing.

One day they had lunched at Regali's, that esoteric Italian restaurant
wherein disciples of all the Arts congregate to pay tribute to good cooking
and modest bills.

Don, who seemed to know everybody, presented the great Severus
Regali himself, a vast man ponderously moustached and endowed with a
mighty voice and the fierce bearing of a Bellino; a figure in *bravura* with the
heart of a child. He bowed low before Flamby, one huge hirsute hand
pressed to his bosom.

'Ragout Regali is on today,' he said; no more—but those words constituted an initiation, admitting Flamby to the epicurean circle.

Of Severus Regali and his famous ragout a story was told, and this was the story as related by Don: No other chef in Europe (Regali had formerly been chef to a Personage) could make a like ragout, and Regali jealously retained the secret of the preparation, which he only served to privileged guests. To him came M. Sapin, the great artist responsible for the menus of a certain peer far-famed as the foremost living disciple of Lucullus. A banquet extraordinary was shortly to take place, and M. Sapin, the mastermind, came to beg of Regali the recipe for his ragout. Wrapped in a fur-lined coat, the immortal Sapin descended from his car (for his salary was that of a Cabinet Minister). Hollow-cheeked, sallow, and having death in his eyes, he begged this favour of his modest rival.

'It shall never be prepared by my hand again, Regali,' he said. 'My physician gives me but one month of life.'

'What!' cried Regali. 'It is then a dying request?'

'It is indeed,' was the mournful reply. 'For this great affair I have sought inspiration from all the classic authorities. I have considered the dormice served with honey and poppy-seed and the grape-fed beccafico dressed with *garum piperatum*, which, according to Petronius, were served at Trimalchio's banquet. But neither of these rare dishes can compare with Ragout Regali.' Regali bowed. 'Therefore, I beg of you, grant me permission to prepare that supreme triumph of our beautiful art, and in honour of the guest of the evening, to present it for the first and, alas! the last time as "Ragout Prince Leopold!"'

Regali consented, and that night after closing-time a strange scene was enacted. Outside the restaurant stood the luxurious car of M. Sapin, and downstairs in the kitchen, behind double-locked doors, the two chefs made Ragout Regali, M. Sapin noting the method of preparation with those pathetic dying eyes. But at the great banquet following the appearance of 'Ragout Prince Leopold,' M. Sapin was summoned to the dining-room and toasted by the epicures there gathered. This was his final triumph. He died a few weeks later. But of such dream stuff was the wonder-dish to whose mystery Regali had admitted Flamby with the words 'Ragout Regali is on today.'

Another morning they went to Guilder's the art school of which Don had said, 'They teach you everything except how to sell your pictures', and Flamby made the acquaintance of Hammett, famous as a painter of dogs, velvet and lace, under whom she was to work. The school surprised her. It was so extremely untidy, and the big windows were so very dirty. Busts and plaster casts, canvas-stretchers, easels, stools and stacks of sketches littered the first, or 'antique' room, and they were all mantled in dust. There was no one in the 'life' room at the time of Flamby's visit, except an old Italian, who was a model, but who looked like an organ-grinder. The suspended lamps, with their huge ugly shades, had an ominous appearance by daylight, and Flamby found herself considering the unfinished drawings and paintings which were visible about the large bleak room, and trying to conjure up thought-forms of the students who had executed them. Later she learned that there were a number of smaller painting-rooms right and left, above and below, but the dirtiest room of all was that in which lumps of clay lay casually about on tables and rests and on the floor, where embryonic things perched upon tripods, like antediluvian birds and saurians, and where the daughters of Praxiteles and sons of Phidias pursued their claggy but fascinating studies under a sculptor who possessed the inestimable gift of teaching more than he knew himself. It was all very unromantic. Strange how ugliness is the mother of beauty, and the sacred fairy-winged scarab of Art comes forth from dirt.

One day Paul came to the Hostel. Flamby was engaged in hanging pictures when she heard his voice in the courtyard below. She was standing on a chair, but her heart began to beat so ridiculously that she was compelled to sit down. She swore with a fluency and resource worthy of her father, then in feverish haste attempted to strip off her overall and wash her hands and adjust her unruly hair at one and the same time. She ceased her frantic efforts as suddenly as she had begun them, drying her hands and tousling her hair fiercely. What did she care? Let him find her looking like a freak; it did not matter. 'You are a little ass,' she told herself bitterly; 'a silly little donkey! Have you *no* brains? He doesn't care how you look. You should not care what he thinks about you. Why don't you get in a panic when Don comes alone? You were as red as a tomato half a minute ago; now you are as white as a ghost. You poor contemptible little idiot!'

She snatched up the hammer which she had dropped and resumed the task of attaching a picture fastener to the wall; but as she passed the mirror above the fireplace she raised her disengaged hand and pulled a curl into place. She banged a little brass nail so hard that it bounced out of the plaster and fell upon the floor. Paul and Don were at the door and the bell was ringing. Flamby achieved composure, and hammer in hand she went to admit her visitors.

One swift glance she ventured, and in Paul's eyes she read that which none could have deduced from his manner. The shameful phantom which had pursued her so long had not been illusory; the photographs taken by Sir

Jacques had survived him. Paul had seen them. Momentarily she almost hated him, and she found a savage and painful satisfaction in the discovery that there was something in his nature less than godlike. It should be easy to forget a man capable of believing that of her which Paul believed. She longed to hide herself from his sight. But almost with his first word of charming greeting came the old joy of hearing him speak, the old foolish sense of inferiority, of helpless gladness. Flamby even ceased to resist it, but she noted that Don was more silent than usual; and once in his grey eyes she detected a look almost of sadness. In the very charm of Paul's unchanged manner there lay a sting, for if he had cared he could not have believed that which Flamby was convinced he did believe and have dismissed the matter thus. But, of course, he did not care.

'Why should he care?' she asked aloud, when again she found herself alone. 'He is just sorry that I am not a good girl. Dad saved the life of his dearest friend, and therefore he considers it his duty to be kind to me. But that is all.'

In vain Flamby sought to reason with her unreasonable heart. What did she desire?—that Paul should love her? A hot flush crept all over her body. That his wife should die? Oh! what a coldly merciless thing was logic! Flamby at this point discovered that she had been weeping for quite a long time. She was very sorry for herself indeed; and recognizing this in turn she began to laugh, perhaps rather hysterically. She was laughing when Mrs. Chumley came to look for her, nor could she stop.

'Whatever are you laughing about, dear? Has Don been telling you one of his ridiculous stories?'

'No. I just thought of a silly trifling thing, and began to laugh and couldn't leave off.'

'Quite understand, dear. I've been like that. I once began laughing in the Tube; so unfortunate. And a man sitting opposite became really annoyed. He had a very odd nose, you see, and he thought I was laughing at it. I could see he thought so, which made me laugh all the more. I had to get out at the next station, dear. Most ridiculous, because I wasn't laughing at the poor man's nose at all, I was laughing at his funny umbrella.'

X

Six months stole almost unobserved into a dim land of memories. The war, which ate up all things, did not spare the almanack; and what should appear to later generations as the most stirring period in the world's history, appeared to many of those who lived through it in London as a dreary blank in their lives, a hiatus, an interval of waiting—a time to be speedily forgotten when its dull aches were no more and absent dear ones again worked side by side for simple ends, and the sweeter triumphs of peace. Some there were whose sorrows drove them like Sarak in quest of the Waters of Oblivion, but, to all, those days were poppy days, unreal and meaningless; transitory, as a bridge between unlike states.

Flamby made progress at Guilder's, growing more and more familiar with the technique of her art, but, under the careful guidance of Hammett, never losing that characteristic nonchalance of style which was the outstanding charm of her work. So many professors seem to regard their pupils as misshapen creatures, who must be reduced to a uniform pattern, but Hammett was not as one of these. He encouraged originality whilst he suppressed eccentricity, and although, recognizing the budding genius in the girl's work, he lavished particular care upon her artistic development, he never tried to make love to her, which proved that he was not only a good painter, but also a sound philosopher. He took her to lunch once or twice to Regali's, which created a coterie of female enemies, but Flamby regarded all women in a more charitable manner since her meeting with Mrs. Chumley, and some of her enemies afterwards became her friends, for she bore them no malice, but sought them out and did her utmost to understand them. Her father had taught her to despise the pettiness of women, but in Mrs. Chumley's sweet sympathy she had found a new model of conduct. Her later philosophy was a quaint one.

'It isn't fair, Mrs. Chumley,' she said one day, sitting on the settee in her little room, knees drawn up to chin and her arms embracing them—'it isn't fair to hate a girl for being spiteful. You might as well hate a cat for killing mice.'

'Quite agree, dear. I am glad you think so.'

'Women are different from men. They haven't got the same big interests in life, and they are not meant to have. I am sorry for women who have to live alone and fight for themselves. But I can't be sorry for those who *want* to fight. Loneliness must be very terrible, and there is really no such thing as a girl friend after school days, is there? Except for very ugly girls or very daft ones.'

'I am sure you would be a staunch friend to anyone, dear.'

'Yes; but they don't know it, you see. Naturally they judge me by themselves,' said Flamby wistfully. 'I used to hate being a woman before I met you, Mrs. Chumley, but I am not quite so sorry now.'

'I am glad, dear. So nice of you to say so.'

'If there were no men in the world I think women might be nicer,' continued Flamby the philosopher—'not at first, of course, but when they had got over it. Nearly all the mean things girls do to one another are done because of men, and yet all the splendid things they do are done for men as well. Aren't we funny? Three of the girls from the school went to be nurses recently, one because her boy had been killed, another because she was in love with a doctor, and the third because she had heard that a great many girls became engaged to Colonials in France. Not one of them went because she wanted to be a nurse. Now, if *you* went, Mrs. Chumley, you would go because you were sorry for all the poor wounded, I know. It would have been just the same when you were eighteen, and that's why I think you are so wonderful.'

Mrs. Chumley became the victim of silent merriment, from which she recovered but slowly. 'You are a really extraordinary child, dear,' she said. 'Yet, you seem to have quite a number of girl friends come to see you as well as boys.'

'Yes. You see I make allowances for them and then they are quite good friends.'

'Who was that fair man who took you to the theatre last night, and brought you home in a lovely car?'

'Orlando James. He has the next studio to Mr. Chauvin. I hate him.'

Mrs. Chumley's blue eyes became even more circular than usual. 'But you went to the theatre with him?'

'Yes; that was why I went. He buys me nice presents, too. I wouldn't take them if I liked him.'

Presently, retiring to her own abode, Flamby picked up a copy of a daily paper and stared for a long time at two closely-printed columns headed, 'Mr. Paul Mario's Challenge to the Churches'. The article was a commentary by a prominent literary man upon Paul's second paper, *Le Monde*, which had appeared that week and had occasioned even wider comment than the first, *Le*

Bateleur. Long excerpts had been printed by practically every journal of note in Great Britain. It had been published in full in New York, Paris, Rome, Stockholm, Christiania and Copenhagen, and had been quoted at great length by the entire colonial Press. It was extraordinary; revolutionary, but convincing. It appealed to every man and woman who had loved, lost and doubted; it was written with conviction and displayed knowledge beyond the compass of ordinary minds. Touching as it did upon mysteries hitherto veiled from public ken, it set the civilized world agog, hoping and questioning, studying the secrets of Tarot and seeking to divine the hidden significance of the word of power, *Yod-he-vau-he.*

Flamby, disciple of the Greek sages, could face the truth unflinchingly, and now she recognized that to endeavour to battle against the memory of Paul Mario was a waste of energy. But because her pride was lofty and implacable she avoided meeting him, yet could not avoid following all that he said and wrote, nor could her pride withhold her from seeking glimpses of him in places which she knew him to frequent. *Le Monde* frightened her. It had the authority of conviction based upon knowledge, and it slew hope in her breast. If nothing was hidden from this wonderful man, why did he omit to explain the mystery of unrequited love?

On more than one occasion Flamby had found herself in that part of Chelsea where Paul's house was situated, and from a discreet distance she had looked at his lighted windows, and then had gone home to consider her own folly from a critical point of view. Flamby, the human Eve, mercilessly taxed by Flamby, the philosopher, pleaded guilty to a charge of personal vanity. Yes, she had dared to think herself pretty—until she had seen Yvonne Mario. Flamby, the daughter of Michael Duveen, had defined Yvonne's appearance as 'a slap in the face.' She no longer expected any man who had seen Yvonne Mario to display the slightest interest in little insignificant Flamby Duveen; for Yvonne possessed the type of beauty which women count irresistible, but which oddly enough rarely enchains the love of men, which inflames the imagination without kindling the heart. Thus was the fairness of the daughter of Icarius, which might not withhold Ulysses from the arms of Calypso, and of this patrician beauty was Fluvia, whom Antony forgot when the taunting smiles of Cleopatra set his soul on fire.

That Paul's esteem was diminished Flamby had known from the very hour that he had quitted Lower Charleswood without word of farewell. His first visit to The Hostel had confirmed her opinion, although confirmation was not needed. He had visited her twice since then; once at Chauvin's studio and once at Guilder's. She had met him on a third occasion by chance. His manner had been charming as ever but marked by a certain gravity, and as Flamby thought, by restraint. Sense of a duty to Don alone had impelled him to see her. He had never mentioned his wife.

Flamby first saw Yvonne in the cloisteresque passage into which Chauvin's studio opened, for the studio was one of a set built around three sides of a small open courtyard in the centre of which was a marble faun. Orlando James, the fashionable portrait painter, occupied the studio next to Chauvin. Flamby had been rather anxious to meet James because Chauvin had warned her to avoid him, and one afternoon as she was leaving for home, she came out into the passage at the same moment that a man and a woman passed the studio door on their way to the gate. The woman walked on without glancing aside, but the man covertly looked back, bestowing a bold glance of his large brown eyes upon Flamby. It was Orlando James. She recognized him immediately, tall, fair, arrogantly handsome and wearing his soft hat B *la Mousquetaire.* But, at the moment, Flamby had no eyes for the debonair Orlando. Stepping back into the shadow of the door, she gazed and gazed, fascinatedly, at the tall, graceful figure of his companion whose slim, daintily shod feet seemed to disdain the common pavement, whose hair of burnished gold gleamed so wonderfully in the wintry sunlight. Flamby's heart would have told her even if she were not familiar with the many published photographs that this elegant woman was Yvonne Mario. Opening the gate, Orlando James held it whilst Yvonne passed out; then ere following her he looked back again smiling destructively at Flamby.

He was painting Yvonne's portrait, as Flamby had pointed out to Chauvin when Chauvin had uttered veiled warnings against his neighbour.

'I know, my dear kid,' Chauvin had replied, peering over his horn-rimmed spectacles; 'but Mrs. Paul Mario can walk in where angels fear to tread. She is Mrs. Paul Mario, my dear kid, and if Mr. Paul Mario approves it is nobody else's business. But your Uncle Chauvin does not approve and your Uncle Chauvin is responsible to your Uncle Don.'

'Don't call him that!' Flamby had cried, with one of her swift changes of mood. 'It sounds damned silly.'

Thereupon Chauvin had laughed until he had had to polish his spectacles, for Chauvin was a cheery soul and the embodiment of all that Mürger meant when he spoke of a Bohemian. 'Oh! oh!' he had chuckled—'you little devil! I must tell Hammett.' And he had been as good as his word; but that same day he had bought Flamby a huge box of chocolates which was a direct and highly immoral encouragement of profanity.

Nevertheless Flamby managed to make the acquaintance of Orlando James, but she did not tell Chauvin. She detested James, but it had been very gratifying to be noticed by a man actually in the company of the dazzling Yvonne Mario. Flamby had profound faith in her ability to take care of herself and not without sound reason, for she was experienced and wise beyond her years, and James's pride in his new conquest amused her vastly because she knew it to be no conquest at all. Only with age do women learn that the foolish world judges beauty harshly and that the judgment of the foolish world may not wholly be neglected. Thus, for human life is a paradox, this knowledge comes when it is no longer any use, since every woman is not a Ninon de Lenclos.

Of such-like matters were Flamby's thoughts as she sat squeezed up into the smallest possible compass upon her settee, arms embracing knees; and, as was so often the case, they led her back to Paul Mario. It was wonderful how all paths seemed to lead to Paul Mario. She sighed, reaching down for the newspaper which had slipped to the floor. As her fingers touched it, the door-bell rang.

Flamby jumped up impetuously, glancing at the celebrated china clock, which recorded the hour of ten p.m. She assumed that Mrs. Chumley had called for what she was wont to describe as 'a goodnight chat.' Flamby opened the door, and the light shone out upon Paul Mario.

XI

There are surprises which transcend the surprising, and as the finer tones of music defeat our ears and pass us by unnoticed so do these super-dramatic happenings find us unmoved. Flamby was aware of a vague numbness; she felt like an automaton, but she was quite composed.

'Good evening, Mr. Mario,' she said. 'How nice of you to call.'

The trite precision of her greeting sounded unfamiliar—the speech of a stranger.

'May I come in, or will the lateness of my visit excite comment among your neighbours?'

'Of course you may come in.'

Paul walked into the cosy little sitting-room and Flamby having closed the door contrived to kick the newspaper under the bureau whilst placing an armchair for Paul. Paul smiled and made a nest of cushions in a corner of the settee. 'Sit there, Flamby,' he said, 'and let me talk to you.'

Flamby sat down facing him, and her nerves beginning to recover from the shock imposed upon them, she found that her heart was really beating, and beating rapidly. Paul was in evening dress, and as the night was showery, wore a loose Burberry. A hard-working Stetson hat, splashed with rain, he had dropped upon the floor beside his chair. His face looked rather gaunt in the artificial light, which cast deep shadows below his eyes, and he was watching her in a way that led her to hope, yet fear, that he might have come to speak about the Charleswood photographs. He was endowed with that natural distinction whose possessor can never be ill at ease, yet he was palpably bent upon some project which he scarcely knew how to approach.

'Will you have a cigarette?' asked Flamby, in a faint voice. 'You may smoke your pipe if you would rather.'

'May I really?' said Paul buoyantly. 'It is a very foul pipe, and will perfume your curtains frightfully.'

'I like it. Lots of my visitors smoke pipes.'

'You have a number of visitors, Flamby?'

'Heaps. I never had so many friends in my life.'

Paul began to charge his briar from a tattered pouch. 'Have you ever thought, Flamby, that I neglected you?' he asked slowly.

'Neglected me? Of course not. You have been to see me twice, and I felt all the time that I was keeping you from your work. Besides—why should I expect you to bother about me?'

'You have every reason to expect it, Flamby. Your father was—a tenant of my uncle, and as I am my uncle's heir, his debts are mine. Your father saved me from the greatest loss in the world. Lastly'—he lighted his pipe—'I want you to count me amongst your friends.'

He held the extinguished match in his fingers, looking around for an ash-tray. Flamby jumped up, took the match and threw it in the hearth, then returned slowly to her place. Her hands were rather unsteady, and she tucked them away behind her, squeezing up closely against the cushions. 'We *are* friends,' she said. 'You have always been my friend.'

'I don't want you to feel alone in the world, as though nobody cared for you. When Don is home I have no fear, but when he is away there is really no one to study your interests, and, after all, Flamby, you are only a girl.'

'There *is* Mrs. Chumley and Mr. Hammett and Claude Chauvin.'

'Three quite delightful people, Flamby, I admit. But Hammett and Chauvin cannot always be with you, and Mrs. Chumley's sweet and unselfish life affords nothing but an illustration of unworldliness. Yet, if these were your only friends, I should be more contented.'

Flamby tapped her foot upon the carpet and stared down at it unseeingly. 'Are there some of my friends you don't think quite nice?' she asked. Her humility must have surprised many a one who had thought he knew her well.

Paul bent forward, resting one hand upon the head of the settee. 'I know very little about your friendships, Flamby. That is why I reproach myself. But a girl who lives alone should exercise the greatest discretion in such matters. You must see that this is so. Friends who would be possible if you were under the care of a mother become impossible when you are deprived of that care. It is not enough to know yourself blameless, Flamby. Worldly folks are grossly suspicious, especially of a pretty girl, and believe me, life is easier and sweeter without misunderstanding.'

'Someone has been telling you tales about me,' said Flamby, an ominous scarlet enflaming her cheeks.

Paul laughed, bending further forward and seeking to draw Flamby's hands out from their silken hiding-place. She resisted a little, averting her flushed face, but finally yielded, although she did not look at Paul. 'Dear little Flamby,' he said, and the tenderness in his voice seemed now to turn her cold. 'You are not angry with me?' He held her hands between his own, looking at her earnestly. She glanced up under her lashes. 'If I had not cared I should have said nothing.'

'Everybody goes on at me,' said Flamby tremulously. 'I haven't done any harm.'

'Who has been "going on" at you, little Flamby?'

'*You* have, and Chauvin, and everybody.'

'But what have they said? What have *I* said?'

'That I am no good—an absolute rotter!'

'Flamby! Who has said such a thing? Not Chauvin, I'll swear, and not I. You are wilfully misjudging your real friends, little girl. Because you are clever—and you are clever, Flamby—you have faith in your judgment of men yet lack faith in your judgment of yourself. Now, tell me frankly, have you any friends of whom Don would disapprove?'

'No. Don trusts me.'

'But he does not trust the world, Flamby, any more than I do, and the world can slay the innocent as readily as the guilty.'

'*I* know!' cried Flamby, looking up quickly. 'It was Mr. Thessaly who told you.'

'Who told me what?'

'That he had seen me at supper with Orlando James. I didn't see him, but James said he was there.'

She met Paul's gaze for a moment and tried to withdraw her hands, but he held them fast, and presently Flamby looked down again at the carpet.

'Whoever told me,' said Paul, 'it is the truth. Do you write often to Don?'

'Yes—sometimes.'

'Then write and ask him if he thinks you should be seen about with Orlando James and I shall be content if you will promise to abide by his reply. Will you do that, Flamby? Please don't be angry with me because I try to help you. I have lived longer than you and I have learned that if we scorn the world's opinion the world will have its revenge. Will you promise?'

'Yes,' said Flamby, all humility again.

Paul stood up, taking his hat from the floor and beginning to button his Burberry. 'I am coming to see you at the school one day soon, but if ever there is anything you want to tell me or if ever I can be of the slightest use to you, telephone to me, Flamby. Don't regard me as a bogey-man.' Flamby had stood up, too, and now Paul held her by the shoulders looking at her charming downcast face. 'We are friends, are we not, little Flamby?'

Flamby glanced up swiftly. 'Yes,' she said. 'Thank you for thinking about me.'

XII

The rain-swept deserted streets made a curious appeal to Paul that night—an appeal to something in his mood that was feverish and unquiet, that first had stirred in response to an apparently chance remark of Thessaly's and that had sent him out to seek Flamby in despite of the weather and the late hour. He did not strive to analyse it, but rather sought to quench it, unknown, and his joy in the steady downpour was a reflection of this subconscious state. Self-distrust, vague and indefinite, touched him unaccountably. He considered the intellectual uproar (for it was nothing less) which he had occasioned by the publication of his two papers—comprising as they did selections from the first part of his book. The attitude of the Church alone indicated how shrewdly he had struck. He had bred no mere nine days' wonder but had sowed a seed which, steadily propagating, already had assumed tall sapling form and had unfolded nascent branches. The bookstalls were beginning to display both anonymous pamphlets and brochures by well-known divines, not all of them directly attacking Mario nor openly defending dogma, but all of them, covertly or overtly, being aimed at him and his works. He had been inundated with correspondence from the two hemispheres; he had been persecuted by callers of many nationalities; a strange grey-haired woman with the inspired eyes of a Sita who had addressed him as *Master* and acclaimed him one long expected, and a party of little brown men, turbaned and urbane, from India, who spoke of the *Vishnu-Purana,* hailing him as a brother, and whose presence had conjured up pictures of the forests of Hindustan. A dignified Chinaman, too, armed with letters of introduction, had presented him with a wonderful book painted upon ivory of the *Trigrams of Fo-Hi.* But most singular visitor of all was a sort of monk, having a black, matted beard and carrying a staff, who had gained access to the study, Paul never learned by what means, and who had thundered out an incomprehensible warning against 'unveiling the shrine,' had denounced what he had termed 'the poison of Fabre d'Olivet' and had departed mysteriously as he had come.

There had been something really terrifying in the personality of this last visitor, power of some kind, and Paul, whose third paper, *La Force,* was in the press, seemed often to hear those strange words ringing in his ears, and he hesitated even now to widen the chasm which already he had opened and which yawned threateningly between the old faith and the new wisdom which yet was a wisdom more ancient than the world. He was but a common man, born of woman; no Krishna conceived of a Virgin Devâki, nor even a Pythagoras initiate of Memphis and heir of Zoroaster; and this night he distrusted his genius. What if he should beckon men, like a vaporous will-o'-the-wisp, out into a morass of error wherein their souls should perish? His power he might doubt no longer; a thousand denunciations, a million acclamations, had borne witness to it. And he had barely begun to speak. Truly the world awaited him and already he bent beneath the burden of a world's desire.

Few pedestrians were abroad and no cabs were to be seen. Every motor-bus appeared to be full inside, with many passengers standing, and even a heroic minority hidden beneath gleaming umbrellas on top. Paul had found the interiors of these vehicles to possess an odour of imperfectly washed humanity, and he avoided the roof, unless a front seat were available, because of the existence of that type of roof-traveller who converts himself into a human fountain by expectorating playfully at selected intervals. Theatre audiences were on their several ways home, and as Paul passed by the entrance to a Tube station he found a considerable crowd seeking to force its way in, a motley crowd representative of every stratum of society from Whitechapel to Mayfair. Women wearing opera cloaks and shod in fragile dress-shoes stood shivering upon the gleaming pavement beside Jewesses from the East End. Fur-collared coats were pressed against wet working raiments, white gloved hands rested upon greasy shoulders. Officers jostled privates, sailors vied with soldiers in the scrum before the entrance to the microbic land of tunnels. War is a potent demagogue.

Isolated standard lamps whose blackened tops gave them an odd appearance of wearing skull caps, broke the gloom of the rain mist at wide intervals. All shops were shut, apparently. One or two cafés preserved a ghostly life within their depths, but their sombre illuminations were suggestive of the Rat Mort. Musicians from the theatre orchestras hurried in the direction of the friendly Tube, instrument cases in hand, and one or two hardy members of the Overseas forces defied the elements and lounged about on corners as though this were a summer's evening in Melbourne. Policemen sheltered in dark porches. Paul walked on, his hands thrust into his coat pockets and the brim of his hat pulled down. He experienced no discomfort and was quite contented with the prospect of walking the remainder of the way home; he determined, however, to light his pipe and in order to do so he stepped into the recess formed by a shop door, found his pouch and having loaded his briar was about to strike a match when he saw a taxi-cab apparently disengaged and approaching slowly. He stepped out from his shelter, calling to the man, and collided heavily with a girl wearing a conspicuous white raincoat and carrying an umbrella.

She slipped and staggered, but Paul caught her in time to save her from a fall upon the muddy pavement. 'I am sincerely sorry,' he said with real solicitude. 'I know I must have hurt you.'

'Not in the least,' she replied in a low tone which might have passed for that of culture with a less inspired observer than Paul. A faint light from the head-lamp of the cab which had drawn up beside the pavement, touched her face. She was young and would have been pretty if the bloom of her cheeks and the redness of her lips had not been due to careful make-up; for her features were good and, as Paul recognized, experiencing a sensation of chill at his heart, not unlike those of his wife. If he could have imagined a debauched Yvonne, she would have looked like this waif of the night who now stood bending beneath the shelter of her wet umbrella upon which the rain pattered, ruefully rubbing a slim silken-clad ankle.

'I can only offer one reparation,' Paul persisted. 'You must allow me to drive you home.'

The cabman coughed dryly, reaching around to open the door. 'It's a rotten night, sir,' he said, 'and I'm short of petrol. Make it a double fare.'

'Really,' declared the girl with that exaggerated drawling accent, 'I can manage quite well.'

'Please don't argue,' said Paul, smiling and assisting her into the cab. 'Tell me where you want to go.'

She gave an address near Torrington Square and Paul got in beside her. 'Now,' he said as the cab moved off, 'I want to talk to you. You must not be angry with me but just listen! In the first place I know I collided with you roughly and I am sorry, but you deliberately got in my way, and I did not hurt your ankle at all!'

'What do you mean?' she cried, the accent more overdone than ever. 'I thought you were a gentleman!'

'Perhaps you were wrong. It is one of the most difficult things in the world to recognize a gentleman. But we can all recognize the truth and I want you to admit that I have told you the truth.'

'Did you get me in here to start the Bible-banging business?' inquired the girl, her factitious refinement deserting her. 'Because if you did I'm getting out.'

'You are going to do nothing of the kind,' said Paul, patting her white-gloved hand. 'You are going to tell me all about yourself and I am going to show you your mistakes and see if some of them cannot be put right.'

'You're nothing to do with the Salvation Army, are you?' she asked sarcastically. But already she was half enslaved by the voice and manner of Paul. 'Do you think I don't know my mistakes? Do you think preaching can do me any good? Are you one of those fools who think all women like me only live the way we do because we can't see where it will end? I know! I know! And I don't care! See that? The sooner the better!' Her sudden violence was that of rebellion against something akin to fear which this strange picturesque-looking man threatened to inspire in her—and it formed no part of her poor philosophy to fear men.

Paul took her hand and held it firmly. 'Little chance acquaintance,' he said, 'was there never anyone in the world whom you loved?—never anyone who was good to you?' She turned aside from him, making no reply. 'If ever there was such a one tell me.'

The cab had already reached the Square, and now the man pulled up before a large apartment-house, and the girl withdrew her hand and rose. 'It's no good,' she said. 'It's no good. I think you mean to be kind, but you're wasting your time. Good night.'

'I have not finished,' replied Paul, opening the door for her. 'I am coming to see where you live before I say good night.'

He followed her out, directing the man to wait and smiling grimly at the thought of his own counsel to Flamby anent giving the world cause for suspicion.

The room in which Paul found himself was on the first floor, overlooking the square, and was well but conventionally furnished. A fire blazed in the grate, and the draped mantelpiece was decorated with a number of photographs of junior officers, many of them autographed. His companion, who said her name was Kitty Chester, had discarded her raincoat and hat, and now stood before the fire arrayed in a smart plaid skirt and a white silk blouse, cut very low. She had neat ankles and a slim figure, but her hands betrayed the fact that she had done manual work at some time in her career. She was much more haggard than he had been able to discern her to be in the dim light of the cab lamp. Taking a cigarette from a box upon the table she lighted it and leaned back against the mantelpiece.

'Well,' she said, 'another blank day'; and obviously she was trying to throw off the spell which Paul had almost succeeded in casting upon her in the cab. 'Barred the Empire, barred the Alhambra, and now the old Pav. is a thing of the past, too. I never thought I should find myself blowing through the rain all dressed up and nowhere to go.'

Paul watched her silently for a moment. In Kitty Chester he recognized the answer to his doubts, and because that answer was yet incomplete, his ge-

nius responded and was revivified. As of old the initiate was tested in order
that he might learn the strength of his wisdom, so now a test was offered to
the wielder of the sword of truth. Paul did not immediately seek to re-estab-
lish control of this wayward spirit, but talked awhile lightly and sympathetically of her life and its trials. Presently: 'I suppose you are sometimes hard
up?' he said.

'Sometimes!'

'But I can see that you would resent an offer of help.'

'I should. Cut it out.'

'I have no intention of pressing the point. But have you no ambition to
lead any different life?'

'My life's my own. I'll do what I like with it. I'd have ended it long ago,
but I hadn't got the pluck. Now you know.'

'Yes,' replied Paul—'now I know. Come and sit down here beside me.'

'I won't.'

'You will. Come and sit down here.'

Kitty Chester met the fixed gaze of his eyes and was lost. With the ghost
of a swagger in her gait she crossed to the red plush sofa upon which Paul
was seated and lounged upon the end of it, one foot swinging in the air. She
had a trick of rubbing the second finger of her left hand as if twisting a ring,
and Paul watched her as she repeated the gesture. He rested his hand upon
hers.

'Did you love your husband?' he asked.

Kitty Chester stood up slowly. Her right hand, which held the lighted
cigarette, went automatically to her breast. She wore a thin gold chain about
her neck. She was staring at Paul haggardly.

'You did love him,' he continued. 'Is he dead?'

Paul's solicitude, so obviously real, so wonderfully disinterested and so
wholly free from cant, already had kindled something in the girl's heart
which she had believed to be lifeless, and for ever cold. Now, his swift intuition and the grave sympathy in his beautiful voice imposed too great a test
upon the weakened self-control of poor Kitty. Without even a warning
quiver of the lips she burst into passionate sobs. Dropping weakly down
upon the sofa she cried until her whole body shook convulsively. Paul
watched her in silence for some time, and then put his arm about her bowed
shoulders.

'Tell me,' he said. 'I understand.' And punctuated by that bitter weeping
the story was told. Kitty had been in the service of a county family and had

married a young tradesman of excellent prospects. Two short years of married life and then the War. Her husband was ordered to France. One year of that ceaseless waiting, hoping, fearing, which war imposes upon women, and then an official telegram. Kitty returned to service—and her baby died.

'What had I done,' she cried wildly. 'What had I done to deserve it? I'd gone as straight as a girl can go. There was nobody else in the world for me but him. Then my baby was taken, and the parsons talk about God! What did anything matter after that! Oh, the loneliness. The loneliness! Men don't know what that loneliness is like—the loneliness of a woman. They have their friends, but nobody wants to be friends with a lonely woman. There are only two ways for her. I tried to kill myself, and I was too big a coward, so I took the easy way and thought I might forget.'

'You thought you might forget. And did you think your husband would ever forget?'

'Oh, my God! don't say that!'

'You see, the name of God still means something to you,' said Paul gently. 'Many a soldier's wife has become a believer, and you are not the first who has shuddered to believe.' He saw his course clearly, and did not hesitate to pursue it. 'The parsons, as you say, talk about God without knowing of What or of Whom they speak, but I am not a parson, and I know of What I speak. Look at me. I have something to ask you.'

She turned her eyes, red with weeping, and was fascinated by Paul's concentrated gaze.

'Do you ever dream of your husband?' he asked.

'Oh! you'll drive me mad!' she whispered, trembling violently. 'For the first six months after . . . I was afraid to close my eyes. I am frightened. I am frightened.'

'You are frightened because he is here, Kitty; but he is here to guard you and not to harm you. He is here because tonight you have done with that life of forgetfulness which is worse than the memories of those you loved. He will always come when you call him, until the very hour that you are ready to join him again. But if you do wrong to the memory of a man who was true to you, even I cannot promise that he will ever hold you in his arms again.'

'But can you promise? —Oh! you seem to *know!* You seem . . . Who are you? Tell me who you are—'

She stood up and retreated from Paul, the pallor of her face discernible through the tear-streaked make-up. He smiled in his charming fashion, holding out his hands.

'I am one who has studied the secrets of nature,' he replied. 'And I promise you that you shall live again as a woman, and be loved by those whom you think you have lost. Look at your locket before you sleep tonight and dream, but do not be afraid. Promise, now, that you will always be faithful in the future. You shall give me the names of your old friends and I shall see if all this great mistake cannot be forgotten.'

XIII

Turning up the lights in his study, Paul seated himself in the great carved chair before his writing-table, and looked for a long time at a set of corrected proofs which lay there. Then, leaning back in the chair he stared about the room at the new and strange ornaments which he had collected in accordance with his system of working amid sympathetic colour. His meeting with Kitty Chester he accepted as a message of encouragement designed to restore his faith in himself and his mission. That he had accomplished her redemption he did not dare to believe, but at least he had rendered it possible. He readily recognized the symbolical significance of their meeting, and it tinged his reflections and quickened his genius, so that a new light was shed thereby upon some of the darker places of the religious past.

Close to his hand, upon an ebony pedestal, stood a squat stone figure having the head of a man with the face of a bull. It was an idol of incalculable age, from Jules Thessaly's collection, a relic of prehistoric Greece and the ancient worship of the threefold Hecate. Set in some remote Thracian valley, it had once looked down upon orgies such as few modern minds can imagine, had seen naked Bacchantes surrounded by tamed jungle beasts and having their arms enwreathed with living serpents, flinging themselves prostrate before its altar, and then amid delirious dances calling upon the Bull-faced Bacchus of whom we read in one of the Orphic hymns. . . .

Dimly visible in a recess of the black-oak bureau was Kali, goddess of Desire, and near her, in a narrow cupboard, the light impinged upon a white, smooth piece of stone which was attached to a wooden frame. It was the emblem of Venus Urania from the oldest temple in Cyprus. These priceless relics were all lent by Thessaly, as were an imperfect statuette in wood, fossilised with age and probably of Moabite origin, representing Ashtaroth, daughter of Sin, and a wonderfully preserved ivory figure, half woman and half fish, of Derceto of Ascalon. The sacred courtesans of the past and the Kitty

THE ORCHARD OF TEARS

Chesters of the present (mused Paul) all were expressions of that mystic principle, IEVE, upon which the universe turns as a compass upon its needle, and which, reproduced in our gross bodies, has led to the creation of the Groves of Paphos. That sublime Desire which should lead us to the great Unity and final fulfilment, would seem through all the ages to have driven men ever further from it. Would a day never dawn when all that uncontrolled Force should be contained and directed harmoniously, when the pure Isis of the Egyptian mysteries should cast down the tainted Isis lascivious rites were celebrated in Pompeii? Scarcely perceptible was the progress of mankind. In every woman was born a spark of Bacchic fire, which leapt up sweetly at the summons of love or crimson, shameful, at the beck of lust. There were certain conditions peculiarly favourable to its evil development; loneliness, according to Kitty Chester, a loneliness beyond man's undersstanding. . . .

Paul aroused himself from a reverie and remembered that he had been thinking of Flamby with a strange and lingering tenderness. The clock on the mantelpiece recorded the hour of two a.m., and he turned out the lights in the study and made his way upstairs. He had told Eustace not to wait up for him, and the house was in darkness. Before Yvonne's room Paul stopped, and gently opened the door. A faint sound of regular breathing, and the scent of jasmine came to him. He closed the door as quietly as he had opened it, and proceeded to the next, which was that of his own room.

When he retired he threw open the heavy curtains draped before the windows, and saw that the weather had cleared. White clouds were racing past the face of the moon. He fell asleep almost immediately, and the moon pursuing her mystic journey, presently shone fully in upon the sleeper. Unwittingly Paul was performing one of the rites of the old Adonis worshippers in sleeping with the moonlight upon his face, and thus sleeping he was visited by a strange dream. . . .

Drunk with the wine of life, he ran through a grove of scented pines, flanked by thickets of giant azaleas and taunting one onward and upward to where faint silver outlines traced upon the azure sky lured to distant peaks. Etherealized shapes of haunting beauty surrounded him, and sometimes they seemed to merge into the verdure and sometimes it was a cloud of blossom that gave up an airy form as a lily gives of its sweetness, now bearing a white nymph, now an Apollo-limbed youth, sun kissed and godlike. Gay hued, four footed creatures mingled with the flying shapes, and all pressed onward; things sleek and eager hastening through the grove, swiftly passing, hoof and pad; leaping girls and laughing youths; amid sentient flowers and trees whose life was joy. Earth's magic sap pulsed through them all and being was an orgy of worship—worship of a bountiful Mother, of Earth in her golden youth. . . .

He passed thence to the banks of Egypt's Nile, and heard the lamentations of priests and wailing of women as a black ox, flower bedecked and wearing a collar encrusted with gems, was drowned in the turgid stream. Time and space ceased to exist for him. Through the murk of cavernous passages he paced, pausing before a pit in which reposed a sarcophagus of huge dimensions; and when the dim company and he had paid tribute to that which lay there, all ascended to a temple, lofty and awesome, its dizzy roof upheld by aisles of monstrous granite. To an accompaniment of sorrowful chanting, the doors of the altar were opened, and within upon the shrine rested a square-hewn statue. Jewelled lamps glowed and censers smoked before the image of the bull, Apis.

The sistrums called him to a shrine of Isis, where *kyphi* was burning, and priestesses, fair royal virgins, made lotus offerings to the mother of light; but magic of old Nileland might not withhold him from the Rites of Ceres when the *Hymn to Demeter* arose within those wonder halls of Ictinus. He saw the blood of a white kid flow upon the altar of Diana at Ephesus and with his own hands laid poppy and dittany at the pearly feet of the Huntress. The *Lament of Adonis* wooed him to the Temple of the Moon, the *Hymn to Râ* won him back to Egypt's god of gods. He lighted *Tsan Ihang*, sweet perfume of Tibet, before Gautama Buddha in Canton's Temple of Five Hundred Ginns and kissed the sacred covering of the Kaaba at Mecca.

Consciousness intruding upon subconsciousness, the mind calling upon the spirit, he found himself questing a likeness, a memory, a furtive thought; and partly it took shape, so that it seemed to him that Apis, Isis, Orpheus and the Buddha had a common resemblance to some person living and human, known to him; whose voice he had heard, and heard again leading the Orphic hymn, chanting the Buddhist prayers and bewailing the passing of Adonis. A man it was his memory sought, and alike in granite statue and golden idol he had detected him; in the silver note of the sistrum, in the deeps of the *Hymn to Râ*. . . .

All blended into one insistent entreaty, voices, music, perfumes, calling upon him to return, but he forced his way through a passage, stifling, low and laden with the breath of remote mortality like those in the depths of Egypt's pyramids. He came forth into a vast cathedral and stood before the high altar. As the acolyte swung the thurible and incense floated upward to the Cross, he, too, arose seraphic and alighted upon the very top of the dome. Below him stretched a maze of tortuous streets, thronged with men and women of a thousand ages and of all the races of mankind. Minaret, pagoda, dome, propylon, arch, portico jutted up from the labyrinth like tares amid a cornfield. Then a mist crept darkly down and drew its mantle over them all. A golden crescent projected above the haze, but it was swallowed up; a slender spire for long remained but finally was lost. He looked down at the basilica upon which he stood. It had vanished. He raised his eyes, and the mist was gone, but an empty world lay where a teeming world had been; a desert wherein no living thing stirred. A voice, a familiar voice, spoke, and the words were familiar, too. They melted into the sweet melancholy of the *Lament for Adonis,* and he awoke, dazzled, half blinded by the brilliancy of the moonlight.

PART THIRD

THE KEY

I

Paul's book, *The Gates,* was published in the spring. Answering, as it did, if not completely, the question upon the solution of which the course of so many human lives depended, it was received as great works were received in the Arcadian days of Victorian literature. It silenced Paul's contemporaries as thunder silences a human orchestra. Only two critics retained sufficient composure to be flippant. No living man commanded so vast an audience as Paul Mario, and now his voice spoke in a new tone. To some it came as a balm, to some it brought disquiet; in each and everyone it wrought a change of outlook. Following a period of strife wherein all save brute force seemed to have perished, it vindicated the claims of him who said that the pen was mightier than the sword. Copies found their way to Berlin but were confiscated by the police. A Vienna firm printed an edition and their premises were raided by the authorities. To the meanest intelligence it was apparent that one had arisen who had something new to say—or something so old that the world had forgotten it. By means of sacrificing half of his usual royalty Paul had contrived that *The Gates* should be published at a price which placed it within reach of popular purchase. What profits still accrued to him, and these were considerable, he devoted to institutes for the wounded and to the maintenance of Hatton Towers as an officers' convalescent home.

Because he did not seek to depict a modern battlefield, knowing that Shakespeare himself must have waxed trite upon such a theme, the hell-pit of Flanders and the agony of France were draped behind his drama like a curtain. No man had come so near to the truth in naked words. His silence was the silence of genius. The tears of the world flowed through his work, yet no weeping woman was depicted. The word of Christ and the message of Mohammed alike were respected and upheld, but priest and *imâm* conspired to denounce him. Rebirth in the flesh he offered as a substitute for heaven and hell. Love and reunion were synonymous. Not for ages unimaginable could man hope to gain that final state which is variously known as Heaven, Paradise and Nirvana; only by the doing of such evil as rarely lies within human compass could he be judged worthy of that extinction which is Hell. No soul could sink thus low whilst another mourned it; and was there a man so vile that no woman loved him? Whilst there was love there could be no Hell, for in Hell there was no reunion. Pestilence and war on earth corresponded with undivinable upheavals on another planet. 'Ere a man's body has grown cold on earth he has stirred again in the womb of his mother.'

Only by means of certain perversions of natural law of which suicide was one, could man evade rebirth, and even thus only for a time. Sorrow was not a punishment but merely a consequence. Punishment was man-made and had no place in the wider scheme, could have no place in a universe where all things were self-inflicted. Germany symbolized the culmination of materialism, 'the triumph of the Bull.' To Germany had been attracted all those entities, converging through the ages, whose progress had been retarded by abandonment to materialism. 'Caligula and Nero defile the earth today, and others even mightier in evil. A Messalina and a PoppF do not survive individually, for such as these are not human in the strictest sense, in that they lack what is called a soul which is a property common to humanity. The parable of the woman of Corinth who seduced Menippus, a disciple of Apollonius, is misunderstood. We have come to regard all mortal bodies as the tenements of immortal souls. This is true of men but is not always true of women. Such women are not strictly mortal: they are feminine animals and their place in the scheme will be discussed later. To speak of their sins is to misuse the word. They are sinless, as the serpent and the upas tree are sinless. . . .'

Paul had discovered that his vast scheme might not be compassed in a single book. *The Gates* was the first drama of a trilogy. In it he outlined the universal truth of which the churches had lost sight or which they had chosen to obscure. He offered a glimpse of the shrine but laid down no doctrine nor did he seek to impose a new philosophy upon the world. In his second book he proposed to furnish proofs of the claims advanced in the first, and in his third to draw deductions from the foregoing. In this he had made Euclid his model. Upon the necessity for a hierarchy and a mystic ritual he insisted. He maintained that orthodox Christianity had lost its hold upon Europe, touched upon causes and indicated how the world upheaval was directly due to the failing power of the churches. He proposed to remodel religion upon a system earlier than but not antagonistic to that of Christ. His claim that the systems of Heremes, Krishna, Confucius Moses, Orphesus and Christ were based upon a common primeval truth he supported by an arresting array of historical facts. All of them had taught that man is re-incarnated, and because Western thought had been diverted from the truth and the fallacies of Heaven, Hell and Purgatory substituted for simple Rebirth, Western thought had become chaotic. The figure of the Pope and the maintenance of a celibate priesthood had prolonged the life of the Church of Rome because, in Paul's opinion, these were survivals of that mysticism upon which the remote hierarchies were builded. 'No religion in the world's history has held such absolute sway over a people as that of Ancient Egypt; no figure living in the memory of man has such majesty of awe as that of the royal high-priest of Amen Râ . . .'

On the day that *The Gates* was published, Yvonne came down late to breakfast, a gossamer study all filmy lace, with the morning sun in her hair. The windows were open, and a hint of spring lent zest to every joy, the loamy fragrance of nascent plant life stealing into the room from the little garden. Tulips decorated the sideboard, for Yvonne loved tulips, and a big bowl of pink roses stood upon the centre of the breakfast table. Paul, glancing up from the pages of the *Daily Telegraph,* became aware of something vaguely familiar yet unexpected in his wife's face. She seemed listless, even slightly pale, and he experienced a sudden pang of an indefinable nature. Looking back over the past two years, he wondered if they had been as significant, as fully crowded with reality, for Yvonne as they had been for him. In Don's manner, when speaking of Yvonne he had more than once detected a sort of gentle reproof and had wondered why Don, who understood most things, failed to perceive that Yvonne's happiness lay in her husband's work. But, this morning, Paul was thinking more particularly about a remark of Jules Thessaly's. Thessaly had urged him, before commencing his second volume to spend a month in Devon. 'You need it, Mario, and your wife needs it more than you do.'

Paul did not immediately broach the subject which now became uppermost in his mind, but following some desultory conversation, he said, 'I should think Devon would be delightful just now. Suppose we run down for a week or two.'

'I should be glad,' replied Yvonne. 'I should have suggested it earlier, only I knew that you could not finish *The Gates* away from your library.' She spoke in a curiously listless way.

'Could you be ready to go on Thursday, Yvonne?'

'Yes, quite easily.'

'I can work upon my notes for the autumn book, in Devon better than in London.'

'But,' began Yvonne, and stopped, staring unseeingly at the roses in the bowl upon the table.

'But what, Yvonne?'

'I was about to propose a complete rest, Paul, but I know it would be useless if the working mood is upon you.'

'You realize what it means to me, Yvonne. I should no more be justified in laying down my pen whilst there was more work to do than a soldier would be justified in laying down his sword in the heat of battle. You do not feel that this task which I have taken up has made a gulf between us?'

'It has done so in a sense,' replied Yvonne, crumbling a fragment of bread between her fingers. 'But I have never been so foolish as to become jealous of your work.'

'I might have been in the army and stationed on the other side of the world,' said Paul laughing.

'I am not complaining about your work, Paul.'

'Yet you are not entirely happy.'

'What makes you think so?'

'I don't know. I sometimes feel that you are not.'

'I am quite happy,' said Yvonne in the listless voice, and presently she went up to her room, Paul looking after her in a troubled way. He was uneasily searching his memory for a clue to the significance of that expression, vaguely familiar but unexpected, which he had noticed in Yvonne's face. He lighted his pipe and went into the study.

Paul already was at work on the second phase of his huge task. He was seeking to prove that the arts had taken the place of the inspired prophets and sibyls of old, that they were not reflections of the souls of a nation but were expressions of the creative Will—the *Od* of Baron Reichenbach—and were in fact not effects but causes. Not only did he claim this for the avowed philosophers, but also, in some degree, for every writer, composer, painter or sculptor. In Russian literature he perceived a forshadowing of the doom of Tzardom and imminent catastrophe. In the literature of France and England he sought to divine the future. The fervent imperialism of Kipling stirred his emotions, but left him spiritually cold. Patriotism was the mother of self-sacrifice, but also of murder, and Paul distrusted all forces which made for intolerance. The delicate word-painting of Pierre Loti, with its typically French genius for exalting the trivial, Paul studied carefully. He found it to resemble the art of those patient, impassive Japanese craftsmen, who draw and colour some exquisite trifling design, a bird, a palm tree, and then cut the picture in half in order to fit it into a panel of some quaint little lacquered cabinet as full of unexpected cupboards and drawers as the Cretan Labyrinth was full of turnings. He studied the books of the living as Egypt's priests were wont to study *The Book of the Dead*, pondering upon Arnold Bennett, who could produce atmosphere without the use of colour, and H. G. Wells who thought aloud. In the hectic genius of D'Annunzio he sought in vain the spirit of Italy. He perceived in those glowing pages the hand of a man possessed, and who should have been prepared to find his MSS. written in penmanship other than his own, like those of Madam Blavatsky's *Isis Unveiled*.

'It all means something, Don,' he said one day. 'We have been granted an insight to the psychology of the German people, which has enabled us to trace the thread running through their literature, art and music, Oscar Wilde, who wrote with a stylo dipped in ambergris, was truly a manifestation of the German spirit which began to invade us subtly at about that time. His scented prose could not conceal this spirit from the perception of Richard Strauss. Strauss recognized it and welcomed it with the music of *nebels, kinnors* and *tabors,* as the misguided Children of Israel welcomed the golden calf. Nietzche's "Thou goest among women?—Take thy whip" we see now to be no mere personal expression but the voice of the soul of Germany, a black thread interwoven in their creative art. There is a similar thread, but perhaps of silver, interwoven in our own and in the French art. Where does it begin and whither does it lead?'

Yet those days throughout which Paul laboured unceasingly for the greatest cause of humanity were lotus days for many. London was raided and rationed; London swore softly, demanded a change of government, turned up its coat collar and stumped doggedly along much as usual. Men fought and women prayed, whilst Paul worked night and day to bring some ray of hope to the hearts of those in whom faith was dead. The black thread crept like an ebon stain into the wool of the carpet. The image of the Bull was set up in many a grove hitherto undefiled, and Paul worked the more feverishly because it was one of the inscrutable cosmic laws that the black should sometimes triumph over the white.

Paul's intimacy with Jules Thessaly had grown closer than he realized. Thessaly was become indispensable to him. Paul, had he essayed the task, must have found it all but impossible to disentangle his own ideas, or those due to direct inspiration, from the ideas of Thessaly or those based upon inquiries traceable to the astonishing data furnished by his collection. Item by item he had revealed its treasures to the man who alone had power to wield them as levers to move the world. Remote but splendid creeds, mere hazy memories of mankind, were reconstructed upon these foundations. The Izamal temples of Yucatan were looted of their secrets—the secrets of a great Red Race, mighty in knowledge and power, which had sought to look upon the face of God before the Great Pyramid was fashioned, whose fleets had ruled the vanished seas known to us as the Sahara and North Africa, whose golden capital had looked proudly put upon an empire mightier than Rome—an empire which the Atlantic Ocean had swallowed up. The story of this cataclysm which had engulfed Atlantis, brought to new lands by a few survivors, had bequeathed to men the legend of the Deluge. The riddle of The Sphinx, most ancient religious symbol in the known world, was resolved; for Paul saw it to represent man emerging from the animal and already aspiring to the spiritual state.

War, pestilence and vast geographical upheavals alike were manifestations of spiritual conflict physically reflected. Some of the German philosophers had perceived this dimly, but as one born in blindness fails to comprehend light, their vision was no more than hereditary memory of another pit of doom which had engulfed them. Those who spoke of casting down the spirit of Prussian militarism used metaphor veiling a truth as profound as that which underlies the Holy Trinity, and which is symbolized by the Sphinx. As vultures swooped to carrion, as harlots flocked to Babylon, so had the unredeemed souls of the universe descended upon Germany. . . .

Thus his concept of evil was universal, and to those who sought to fix 'responsibility' for the war upon this one or that he raised a protesting hand. No man made the Deluge.

By subtle means, insidious as the breath of nard, corruption of primeval sin was spread from race to race. By like means it must be combated, Truth must be disguised if it should penetrate to enemy darkness. A naked truth is rarely acceptable, or, as Don expressed it, 'Truth does not strip well.' Paul discussed this aspect of the matter with Don and Thessaly one day. 'We are all children,' he said. 'If it were not for such picturesque people as Henry VIII and Charles II we should forget our history for lack of landmarks. Carefully selected words are writer's landmarks, and in remembering them one remembers the passage which they decorated. I can conjure up at will the entire philosophy of Buddha as epitomized in the *Light of Asia* by contemplation of such a landmark; Arnold's expression for a sheep, "woolly mother." There are other words and phrases which the art of then-users in the same way has magically endowed: "Totem" is one of these. It is for me a Pharos instantly opening up the fairway to a great man's philosophy. "Damascus," too, has such properties, and the phrase "cherry blossom in Japan" bears me upon a magical carpet to a certain street in Yokohama and there unveils to me all the secrets of Japanese mysticism.'

'I quite see your point,' Don replied. 'In the same way I have never ceased to regret that I was not born in Ashby-de-la-Zouch. The possession of such a euphonious birthplace would have coloured all my life.'

'But like the Scotsman you would have revered your home from a distance,' said Thessaly. 'I agree with you that it would have been an ideal birthplace if you had left it at so tender an age that you failed to recall its physical peculiarities. It is the same with women. In order that one should retain nothing but fairy memories of a woman—memories of some poetic name, of the perfume of roses, of beauty glimpsed through gossamer—it is important that one should not have lived with her. Herein lies the lasting glamour of the woman we have never possessed.'

II

The world had been discussing Paul Mario's New Gospel as enunciated in *The Gates* for three weeks or more. On a bright morning when sunbeams filtered through the dust which partly curtained the windows of Guilder's and painted golden squares and rectangles upon the floor, Flamby stood where the light touched her elfin hair into torch-like flame, removing a very smart studio smock preparatory to departing to Regali's for lunch. There was no one else in the small painting-room, except a wondrous-hued parrakeet upon a perch, from which he contemplated his portrait in oils, head knowingly tilted to one side with solemn disapproval, for Flamby had painted his bill too red and he knew it, apparently.

'Bad,' he remarked. 'Damn bad.'

He belonged to Crozier, the artist famed for 'sun-soaked flesh,' and Crozier's pupils were all too familiar with this formula. It was so often upon Crozier's lips that Lorenzo the Magnificent (the parrakeet) had acquired it perfectly.

'Quite right, Lorenzo,' said Flamby, throwing her smock on to a stool. 'It's blasted bad.'

'Damn bad,' corrected Lorenzo. 'No guts.'

'I don't agree with you there, Lorenzo. It's your nose that I hate.'

'No sun!' screamed Lorenzo excitedly. 'The bloodsome thing never saw the sun!'

'Oh, please behave, Lorenzo, or I shall not share my sugar ration with you any more.'

'Sugar?' inquired Lorenzo, head on one side again.

Flamby held up a lump of sugar upon her small pink palm, and a silence of contentment immediately descended upon Lorenzo, only broken by the sound of munching. Flamby was just going out to wash the paint from her hands, for she always contrived to get nearly as much upon her fingers as upon the canvas, when a cheery voice cried: 'Ha! caught you. I thought I might be too late.'

She turned, and there in the doorway stood Don. Less than three months had elapsed since his last leave and Flamby was intensely surprised to see him. She came forward with outstretched hands. 'Oh, Don,' she cried. 'How lovely! However did you manage it?'

An exquisite blush stained her cheeks, and her eyes lighted up happily. Glad surprises made her blush, and she was very sincerely glad as well as surprised to see Don. She had not even heard him approach. She had been wondering what Devonshire was like, for Paul was in Devonshire. Now as Don took both her hands and smiled in the old joyous way she thought that he looked ill, almost cadaverous, in spite of the tan which clung to his skin.

'Craft, Flamby, guile and the subtlety of the serpent. The best men get the worst leave.'

'I don't believe it,' said Flamby, watching him in sudden anxiety. 'You have been ill. Oh, don't think you can pretend to *me*; I can see you have.'

'Bad,' remarked Lorenzo in cordial agreement. He had finished the sugar. 'Damn bad.'

'What!' cried Don—'have you got old Crozier's Lorenzo down here? Hullo! let us see how you have "percepted" him.' He crossed to the easel, surveying Flamby's painting critically. 'Does Hammett still talk about "percepting the subject" and "emerging the high-lights" and "profunding the shadows"?'

'He does. You're mean not to tell me.'

'What do you want me to tell you, Flamby?—that the drawing is magnificent and the painting brilliant except for the treatment of the bill, which is *too* brilliant.' He turned and met her reproachful gaze. 'Perhaps I *am* mean,

Flamby, to frighten you by not replying to your question, but really I am quite fit. I have had a touch of trench fever or something, not enough to result in being sent home to hospital, and have now got a few days' sick-leave to pull round after a course of weak gruel.'

'That's very unusual, isn't it?'

'What, Flamby?'

'To get home leave after treatment at a base hospital? I mean they might as well have sent you home in the first place.'

Don stared at her long and seriously. 'Flamby,' he said, 'you have been flirting with junior subalterns. No one above the rank of a second-lieutenant ever knew so much about King's Regulations.'

'Own up, then.'

Don continued the serious stare. 'Flamby,' he said, 'your father would have been proud of you. You are a very clever girl. If art fails there is always the Bar. I am not advising you to take to drink; I refer to the law. Listen, Flamby. I was wrong to try to deceive you as well as the others. Besides, it is not necessary. You are unusual. I stopped a stray piece of shrapnel a fortnight after I went back and was sent to a hospital in Burton-on-Trent. The M.O.'s have a positive genius for sending men to spots remote from their homes and kindreds—appalling sentence. In this case it was a blessing in disguise. By some muddle or another my name was omitted from the casualty list, or rather it was printed as "Norton," and never corrected publicly. I accepted the kindness of the gods. Imagine my relief. I had pictured sisters and cousins and the dear old Aunt dragging themselves to Burton-on-Trent—and I am the only beer drinker in the family. I know you won't betray my gruesome secret, Flamby.'

Flamby's eyes were so misty that she averted her face. 'Oh, Don,' she said unsteadily, 'and I wrote to you only three days ago and thought you were safe.'

Don unbuttoned the left breast-pocket of his tunic and flourished a letter triumphantly. 'Young Conroy has been forwarding all my mail,' he explained, 'and I have addressed my letters from nowhere in particular and sent them to him to be posted! Now, what about the guile and subtlety of the serpent! Let us take counsel with the great Severus Regali. I am allowed a little clear soup and an omelette, now.'

Don and Flamby arrived late at Regali's and were compelled to wait for a time in the little inner room. There were many familiar faces around the tables. Chauvin was there with Madame Rilette, the human geranium, and Hammett; Wildrake, editor of the *Quatre d'Arts* revue and the Baronne G., Paris's smartest and most up-to-date lady novelist. The Baronne had been married four times. Her latest hobby was libel actions. Archibald Forester, re-nowned as an explorer of the psychic borderland, and wearing green tabs and a crown upon his shoulder-strap, discussed matters Alpine with an Italian artillery officer. On the whole the atmosphere was distinctly Savage that day. Flamby accepted a cigarette from Don and sat for awhile, pensive. With a jade-green velvet tam-o'-shanter to set off the coppery high-lights of her hair she was a picture worthy of the admiration which was discernible in Don's eyes. Presently she said, 'I found you out a long time ago.'

'Found me out?'

'Yes, found you out. I don't know to this day how much I really receive from the War Office, because Mr. Nevin won't tell me. He just muddles me up with a lot of figures—'

'You have seen him, then?'

'Of course I have seen him. But one thing I do know. I owe you over a hundred pounds, and I am going to pay it!'

'But, Flamby,' said Don, a startled expression appearing upon his face, 'you don't owe it to me at all. You are wrong.'

Flamby studied him carefully for awhile. 'I am going to send it to Mr. Nevin—I have told him so—and he can settle the matter.' She laid her hand on Don's sleeve. 'Don't think me silly, or an ungrateful little beast,' she said, 'but I can't talk about it any more; it makes me want to cry. Did you know that Chauvin got me a commission from the War Office propaganda people to do pictures of horses and mules and things?'

'Yes,' replied Don, guiltily. But to his great relief Flamby did not accuse him of being concerned in the matter.

'I felt a rotten little slacker,' explained Flamby; 'I wrote and told you so. Did you get the letter?'

'Of course. Surely I replied?'

'I don't remember if you did, but I told Chauvin and he recommended my work to them and they said I could do twelve drawings. They accepted the first three I did, but rejected the fourth, which both Hammett and Chauvin thought the best.'

'Probably it was. That was why they rejected it. But about this money—'

'Please,' pleaded Flamby.

Don looked into her eyes and was silenced. He suppressed a sigh. 'Have you seen Paul lately?' he asked.

'No. He is away. His book frightens me.'

'Frightens you,' said Don, staring curiously. 'In what way?'

'I don't know that I can explain. I feel afraid for *him.*'

'For Paul?'

'Yes.'

'Because he has seen the truth?'

Flamby hesitated. 'It must be awful for a doctor who has specialized in some dreadful disease to find—'

'That he suffers from it? This is a common thing with specialists.' Don spoke almost heedlessly, but had no sooner spoken than he became aware of the peculiar significance of his words. He sat staring silently at Flamby. Before he had time for further speech Regali attended in person to announce that places were vacant at one of the tables. This table Don and Flamby shared with a lady wearing her hair dressed in imitation of a yellow dahlia, and with a prominent colourist who was devoting his life to dissipating the popular delusion about trees being green. He was gradually educating the world to comprehend that trees were not green but blue. He had a very long nose and ate French mustard with his macaroni. The conversation became cubical and coloured.

'I maintain,' said the colourist, who was fiercely cynical, as might have been anticipated of one who consumed such large quantities of mustard, 'that humanity is akin to the worm. The myth of Psyche and the idea that we possess souls arose simply out of the contemplation of colour by some primitive sensitive. Very delicately coloured young girls were responsible for the legend, but humanity in the bulk is colourless, and therefore soulless. Large public gatherings fill me with intense personal disgust. From Nelson's point of view, a popular demonstration in Trafalgar Square must unpleasantly resemble a box of bait.'

'Clearly you have never loved,' said Don. 'One day some misguided woman may marry you. You will awaken to the discovery that she is different from common humanity.'

'Nearly every man considers his own wife to be different from other women—until the third or fourth day of the honeymoon.'

He was incorrigible; French mustard had embittered his life. 'Some men are even more gross than women,' he declared thoughtfully. 'Cubically they are stronger, but their colouring is less delicate.'

His yellow-haired companion watched him with limpid faithful brown eyes, hanging upon his words as upon the pronouncements of a CumFan oracle. Having concluded his luncheon with a piece of cheese liberally coated in mustard he rose, shaking his head sadly.

'Don't shake your head like that,' Don implored him. 'I can hear your brains rattling.'

But smileless, the cynic departed, and Flamby looked after him without regret. 'If he painted as much as he talked,' she said, 'he would have to hire a railway station to show his pictures.'

'Yes, or the offices of the Food Controller. His conversation is intensely interesting, but it doesn't mean anything. I have always suspected him of keeping coal in his bath.'

Orlando James came in, standing just by the doorway, one hand resting upon his hip whilst he gnawed the nails of the other with his fine white teeth. He wore the colours of a regiment with which he had served for a time, and a silver badge on the right lapel of his tweed jacket. Presently, perceiving Flamby, he advanced to the table at which she was seated with Don. He had all the arrogance of acknowledged superiority. 'Hullo, kid,' he said, dropping into the chair vacated by the cynical one. 'How do, Courtier. You look a bit cheap—been gassed?'

'No,' replied Don; 'merely a stiff neck due to sleeping with my head above the parapet.'

James stared dully, continuing to bite his nails. 'When are you going back?'

'As soon as my batman wires me that the weather has improved.'

'Have you finished lunch? Let's split a bottle of wine before you go.'

'No bottle of wine for me,' said Flamby, 'unless you want the police in. One glass of wine and you'd be ashamed to know me.' She was uncomfortably conscious of a certain tension which the presence of James had created. 'Isn't it time we started?' she asked, turning to Don. 'Mrs. Chumley will be expecting us.'

'Ah!' cried Don gratefully, glancing at his watch. 'Of course she will. Where is the waiter?'

'You don't like James, do you?' said Flamby, as the car approached The Hostel.

'No. Vanity in a man is ridiculous, and I always endeavour to avoid ridiculous people. James is a clever painter, but a very stupid fellow. Seeing him to-day reminds me of something I had meant to ask you, Flamby. Just before last I came on leave you wrote at Paul's request to enquire if I considered it wise that you should go about with James and we discussed the point whilst I was home. You remember, no doubt?'

Flamby nodded. Her expression was very pensive. 'Then I wrote and asked if you minded my seeing him occasionally for a special purpose, and you wrote back that you had every confidence in my discretion, which pleased me very much. Now I suppose you want to know what the special purpose was?'

'Not unless you wish to tell me, Flamby.'

'I do wish to tell you,' said Flamby slowly. 'That was why I suggested coming here, because I knew all the time of course that Mrs. Chumley was away.'

They entered The Hostel, deserted as it usually was at that hour of the day, passing into the courtyard, which already was gay with the flowers of early spring. The window-boxes, too, and vases within open casements splashed patches of colour upon the old-world canvas, the yellow and purple of crocus and daffodil, modest star-blue of forget-me-nots and the varied tints of sweet hyacinth. Flamby's tiny house, which Mrs. Chumley called 'the squirrel's nest,' was fragrant with roses, for Flamby's taste in flowers was extravagant, and she regularly exhausted the stocks of the local florist. A huge basket of white roses stood upon a side-table, a card attached. Flamby glanced at the card. 'James again,' she said. 'He's some use in the world after all.' She composedly filled a jug with water and placed the flowers in it until she should have time to arrange them.

'Is Chauvin expecting you this afternoon?' asked Don.

'No, not today. I love Chauvin, but I don't think I shall be able to stay on with him if I am to finish the other eight designs for the War Office people in time. Please light your pipe. Would you like a drink? I've got all sorts of things to drink.'

'No, thank you, Flamby. We can go out to tea presently.'

'No, let's have tea here. I have some gorgeous cakes I got at Fullers' this morning.'

'Right. Better still. I will help.'

Flamby tossed her tam-o'-shanter on to a chair, slapped the pockets of Don's tunic in quest of his cigarette-case, found it, took out and lighted a cigarette, and then curled herself up in a corner of the settee, hugging her knees. 'Paul thinks I'm fast,' she said.

Don, who was lighting his pipe, stared at her so long that the match burned his fingers and dropped into his cap, which lay beside him on the floor. Flamby's visitors speedily acquired the homely trick of hanging their hats up on the floor.

'Flamby!' he said reproachfully, 'I know you are joking, but I don't like you to say such a thing even in jest.'

'*Dulce est desipere,*' replied Flamby, 'but I am not jesting. Oh, that beastly Latin! Do you remember when I quoted Portia to you? It makes me go all goosey to think of some of the awful things I have said to people.'

'You have said one thing, Flamby, which I must request you to explain,' said Don gravely. 'Paul is utterly incapable of harbouring an evil thought about anyone, and equally incapable of misjudging character.'

'Ah, I knew you would say that, Don, and it is just that which worries me so.'

'I don't understand.'

Flamby snuggled her knees up tighter against her round chin and stared wistfully straight before her. A ray from the afternoon sun intruded through the window and touched her wonderful hair into magic flame. 'Paul has altered the lives of a lot of people, hasn't he?' she asked.

'He has. I cannot doubt that he will become the centre of a world-wide movement. I received a letter only two days ago from a man who was with us at Oxford, and who entered the Church, assuring me that he had only awaited such a lead to resign his office and seek independently to spread the true doctrine. He is only one of many. I know several Army chaplains who have been troubled with serious doubts for years. They will rally to Paul as the Crusaders rallied to Peter the Hermit.'

'I read his book,' said Flamby, still staring unseeingly before her, 'and something inside myself told me that every word of it was true. I know that I have lived before, everybody knows it, but everybody isn't able to realize it. Dad told me that re-incarnation was the secret of life once when I asked him who his father was. He said, "Never mind about that. Damn your ancestors!..." Oh! I didn't mean to say it! But, really he said that. "It is your *spiritual* ancestry that counts," he told me. "There are plenty of noble blackguards, and it wasn't his parents who made a poet of Keats." Dad convinced me in a wonderful way. He pointed out that a child born of a fine cultured family and one whose father was a thief and his mother something worse didn't start level at all. One was handicapped before he had the sense to think for himself; "be-

fore he weighed in," was how dad put it. "If there is a just God," he said—
"and every man finds out sooner or later that there is, to his joy or to his sorrow—there are no unfair handicaps. It wouldn't be racing. Why should an innocent baby be born with the diseases and deformities of its parents? Why
should some be born blind?" What he called "the hell-fire and brimstone"
theory used to make him sick. He considered that most missionaries ought
to be publicly executed, and said that in the Far East where he had lived you
could see their work "like the trail of a tin tabernacle across a blasted heath."
That sounds like swearing, but it's Shakespeare.'

'I don't see,' said Don, as Flamby became silent, 'what has this to do
with Paul's misjudgment of you, or your misjudgment of Paul. It simply
means that you agree with him. You are such an extraordinarily clever girl,
and have had so extraordinary a training, that I cannot pass lightly by anything you say seriously. What has led you to believe that Paul thinks ill of
you, and why does it worry you that I think him incapable of such a thing?'

Flamby absently flicked cigarette ash upon the carpet. 'According to *The
Gates*,' she said, speaking very slowly and evidently seeking for words where-
with to express her meaning, 'everybody's sorrows and joys and understanding or lack of understanding are exactly in proportion to the use they have
made of their opportunities, not just in one life but in other lives before.'

Don nodded without speaking.

'A man who had come as near to perfection as is possible in this world
would have found his perfect mate, what Paul calls his "Isis-self."'

'Embodied, in Paul's case, in Yvonne.'

'He would be in no doubt about it, and no more would she. If she was
below him he would raise her, if she was above him he might marry, but he
would not mistake another woman for the right one. And things that convinced other men would not convince a true initiate. So I am worried about
Paul, because if he is not a true initiate, where did he learn the things that are
in *The Gates?*'

Don's face was very grave. 'You have been studying strange books,
Flamby. What have you been reading?'

'Heaps of things.' Flamby blushed. 'I managed to get a Reader's ticket
for the British Museum. I am interested, you see. But there are things in
Paul's book and other things promised in the next which—oh!—I'm afraid I
can't explain—'

'You cannot account for such knowledge in an ordinary mortal, and evidently something has occurred which has led you to regard Paul as less than a god. Tell me about it, Flamby.'

III

Don stood up, and walking across the room looked out of the window into the quadrangle. The story of the Charleswood photographs, which Flamby had related with many a pause and hesitance, had seemed to cast upon the room a shadow—the shadow of a wicked hypocrite. Both were silent for several minutes.

'And you are sure that Paul has seen these photographs?' said Don.

'You must have noticed the change in him yourself.'

'I had noticed it, Flamby. I am afraid you are right. I will go down to Devonshire tonight and—'

'You will not!'

Don turned, and Flamby, her face evenly dusky and her eyes very bright, was standing up watching him. 'Please don't be angry,' she said approaching him, 'because I spoke like that. But I could never forgive you if you told him. If he can think such a thing of me I don't care. What have I ever said or done that he should *dare* to think such a thing!'

Don took both her hands and found that she was trembling. She looked aside, biting her lower lip. In vain she sought to control her emotions, knowing that they had finally betrayed her secret to this man in whose steadfast eyes she had long ago read a sorrowful understanding. At that moment she came near to hating Paul, and this, too, Don perceived with the clairvoyance of love. But because he was a very noble gentleman indeed, and at least as worthy of honour as the immortal Bussy d'Amboise, he sought not to advantage himself but to plead the cause of his friend and to lighten the sorrow of Flamby. 'Have you tried hard not to care so much?'

Flamby nodded desperately, her eyes wells of tears.

'And it was useless?'

'Oh!' she cried, 'I am mad! I hate myself! I hate myself!' She withdrew her hands and leapt on to the settee wildly, pressing her face against the cushions.

Don inhaled a deep breath and stood watching her. He thrust his hands into the pockets of his tunic. 'Have you considered, Flamby, what a hopeless thing it is.'

'Of course, of course! I should loathe and despise any other girl who was such a wicked little fool. Dad would have killed me, and I should have deserved it!'

'Don't blame Paul too much, Flamby.'

'I don't. I am glad that he can be so mean,' she sobbed. 'It helps me not to like him any more!'

'Paul is no ordinary man, Flamby, but neither is he a magician. How could you expect him to know?'

'He never even asked me.'

Don, watching her, suddenly recognized that he could trust himself to pursue this conversation no further. 'Tell me why you wanted to see Orlando James again,' he said.

Flamby looked up quickly, and Don's hands clenched themselves in his pockets when he saw her tear-stained face. 'I am afraid,' she replied, 'to tell you—now.'

'Why are you afraid now, Flamby?'

'Because you will think—'

'I shall think nothing unworthy of you, Flamby.'

'I went,' said Flamby, twisting a little lace handkerchief in her hands, 'because I was afraid—for Paul.'

'For Paul!'

'You are beginning to wonder already.'

'I am beginning to wonder but not to doubt. In what way were you afraid?'

'He is so sure.'

'Sure that he has found the truth?'

'Not that, but sure that he is right in making it known.'

Don hesitated. He, too, had had his moments of doubt, but he perceived that Flamby's doubts were based upon some matter which at present he knew nothing. 'Paul believes quite sincerely that he has been chosen for this task,' he said. 'He believes his present circumstances, or *Karma*, to be due to a number of earlier incarnations devoted to the pursuit of knowledge.'

'Do you think if that was true he would make so many mistakes about people?' asked Flamby, and her voice had not yet recovered entire steadiness.

'I have told you that he is not a magician, Flamby, but you have still to tell me why you wanted to see Orlando James.'

'I don't believe I can tell you, after all.' Flamby had twisted the little handkerchief into a rope and was tugging at it desperately.

SAX ROHMER

'Why?'

'Well—I might be wrong, and then I should never forgive myself. It is something you ought to know, but I can see now that I cannot tell you.'

Don very deliberately took up his pipe from the table. 'Here's an ashtray,' said Flamby in a faint voice. 'Shall we go out to tea and see if we can cheer ourselves up a bit?'

'I think we might,' replied Don, smiling in almost the old way. 'Some place where there is a band.'

As a direct result of this conversation, Paul received a letter two days later from Don. It touched whimsically upon many matters, and finally, 'I have decided to add Orlando James to my list of undesirable acquaintances,' wrote Don. 'Don't let this harsh decision influence your own conduct in any way, but if at any time you chance to go walking with him and meet myself, pardon me if I fail to acknowledge either of you.'

Paul read this paragraph many times. He received the letter one morning whilst Yvonne was out, she having gone into the neighbouring village, and when she came back he spoke of it to her. 'Have you seen anything of Orlando James recently?' he asked.

Yvonne turned and began to arrange some fresh flowers in a bowl upon the cottage window-ledge. 'No,' she replied. 'I have seen him rarely since the portrait was finished. Why?'

'I was merely wondering. He seems to be establishing a queer sort of reputation. Thessaly has thrown out hints more than once and Don quite frankly dislikes him.'

'What kind of reputation, Paul?'

'Oh, the wrong kind for a portrait painter,' replied Paul lightly. 'I shall send him a cheque for the picture.'

'But he has refused to accept any payment whatever.'

'It was very flattering on his part to declare that its exhibition was worth so much to him, and to decline a fee, but nevertheless I shall send him a cheque tonight. Did you remember to go to the Post Office?'

'Yes.' Yvonne turned slowly. 'Here are the stamps.'

'I can see,' said Paul, 'that either I must return to London or have Edwards come down here and put up somewhere in the neighbourhood. I have more work than I can handle unassisted.'

'Let us go back to town, then, if you think it is hindering you to stay here.'

'There is no occasion for you to return, Yvonne.'

'Yes, but—I don't want to stay, Paul, if you are going. Really, I would rather not.' There was something pathetic, almost fearful, in the insistency of her manner, and Paul had a glimpse again of that intangible yet tauntingly familiar phantom in his wife's bearing. A revelation seemed to be imminent, but it eluded him, and the more eagerly he sought to grasp it the further did it recede. 'You don't *want* to leave me behind, do you?' said Yvonne.

'Want to leave you behind!' cried Paul, standing up and crossing to where she stood by the window. 'Yvonne!' He held her close in his arms, but there was no fire in the violet eyes, only a tired, pathetic expression.

IV

The pageant proceeded merrily; these were merry days. And because it was rumoured that men who fought hard also drank hard, the brethren of the blue ribbon at last perceived their opportunity and seized upon it with all the vigour and tenacity which belong to those reared upon a cocoa diet. Denying the divinity of the grape, they concealed their treason against Bacchus beneath a cloak of national necessity, and denied others that which they did not want themselves. They remained personally immune because no one thought of imposing a tax upon temperance-meetings, hot-water bottles and air-raid shelters. 'Avoid a man who neither drinks nor smokes,' was one of Don's adages. 'He has other amusements.'

Paul continued his pursuit of the elusive thread interwoven in modern literature, and made several notable discoveries. 'Contemplation of the mountainous toils of Balzac and Dumas fills me with a kind of physical terror,' he said to Don on one occasion. 'It is an odd reflection that they would have achieved immortality just the same if they had contented themselves respectively with the creation of Madame Marneffe and the girl with the golden eyes, D'Artagnan and Chicot. The memory of Pumas is enshrined in his good men, that of Balzac in his bad women. One represents the active Male principle, the Sun, the other the passive Feminine, or the Moon. I have decided that Dumas was the immediate reincarnation of a musketeer, and Balzac of a public prosecutor.'

'Pursuing this interesting form of criticism,' said Don, 'at once so trenchant and so unobjectionable, to what earlier phase should you ascribe the wit of G. K. Chesterton for example?'

SAX ROHMER

'To the personal influence of Dr. Johnson and his contemporaries. H. G. Wells would seem to have had no earthly experiences since he was a priest of Bel, or if he had they were comparatively colourless. Rudyard Kipling knew and loved the spacious times of Elizabeth. How clearly we can trace the Roman exquisite in Walter Pater and the *bravo* in George Moore. Stevenson was a buccaneer in whom repentance came too late, and who suffered the extreme penalty probably under Charles II. The author of *The Golden Bough* was conceivably a Chaldean librarian, and from the writings of Anatole France steps forth shadowy a literary *religieux* of the sixteenth century; but it is when we come to consider such cases as those of Spencer and Darwin that we meet with insurmountable obstacles. The *patientiotype* process of Victor Hugo defies this system of analysis also, as does the glorious humanity of Mark Twain, and although Pinero proclaims himself a wit of the Regency, Bernard Shaw's spiritual pedigree is obscure. Nevertheless, all are weavers of the holy carpet, and our lives are drawn into the loom. All began weaving in the childhood of the world and each has taken up the thread again at his appointed hour.'

Paul spent a great part of his time in Jules Thessaly's company. Thessaly had closed his town house, and was living in chambers adjoining Victoria Street. His windows commanded a view of an entrance to Westminster Cathedral, 'from whence upward to my profane dwelling,' he declared, 'arises an odour of sanctity.' From Thessaly's flat they set out upon many a strange excursion, one night visiting a private gaming-house whose patrons figured in the pages of Debrett, and, perhaps on the following evening, Thessaly's car would take them to a point in the West India Dock Road, from whence, roughly attired, they would plunge into the Asiatic underworld which lies hidden beneath the names of Three Colt Street and Pennyfields. They visited a foul den in Limehouse where a crook-backed Chinaman sat rocking to and fro before a dilapidated wooden joss in the light of a tin paraffin lamp, listened to the rats squealing under the dirty floor and watched men smoke opium. They patronized 'revue' East and West, that concession to the demand of youth long exiled from feminine society which had superseded the legitimate drama. 'There are three ingredients essential to the success of such an entertainment,' Thessaly pronounced: 'fat legs, thin legs, and legs.' They witnessed a knuckle-fight in Whitechapel between a sailorman and a Jewish pugilist. The referee was a member of a famous sporting club, and the purse was put up by a young peer on leave from the bloody shambles before Ypres.

'Our trans-Tiber evenings,' Paul termed these adventures.

He had seized upon a clue to the ills of the world and he pursued it feverishly. 'If men realized, as they realize that physical illness follows physical excess, that for every moment of pain unnecessarily inflicted upon any living creature—a horse, a dog, a cage-bird—they must suffer themselves a worse pang, would not the world be a better place?' he asked. 'That fighting peer is accounted a fine fellow by his companions, and in an earlier life, when the unshaped destinies of men were being rough-hewn with sword and axe, he *was* a fine fellow. But that earlier influence now is checking his development. If he could realize that he will probably be reborn a weakling doomed to surfer the buffets of the physically strong, he would doubtless reconsider his philosophy. He has lost track of himself. Our childish love of animals, which corresponds to a psychic pre-natal phase, is a memory which becomes obscured as the fleshly veil grows denser—which the many neglect, but which the wise man cherishes.'

'Heredity plays its part, too,' said Thessaly.

'Quite so. It is difficult, sometimes almost impossible, to distinguish between the influences of heredity and those of pre-existence.'

'More especially since few of us know our own fathers, and none of us our grandfathers. If our family tree record a line of abstemious forbears, and we mysteriously develop a partiality for neat rum and loose company, we hesitate whether to reproach ourselves for the vices of a previous existence or to disparage the morality of our grandmother.'

Strange stories won currency at this time, too. Arising as he had done out of a cataclysm, Paul Mario by many was accepted as the harbinger of a second Coming. His claims were based upon no mere reiteration of ancient theories, but upon a comprehensible system which required no prayer-won faith from its followers, but which logically explained life, death, and those parts of the Word of Jesus Christ which orthodoxy persisted in regarding as 'divine mysteries.' Paul's concept of God and the Creation was substantially identical with that of Jacob Boehme and the Hermetic Philosophers. He showed the Universe to be the outcome of a Thought. Unexpressed Will desired to find expression, to become manifest. Such was the birth of Desire. Since in the beginning this Will was an Eye which beheld nothing because nothing outside Itself existed. It fashioned a Mirror and therein saw all things in Itself. This Mirror was the Eternal Mother, the Will the Eternal Father. The Eternal Father, beholding Himself and His wonders mirrored in the Eternal Mother, willed that being passive they should become active.

Thought became materialized, force and space begot Motion and the Universe was. As illustrating the seven qualities through which the Divine energy operated, Paul quoted the following lines:—

> 'There are seven degrees in the holy sphere
> That girdles the outer skies;
> There are seven hues in the atmosphere
> Of the Spirit Paradise;
> And the seven lamps burn bright and clear
> In the mind, the heart, and the eyes
> Of angel-spirits from every world
> That ever and ever arise.
>
> There are seven ages the angels know
> In the courts of the Spirit Heaven:
> And seven joys through the spirit flow
> From the morn of the heart till even;
> Seven curtains of light wave to and fro
> Where the seven great trumpets the angels blow.
> And the throne of God hath a seven-fold glow,
> And the angel hosts are seven.
>
> And a spiral winds from the worlds to the suns,
> And every star that shines
> In the path of degrees for ever runs,
> And the spiral octave climbs;
> And a seven-fold heaven round every one
> In the spiral order twines.
>
> There are seven links from God to man,
> There are seven links and a threefold span;
> And seven spheres in the great degree
> Of one created immensity.
>
> There are seven octaves of spirit love
> In the heart, the mind, and the heavens above;
> And seven degrees in the frailest thing,
> Though it hath but a day for its blossoming.'

It seemed as though all mysticism had culminated in Paul Mario, and

THE ORCHARD OF TEARS

so immense was his influence that the English Church was forced into action. Such heterodox views had been expressed from the pulpit since *The Gates* had cast its challenge at the feet of orthodoxy that the bishops unanimously pronounced its teachings to be heretical, and forbade their adoption under divers pains and penalties. A certain brilliant and fashionable preacher resigned his living, and financed by a society established for the purpose, prepared to build a great church upon a site adjoining the Strand, to be called the New Temple. A definite schism thereupon was created, and so insistent became the demand for more light, for a personal message, that Paul was urged by a committee, including some of the foremost thinkers of the day, to deliver a series of addresses at the Albert Hall. He had lighted a veritable bonfire, and its flames were spreading to the four points of the compass. Even Islâm, that fanatic rock against which reform dashes itself in vain, was stirred at last, and the Sherîf of Mecca issued a *firmân* to the mosques within his province authorizing an intensive campaign against the *Korân Inglîsi*—for Paul had embraced the tenets of the Moslem faith within his new Catholic creed.

At one of his clubs, which he visited rarely, he met one evening a bishop famed as a religious educationalist, a large red cleric having bristling eyebrows resembling shrimps and the calculating glance of a judge of good port. This astute man of the world attacked him along peculiar lines. 'There must always be a hierarchy, Mr. Mario,' he said. 'Buddha—if such a personage ever existed—endeavoured to dispense with a priesthood and a ritual, but his followers have been unable to do so. You aver that the Kingdom of God is within ourselves, but if every man were able to find the Kingdom of God within himself he would have no occasion to pay others to find it for him. What would become of the poor churchman?'

'I have not proposed the abolition of the old priesthood,' Paul replied. 'I have proposed the establishment of a new. Only by appreciation of the fact that Man is the supreme Mystery can man solve the Riddle of the Universe, and what is there of mystery about your tennis-playing curate? The gossiper whom we have seen nibbling buttered scones at five o'clock tea mounts the pulpit and addresses us upon the subject of the Holy Trinity. On this subject naturally he has nothing to tell us, and naturally, we are bored. Rather than abolish ritual I would embellish it, calling to my aid all the resources of art and music. I would invest my ritual with awe and majesty, and my priests should be a class apart.'

'Such an appeal is not for every man, Mr. Mario. Your New Temple would be designed to inculcate the truth upon minds which have already received it; a thankless task. We seek the good of the greatest number, and you must bring your gods to earth if you would raise your worshippers to heaven. After all, simplicity rather than knowledge is the keynote of happiness.'

'You would trick your penitents into paradise?'

'Perhaps I am obtuse, but it seems to me that this is *your* design, not mine.'

'What does the Church offer,' said Paul, 'that the human mind can grasp? What hope do you extend to the sorrowing widow of a man who has died unrepentant and full of sin? Eternal loss. Is this to be her reward for years of faithful love? If, upon her death-bed the woman of atrocious life can be bullied into uttering words of penitence she is "saved." If she die as she lived, if a shot, a knife, a street accident cut her off in the midst of her sinning, she is "lost." A moment of panic wins salvation for the one; a life-time of self-denial counts for nothing in the case of another. If I go out into the street and strike down a bawd—a thing lower than the lowest animal and more noxious—I hang. If I don the King's uniform and accept the orders of an officer, I may slay good men and bad, come whom may, and die assured of heaven. It is war. Why is it war? Simply because it is slaughter as opposed to slaying. Our cause, you will say, is just. So is my cause against the pander.'

'You are, then, a novel sort of conscientious objector?'

'Not at all. If at the price of my life I could exterminate every living thing that is Prussian I should do it. But I know *why* I should do it, and why I should be justified. If one troubled with doubts upon such a score were to ask your cloth to resolve them, he would be told that he fought for King and Country, or something equally beside the point. Patriotism, my lord, becomes impossible when we realize that in turn we have inhabited many countries. You were once perhaps an Austrian, and may yet be a Turk.'

'The theory of re-incarnation, Mr. Mario, helps to people our lunatic asylums. I was assured recently by a well-known brain specialist that the claimants to the soul of Cleopatra would out-number the Hippodrome "Beauty Chorus."'

'You speak of the "theory" of re-incarnation, yet it was taught by Christ.'

'There we arrive at a definite point of divergence, Mr. Mario,' said his lordship. 'Let us agree to differ, for I perceive that no other form of agreement is possible between us.'

'There is something frightfully unsatisfactory about bishops,' declared Thessaly, when Paul spoke of this conversation to him. 'Many vicars and deans are quite romantic people, but immediately they are presented with a mitre they become uninteresting and often begin to write to the *Times*. Besides, no one but Forbes Robertson could hope to look impressive in a mitre. It is most unsuitable headgear for an elderly gentleman.'

V

Don remained in London for several months, performing light duties at the War Office. No one but Paul ever knew how far he had penetrated into the grim valley, how almost miraculous had been his recovery. And not even Paul knew that if Flamby's heart had been free Don might never have returned to France. In despite of his shattered health he refused the staff appointment which was offered to him and volunteered for active service, unfit though he was to undertake it.

'We don't seem to be able to realize, Paul,' he said, 'that the possession of an artificial leg and a Victoria Cross does not constitute a staff officer. My only perceptible qualification for the post offered is my crocky condition. The brains of the Army should surely be made up not of long pedigrees and gallant cripples, but of genius fit to cope with that of the German High Command. A cowardly criminal with a capacity for intrigue would probably be a greater acquisition than that of the most gallant officer who ever covered a strategic "withdrawal."'

Poor Flamby smiled and jested until the very moment of Don's departure and cried all day afterwards. Then she sat down at the little oak bureau and wrote a long letter declaring that she had quite definitely and irrevocably decided to forget Paul, and that she should have something 'very particular' to confide to Don when he returned. Whilst searching for a stamp she chanced upon a photograph of Paul cut from a weekly journal. Very slowly she tore the letter up into tiny pieces and dropped them in a Japanese paperbasket. She went to bed and read *The Gates* until she fell asleep, leaving the light burning.

The fear of which she had spoken to Don oppressed her more and more. That Paul had grasped the Absolute Key she could not doubt, but it seemed to Flamby that he had given life to something which had lain dormant, occult, for untold ages, that he had created a thing which already had outgrown his control. In art, literature and music disciples proclaimed themselves. One of France's foremost composers produced a symphony, *Dawn*, directly inspired by the gospel of Paul Mario; in *The Gates* painters found fresh subjects for their brushes, and the literature of the world became a mirror reflecting Paul's doctrine. Here was no brilliant spark to dazzle for a moment and die, but a beacon burning ever brighter on which humanity, race by race, fixed a steadfast gaze. Theosophy acclaimed him the new Buddha, and in Judaism a sect arose who saw, in Paul, Isaiah reborn.

But Flamby was afraid. Paul's theory that the arts had taken the place of the sibyls, that man was only an instrument of higher powers which shaped the Universe, dismayed her; for upon seeking to analyse the emotions which *The Gates* aroused she thought that she could discern the origin of this fear in an unfamiliar note which now and again intruded, a voice unlike the voice of Paul Mario. He was sometimes dominated by an alien influence, perhaps was so dominated throughout save that the control did not throughout reveal its presence. His own work proved his theory to be true. It was a concept of life beyond human ken revealed through the genius of a master mind. Such revelations in the past had only been granted to mystics who had sought them in a life of self-abnegation far from the world. It was no mere reshuffling of the Tarot of the Initiates, but in many respects was a new gospel, and because that which is unknown is thought to be wonderful, in questing the source of Paul's inspiration Flamby constantly found her thoughts to be focussed upon Jules Thessaly.

At this time she had won recognition from the artistic coterie, or mutual admiration society, which stands for English art, although her marked independence of intellect had held her to some extent aloof from their ever-changing 'cults.' But she had met those painters, illustrators, sculptors, critics, dealers and art editors who 'mattered.' Practically all of them seemed to know Thessaly; many regarded him as the most influential living patron of art; yet Flamby had never met Thessaly, had never even seen him. She had heard that he possessed a striking personality, she knew that he often lunched at Regali's and sometimes visited the Café Royal. People had said to her, 'There goes Jules Thessaly'—and she had turned just too late, always too late. Orlando James had arranged for her to meet him at luncheon one day, and Thessaly had been summoned to Paris on urgent business. At first Flamby had thought little of the matter, but latterly she had thought much. To Don she had refrained from speaking of this, for it seemed to savour of that feminine jealousy which regards with suspicious disfavour any living creature, man, woman or dog, near to a beloved object. But she was convinced that Thessaly deliberately avoided her and she suspected that he influenced Paul unfavourably, although of this latter fact she had practically no evidence.

Similar doubts respecting the motive which might be attributed to her had prevented Flamby from telling Don why she wished to keep in touch with Orlando James. Paul's philosophy was a broad one, and imposed few trammels upon social intercourse between the sexes. He regarded early-Victorian prudery with frank horror, and counted the narrowness of middle-class suburban life as directly traceable to this tainted spring. Don had once declared a suburban Sunday to be 'hell's delight. *Rock of Ages*' he said, '(arrangement for piano) has more to answer for than the entire ritual of the Black Mass.' Paul applauded breadth of outlook; nevertheless Flamby doubted if Paul would have approved certain clandestine visits to James's studio. It was Flamby's discovery of the identity of the tall lady, closely veiled, whom she had seen one night descending from a cab and hurrying under the arch into the little courtyard of the faun, which first had awakened that indefinite fear whereof she had spoken to Don. On several successive evenings she had invented reasons for remaining late at Chauvin's, and at last had been rewarded by seeing the veiled visitor admitted to James's studio. The light shining out upon her face had revealed the features of Yvonne Mario. Flamby had spied and had counted her espionage justified. Any other woman in like circumstances would have spied also, justified or otherwise. For women in some respects are wiser than men, and he who counts woman supine has viewed his world awry; but the true deeps of a woman's soul may only be stirred by passion. Honour and those other temporal shadows at whose beck men lay down life leave women unstirred. What man of honour would tear open a letter addressed to another, though he suspected it to contain his death-warrant? What woman, in like case, would hesitate to steam it?

VI

Hight mass in Westminster Cathedral was about to conclude. The air was heavy with incense, and the organ notes seemed to float upon it buoyantly, rebounding from marble wall and Byzantine pillar to remain indefinitely suspended ere sinking into silence. The voice of the officiating priest fascinated Paul Mario strangely. He found himself following the rhythm but not the meaning of the words. That solitary human voice was the complement of a theme whereof the incense and the monotonous music made up the other parts. Comprehension of words and syllables was unnecessary. Detached, no portion of the ritual had meaning; its portent lay in the whole. The atmosphere which it created was not that of the Mount but was purely mediFval, nor had the Roman fashion of the vast interior power to hold one's imagination enchained to the Cross of Calvary. The white robes of the altar servants, broidered vestments of the priests and pallid torches of a hundred candles belonged to the Rome of Caesar Borgia and not to the Rome of Caesar Nero. Into that singular building, impressive in its incompleteness, crept no echo of the catacombs, and the sighing of the reed notes was voluptuous as a lover's whisper, and as far removed from the murmurs of the Christian martyrs. Here were pomp and majesty with all their emotional appeal. Mystery alone was lacking. The robes of Cardinal Pescara lent a final touch of colour to the mediFval opulence of the scene.

It was to hear the Cardinal speak that Paul had come. The occasion was an impressive one, and the great church was sombre with mourning. Men of a famous Irish regiment occupied row after row of seats, and from the galleries above must have looked like a carpet of sand spread across the floor. The sermon had proved to be worthy of the master of rhetoric who had delivered it. The silvern voice of the Cardinal, from the pronouncement of his opening words to the close of his peroration when he stood with outstretched arms and eyes uplifted pitifully in illustration of the Agony of Golgotha, charmed his hearers as of old the lyre of Apollo had power to charm. His genius invested the consolation of the church with a new significance, exalting the majesty of bereavement to a higher sovereignty. His English was faultless, beautified by a soft Italian intonation, and his sense of the dramatic and of the value of sudden silences reminded Paul of Sir Henry Irving, whom he had seen once during his first term at Oxford and had never forgotten. Dramatically it was a flawless performance; intellectually it was masterful. That crucified pitiful figure stood majestic above a weeping multitude dominating them by the sheer genius of oratory. Chord after chord of his human instrument he had touched unerringly, now stirring the blood with exquisite phrases, now steeping the mind in magnetic silence. Paul recognized, and was awe-stricken, that this white-haired ascetic man wielded a power almost as great as his own.

When finally he passed out from the Cathedral, the impression of the Mass had lost much of its hold upon him, but the haunting cadences of that suave Italian voice followed him eerily. Near the open doors a priest, wearing cassock and biretta, stood narrowly scrutinizing each face, and as Paul was about to pass he extended his hand, detaining him. 'Mr. Paul Mario?' he asked.

'I am Paul Mario, yes.'

'His Eminence, Cardinal Pescara, begs the favour of a few moments' conversation.'

Opening a private door the priest led Paul along a bare, tiled corridor. Paul followed his guide in silence, his brain busy with conjectures respecting how and by whom his presence in the Cathedral had been detected. His appearance was familiar to most people, he was aware, but he had entered unostentatiously among a group of black-clad women, and had thought himself unrecognized. In the mode of making his acquaintance adopted by the Cardinal he perceived the working of that subtle Italian intellect. The unexpected summons whilst yet his mind was under the influence of ceremonial, the direct appeal to the dramatic which never fails with one of artistic temperament; it was well conceived to enslave the imagination of the man who had written *Francesca of the Lilies.* He was conscious of nervousness, of an indefinable apprehension, and ere he had come to the end of the bare corridor, the poet, deserting the man, had posted halberdiers outside the door which the priest had unlocked and had set a guard over that which they were approaching. His guide became a cowled familiar of the Holy Office, and beyond the second door in an apartment black-draped and sepulchral and lighted by ghostly candles, inquisitors awaited him who, sweetly solicitous for his spiritual wellbeing, would watch men crush his limbs in iron boots, suspend him by his thumbs from a beam and tear out his tongue with white-hot pincers. Then if spark of life remained in his mutilated body, they would direct, amid murmured *Aves,* that his eyes be burned from their sockets in order that he might look upon heresy no more. His guide rapped upon the door, opened it and permitted Paul to enter the room, closing the door behind him. He found himself in a small square apartment panelled in dark wood. A long narrow oak table was set against the wall facing the entrance, and upon it were writing materials, a scarlet biretta and a large silver crucifix. On the point of rising from a high-backed chair before this table was a man wearing the red robe of a Cardinal. He turned to greet his visitor and Paul looked into the eyes of Giovanni Pescara. There was a clash definite as that of blade upon blade, then the Cardinal inclined his head with gentle dignity and extended a delicate white hand. A padded armchair stood beside the end of the table.

'I am sincerely indebted to you, Mr. Mario, for granting me this unconventional interview. My invitation must have seemed brusque to the point of the uncouth, but chancing to learn of your presence I took advantage of an opportunity unlikely to repeat itself. I return to Rome tonight.'

'Your Eminence's invitation was a command,' replied Paul, and knew the words to be dictated by some former Mario, or by an earlier self in whose eyes a prince of the Church had ranked only second to the King. 'I am honoured in obeying it.'

Giovanni Pescara, in despite of his frail physique, was a man of imposing presence, the aristocrat proclaiming himself in every gesture, in the poise of his noble head, with its crown of wavy silver hair, in the movements of his fine hands. He had the prominent nose and delicate slightly distended nostrils of his family, but all the subtlety of the man was veiled by his widely opened mild hazel eyes. Seen thus closely, his face, which because of a pure white complexion from a distance looked statuesquely smooth, proved to be covered with a network of tiny lines. It was a wonderful face, and his smile lent it absolute beauty.

'I should have counted my brief visit incomplete, Mr. Mario, if I had not met you. Therefore I pray you hold me excused. In Italy, where your fame is at least as great as it is in England, we are proud to know you one of ourselves. Many generations have come and gone since Paolo Mario settled in the English county of Kent, but the olive of Italy proclaims itself in his descendant. No son of the North could have given to the world the beautiful Tarone called *Francesca of the Lilies.* The fire of the South is in her blood and her voice is the voice of our golden nights. I have read the story in English, and it is magnificent, but Italian is its perfect raiment.'

'It is delightful of you to say so,' said Paul, subtly flattered by the knowledge of his ancestry exhibited by the Cardinal, but at the same time keenly on the alert. Giovanni Pescara did not study men at the prompting of mere curiosity.

'It is delightful to have been afforded an opportunity to say so. Your love of Tuscany, which is natural, has sometimes led me to hope that one day you would consent to spend your winters or a part of them amongst us, Mr. Mario. No door in Italy would be closed to you.'

'You honour me very highly, and indeed I know something of your Italian hospitality, but there are so many points upon which I find myself at variance with the Church that I should hesitate to accept it under false pretences.'

Cardinal Pescara gazed at him mildly. 'You find yourself at variance with the Church, Mr. Mario? Frankly, your words surprise me. In which of your works have you expressed these dissensions?'

'Notably in *The Gates.*'

'In that event I have misunderstood your purpose in writing that fine and unusual book. I do not recall that his Holiness has banned it.'

Paul met the questioning glance of the hazel eyes and knew himself foiled. 'I must confess that I have not expressly inquired into that matter,' he said; 'but it was only because I had taken inclusion in the Index for granted.'

'But why should you do so, Mr. Mario? Have you advocated the destruction of the Papal power?'

'Emphatically no. An organization such as that of Rome and resting upon such authority is not lightly destroyed.'

'Have you denied the mission of the heir of St. Peter to preach the Word of the Messiah?'

'I have not.'

'Have you denied the divinity of Christ or the existence of Almighty God?'

'Certainly not.'

'Then why should you expect Rome to place its ban upon your book?'

'I have not questioned the authority of Rome, your Eminence, but I have questioned Rome's employment of that authority.'

'As you are entitled to do being not a priest but a layman. We have many Orders within the Church, and upon minor doctrinal points they differ one from another, but their brotherhood is universal and his Holiness looks with equal favour upon them all. Amongst Catholic laymen we have kindly critics, but Rome is ever ready to reply to criticism and never disregards it. If you are conscious of imperfections in the administration of the Church, the Church would welcome your aid in removing them.'

The facile skill with which the Cardinal had disarmed him excited Paul's admiration even whilst he found himself disadvantaged by it. 'My conception of the life of the spirit differs widely from that of Catholicism,' he said, speaking slowly and deliberately. 'We stand upon opposite platforms, and our purposes are divided. I regard not one man in a million, however admirable his life, as fit for that perfect state called Heaven and not one in a hundred millions, however evil, as deserving of that utter damnation called Hell. I say that there are intermediate states innumerable. Is Rome open to consider such a claim?'

'To consider it, Mr. Mario? Rome has always taught it. Have we not a Purgatory?'

'For the justified, but what of the sinner?'

'Have we no prayers for the dead? You maintain that no man is fit for Heaven; so does Rome—that no soul is lost whilst one prayer is offered for its redemption. We agree with you. In *The Gates* you have done no more than to analyse the symbolism of Roman ritual, defining Purgatory as a series of earthly experiences and Heaven as their termination. Have you considered, Mr. Mario, that whatever a man's belief may be, he can do no more than to be true to himself?'

'And is Rome true to Rome, your Eminence? Before the horrors of war the spirit stands aghast, but are the horrors perpetrated by Prussia reconcilable with the teachings of St. Peter? For lesser crimes, thousands burned at the stake during the Pontificate of Innocent VIII; yet Rome today hears German prelates calling upon God to exalt the murderer, the ravisher, and is silent. If Rome is untrue to Rome the rock upon which the Church of St. Peter stands may yet be shattered.'

Cardinal Pescara twisted the ring upon his finger, regarding Paul with a glance of almost pathetic entreaty. 'You hurt me, Mr, Mario,' he said. 'I do not recall that you have levelled this charge against the Catholic Church in your book. But it seems to me to be rather a criticism of internal administration than of doctrine, after all. If no man be worthy of Hell, why should his Holiness abandon sinful Germany? It is for him to decide, since all laws are locked within the bosom of the Pope.'

'I would unlock those laws, your Eminence, and set them up before the world in place of empty dogmas. I would have open sanctuaries and open minds. Humanity has outgrown its childhood and demands more reasonable fare than that which sufficed for its needs in the nursery.'

'That you honestly suppose this to be so I cannot question; but what you term "open-mindedness"—implying a state of receptivity—is in fact an utter rejection of all established spiritual truths. The open-minded and the atheistical draw dangerously closer day by day. The only thing of which they are sure is that they are sure of nothing and their *credo* is "I do not believe." Broadly speaking, Mr. Mario, our differences may be said to revolve around one point. Of the construction which you place upon the Word of the Messiah I shall say nothing, but it is your projected second book in which, if I understand your purpose, you propose to lay bare the "arcana of the initiates" (the words are your own) which, if it ever be published, will indisputably occasion action by the Holy See. Let me endeavour to bring home to you the fact that I believe you are about to make a dreadful and irrevocable mistake.'

The hazel eyes momentarily lost their softness and the Cardinal's expression grew gravely imperious. Paul felt again the shock of this man's powerful will and braced himself for combat.

'I shall always listen to your Eminence with respect.'

'Respect, Mr. Mario, is due to any man who is sincere in his efforts to promote the well-being of his fellows, even though his efforts be mistaken. In the symbolism of the Church and even in the form of the Papal crown you have recognized the outward form of an inner truth. You have applauded the ritual of the Mass and the traditions of the Catholic priesthood because they approach so nearly to that mystic ideal which gave potency to the great hierarchies of the past, notably to that of Ancient Egypt. I shall venture to ask you a question. Outside the sacred colleges of the Egyptian priesthood what was known in those days of the truth underlying the symbols, Isis, Osiris and Amen-Râ?'

'Nothing.'

'Then why did you admire a system diametrically opposed to that which you would set up?'

'Because it was ideally suited to the age of the Pharaohs. The world has advanced since those days but religion has tried to stand still.'

'The world has advanced, and in *The Gates* we hear the tap of the cripple's crutch upon the pavements of our enlightened cities. The world has advanced, Mr. Mario, and is filled with sad-eyed mothers and with widows who have scarcely known wifehood. Where is your evidence that this generation is ready for the "blinding light of truth"? You believe that you have been given a mission. I do not question your good faith. You believe that throughout a series of earlier physical experiences you have been preparing for this mission. Granting for a moment that this is so, what proof can you offer of your having attained to that state of perfection which you, yourself, lay down as a *sine qua non* of mastership? If it should be revealed to you that you have actually lived before, but as a man enthusiastic, ardent and blinded by those passions which are a wall between humanity and the angels, should you not take pause? You have granted the authority of Rome. Wherein does your own reside? Are you sure that for you the veil is wholly lifted? Are you sure that you have no false friends? Are you sure that you comprehend the meaning of your own tenet—"Perfect Love and Fulfilment"? If you have any doubts upon these points, Mr. Mario, hold your hand. It can profit the world nothing to restir the witches' cauldron. Love must always be the main-spring of life and honour its loftiest ideal. Teach men how to live and leave it to Death to reveal the hereafter. Not for the good of mankind do I tremble—God has the world in His charge—but for yourself. We all are granted glimpses of our imperfections, perhaps in the form of twinges of conscience, or dreams, or as you would say in the form of hazy memories inherited from earlier imperfect lives. If these gentle lessons fail, swift blows rain upon us. But we are never permitted to fall into error unchecked. Read well the tablet of your soul and read between the lines. Measure your strength and test your purity ere you dare to attempt to shatter at a blow the structure of the ages. When Lucifer fell from the Divine order, it was lust of knowledge that prompted him to set his own will in opposition to the Almighty. I speak in figures which you will understand. Lucifer became the great Self-Centre as opposed to the greater God-Centre. He is more active amongst us today than he has been for many ages. He has numerous servants and handmaidens. Are you sure, Mr. Mario, that you can recognize them when they pass you by? Remember that the Devil is a philosopher. If we may learn anything from the ancient creeds surely it is that the secret of governing humanity is never to tell humanity the truth.'

VII

Some days later Flamby was taking tea by appointment in Orlando James's studio. Don had written from France urging her to divulge the nature of her misgivings respecting Paul and their connection with James, and Flamby, greatly daring, had determined to obtain confirmation of the doubts which troubled her. She wore the Liberty dress of grey velvet, and as she bent over an Arab coffee-table and her pretty hands busied themselves amid the old silver of the tea-service, Flamby made a delectable study which Orlando James who watched her found to be exceedingly tantalizing. He flicked cigarette ash on to the floor and admired the creamy curve of Flamby's neck as she lowered her head in the act of pouring out tea.

'What a pretty neck you have, kid,' he said in his drawling self-confident way.

'Yes,' replied Flamby, dropping pieces of sugar into the cups, 'it isn't so bad as necks go. But I should have liked it to be white instead of yellow.'

'It isn't yellow: it's a delicious sort of old-ivory velvet which I am just itching to paint.'

'Then why don't you?' inquired Flamby, composedly settling herself in a nest of cushions on the floor.

'Because you will never pose for me.'

'You have never asked me.'

'Why I asked you only a few days ago to pose for my next big picture.'

Flamby sipped hot tea and looked up at James scornfully. 'Do you think I'm daft!' she said. 'I am a painter, not a model. If you want to paint my portrait I don't mind, but if you've got an idea in your head that I am ever likely to pose for the figure you can get it out as quick as lightning.'

James lounged in a long rest-chair, watching her languidly. 'You're a funny girl,' he said. 'I thought I was paying you a compliment, but perhaps it's a sore point. Where's the flaw, kid?'

'The flaw?'

'Yes, what is it—knotty knees? It certainly isn't thick ankles.'

Flamby had much ado to preserve composure; momentarily her thoughts became murderous. This was truly a "sore point," but mentally comparing Orlando James with Sir Jacques she was compelled to admit that the bold roué was preferable to the masked satyr. She placed her tea cup on a corner of the Arab table and smoothed her skirt placidly.

'Spotty skin,' she replied. 'Haven't you seen my picture in the newspapers advertising somebody's ointment?'

James stared in the dull manner which characterized his reception of a joke. 'Is that funny, Flamby?' he said, 'because I don't believe it is true.'

'Don't you? Well, it doesn't matter. Do you want any more tea?'

He passed his cup, watching her constantly and wondering why since he had progressed thus far in her favour not all his well-tried devices could advance him a single pace further. He had learned during a long and varied experience that the chief difficulty in these little affairs was that of breaking down the barrier which ordinarily precludes discussion of such intimately personal matters. Once this was accomplished he had found his art to be a weapon against which woman's vanity was impotent. Unfortunately for his chances of success, Sir Jacques had also been a graduate of this school of artistic libertinage.

'There is something selfish about a girl who keeps her beauty all to herself when it might delight future generations,' he said, taking the newly filled cup from Flamby. 'Besides, it really is a compliment, kid, to ask you to pose for a big thing like *The Dreaming Keats*. It's going to be my masterpiece.'

'Our next picture is always going to be our masterpiece,' murmured Flamby wisely, taking an Egyptian cigarette from the Japanese cabinet on the table.

'But I think I can claim to know what I'm talking about, Flamby. It means that I regard you as one of the prettiest girls in London.'

'Your vanity is most soothing,' said Flamby, curling herself up comfortably amid the poppy-hued cushions and trying to blow rings of smoke.

'Where does the vanity come in?'

'In your delightful presumption. Do you honestly believe, Orlando, that any woman in London would turn amateur model if you asked her?'

'I don't say that *any* woman would do so, but almost any pretty woman would.'

'I don't believe it.'

'You know who my model was for *Eunice*, don't you?'

'I have heard that Lady Daphne Freyle posed for it and the hair is like hers certainly, but the face of the figure is turned away. Oh!—how funny.'

'What is funny?'

'It has just occurred to me that a number of your pictures are like that: the figure is either veiled or half looking away.'

'That is necessary when one's models are so well-known.'

Flamby hugged her knees tightly and gazed at the speaker as if fascinated. She was endeavouring to readjust her perspective. Vanity in women assumed many strange shapes. There were those who bartered honour for the right to live and in order that they might escape starvation. These were pitiful. There were some who bought jewels at the price of shame, and others who sold body and soul for an hour in the limelight. These were unworthy of pity. But what of those who offered themselves, like *ghawâzi* in a Keneh bazaar, in return for the odious distinction of knowing their charms to be 'immortalized' by the brush of Orlando James? These were beyond Flamby's powers of comprehension.

'But Lady Daphne is an exception. I am only surprised that she did not want a pose which rendered her immediately recognizable.'

'She did,' drawled James, 'but *I* didn't.'

'Was she really an ideal model or did you induce her to pose just to please your colossal vanity?'

'My dear Flamby, it is next to impossible to find a flawless model among the professionals. Hammett or anybody will tell you the same. They lack that ideal delicacy, what Crozier calls "the texture of nobility," which one finds in a woman of good family. Half the success of my big subjects has been due to my models. This will be recognized when the history of modern art comes to be written. I am held up at the moment, and that is the reason why I am anxious to start on *Keats.*'

'What is holding you up?'

'My model for *The Circassian* has jibbed. Otherwise it would be finished.'

'There are disadvantages attaching to your method after all?'

'Yes. I shall avoid married models in future. Husbands are so inartistic.'

'You don't want me to believe that some misguided married woman has been posing for *The Circassian?*'

'Why misguided? It will be a wonderful picture.'

'It is that Eastern thing is it not?—the marble pool and the half veiled figure lying beside it with one hand in the water?'

'Yes, but I've had to shelve it. Did I show you that last sketch for the Keats picture?'

'You did, Orlando; but dismiss the idea that I am going to play Phyrne to your Apelles. It won't come off. It may work successfully with daft society women who have got bored with pretending to be nurses and ambulance drivers but you really cannot expect Flamby Duveen to begin competing with the professional models. I could quote something from Ovid that would be quite to the point but you wouldn't understand and I should have to laugh all by myself.'

'You are a tantalizing little devil,' said James, his dull brain seeking vainly a clue to the cause of Flamby's obduracy.

Flamby, meanwhile maturing her plan, made the next move. 'Is the Keats picture to be more important than *The Circassian?*' she asked naïvely.

'Of course,' James replied, believing that at last a clue was his. 'I have told you that it will be my masterpiece.' He had offered an identical assurance to many a hesitant amateur.

'Is your model for *The Circassian* really very pretty?'

'She is; but of a more ordinary type than you, kid. You are simply a nymph in human shape. You will send the critics crazy.'

He watched her with scarcely veiled eagerness, and Flamby, placing the end of her cigarette in a silver ash-tray, seemed to be thinking.

'Is she—well-known?'

James recognized familiar symptoms and his hopes leapt high. 'If I show you the canvas and you recognize the model will you promise not to tell anybody? I am painting it by a new process. I got the idea from Wiertz. The violet gauze of the veil is only indicated yet.'

Flamby nodded, watching him wide-eyed. Her expression was inscrutable. He crossed the big studio and wheeled an easel out from the recess in which it had been concealed. The canvas was draped and having set it in a good light he turned, taking a step forward. 'No telling,' he said.

'No,' replied Flamby, rising from her extemporized *diwân*.

James towered over her slight figure vastly. 'Give me a kiss and I will believe you,' he said.

Flamby felt a tingling sensation and knew that a flush was rising from her neck to her brow, but with success in view she was loth to abandon her scheme. 'Show me first,' she said.

'Oh, no, Be a sport, kid. You might do me no end of harm if you blabbed. Give me a kiss and I shall know we are pals.' He placed his hand on Flamby's shoulder and she tried not to shrink. The rich colour fled from her cheeks and her oval face assumed that even, dusky hue which was a danger signal, but which Orlando James failed to recognize for one.

'I don't want to kiss you; I want to see the picture.'

'And I don't want you to see the picture until you have kissed me,' replied James, smiling confidently and clasping his arm around Flamby's shoulders. 'Only one tiny kiss and I shall know I can trust you.'

He drew her close, and Flamby experienced a thrill of terror because of the strength of his arm and her own helplessness. But she averted her face and thrust one hand against James's breast, fighting hard to retain composure. He bent over her and thereupon Flamby knew that the truce must end. Her heart began to throb wildly.

'I won't kiss you!' she cried. 'Let me go!'

Orlando James looked into her face, now flushed again and found the lure of Flamby's lips to be one beyond his powers of rejection. 'Don't get wild, kiddie,' he said softly. 'You need not be cruel.'

'Let me go,' repeated Flamby in a low voice.

He held her closer and his face almost touched hers. Whereupon the storm burst. 'Are you going to let me go?' said Flamby breathlessly; and even as she spoke James sought to touch her lips. Flamby raised her open hand and struck him hard upon the cheek. '*Now* will you let me go!'

Orlando James laughed loudly. 'You lovely little devil,' he cried. 'I shall kiss you a hundred times for that.'

Backward swung Flamby's foot and James received a shrewd kick upon his shin. But the little *suPde* shoes which Flamby wore were incapable of inflicting such punishment as those heavy boots which once had wrought the discomfiture of Fawkes. James threw both arms around her and lifted her bodily, as one lifts a child, smiling into her face. She battled against him, hand and foot, but could strike with slight force because of her helpless position. He crushed her to him and kissed her on the lips. As he did so she remembered the form of her French shoes and raising her right foot she battered madly at his knee with the high wooden heel. One of the blows got home, and uttering a smothered curse James dropped her, but did not release her.

'You low dirty swine!' she cried at him.

He held her by her arms and now she suddenly twisted violently, writhed and wrenched herself free, leaving a velvet sleeve in James's grasp and leaping back from him, one creamy shoulder bared by the tattered gown and her wonderful hair loosened and foaming about her head to lend her the aspect of a beautiful Bisharîn girl, wild as the desert gazelle. James saw that she wore an antique gold locket upon a thin chain about her neck. He clutched at her, but she bounded back again, her eyes blazing dangerously and snatched up the Japanese cabinet. With all her strength she hurled it at his head.

'Take that,' she screamed, flushing scarlet—'blast you!'

He ducked, inhaling sibilantly, but a corner of the little cabinet struck his forehead, and he stumbled, caught his foot against a cushion and fell across the table amid a litter of china and silver ware. He clutched at the draped picture, and canvas and easel fell crashing to the floor, revealing the nearly completed *Circassian.* Flamby sprang across the studio, wrenched open the door and ran out banging it behind her. As it closed she fell back against it, panting—and saw Paul Mario approaching from the direction of Chauvin's.

VII

In the glance which Paul gave Flamby there was something odic and strange. He experienced a consciousness of giving and a consciousness of loss. Flamby was aware of intense shame and mad joy. She threw her arm over her bare shoulder to hide it and shrank back against the door not daring to raise her eyes again. She was trembling violently. Beneath her downcast lashed she could see the door of Chauvin's studio, and suddenly she determined to fly there for shelter, as had been her original intention. She started—but Paul held her fast. Flamby hid her face against his coat.

'Flamby—who has done this?' Paul's voice was very low and very steady.

Flamby swallowed emotionally, but already her quick wit was at work again and she realized that Paul must be prevented from entering James's studio, must be spared a sight of the picture which lay upon the floor. 'We were—just ragging,' she said tremulously, 'and it got too rough. So I—ran out. My dress is torn, you see.' She did not look up. Paul's Harris tweed coat had a faint odour of peat and tobacco. She realized that she was clutching him for support.

He was carrying a light Burberry on his arm, and he held it open for her. 'Slip this on, Flamby,' he said, in the same low, steady voice, 'and sit there on the ledge for a moment.' He helped her to put on the coat, which enveloped her grotesquely, led her to the low parapet which surrounded the figure of the dancing faun and stepped toward the door of James's studio.

Flamby leapt up and clutched his arm with both hands. 'No, no!' she cried. 'You must not go in there! Oh, please listen to me. I don't want you to go in.'

Paul half turned, looking down at her. 'Don't excite yourself, Flamby. I shall not be a moment.'

But she clutched him persistently until, looking swiftly up at him, she saw the pallor of his olive skin and the expression in his eyes. She allowed him to unlock her fingers from his arm and she dropped down weakly on to the narrow stone ledge as he crossed to the studio door. It was very still in the courtyard. Some sparrows were chirping up on a roof, but the sounds of the highroad were muted and dim. Paul grasped the brass handle and sought to turn it. As he did so Flamby realized that James had bolted the door. Paul stood for a moment looking at the massive oak and then turned away, rejoining Flamby. 'Come along to Chauvin's,' he said. 'I will get a cab for you.'

The only occupant of Chauvin's studio was a romantic-looking man wearing a very dirty smock, a man who looked like an illustration for *La Vie de BohPme,* so that a stranger must have mistaken him for a celebrated artist although he actually combined the duties of a concierge with those of a charwoman. He displayed no surprise when Flamby came in, wild-haired, arrayed in Paul's Burberry.

'See if you can get a taxi, Martin,' said Flamby, dropping into a huge Jacobean arm-chair over which a purple cloak was draped. A King Charles spaniel who had been asleep on a cushion awoke immediately and jumped on to her knees. Flamby caressed the little animal, looking down at his snubnosed face intently. Paul walked up and down the studio. He began speaking in a low voice.

'I had hoped, Flamby, that you had done as I once asked you to do and dropped—Orlando James.'

'I did,' said Flamby quickly and continuing to caress the spaniel. 'I wrote to Don the very night you told me to.'

'And I am sure that Don agreed with me.'

'He did, yes. But—Don knows I still pretend to be friends with—James.'

Paul stood still, facing her, but she did not look up. 'Don knows this?'

Flamby nodded her head. She did not seem to care that her hair was in disorder. 'He knows that I hate James, though,' she added.

'I don't understand at all. Whatever can have induced you to trust yourself in that ruffian's studio?'

'I've been before. It was my fault. I made him think he was doing fine.'

'He is so infernally conceited. I wanted to let him down. But he got desperate. He is not a man; he's a pig. But I threw a cabinet at him.'

'Did you hit him?' asked Paul grimly.

'Yes; but I wish it had been a brick.'

'So do I,' replied Paul. 'I shall not ask you for particulars, Flamby, but I shall take certain steps which will make London too hot to hold Mr. Orlande James.' His restrained passion was electric and it acted upon Flamby in a curious way and seemed to set her heart singing.

When Martin returned to report that a cab waited, Paul walked out under the arch to the street and having placed Flamby in the cab, he held her hand for a moment and their glances met. 'Dear little wild-haired Flamby,' he said, and his voice had the same note of tenderness which she had heard in it once before and of which she had dreamed ever since. 'Take care of yourself, little girl. You belong to the clean hills and the sweet green woods which I almost wish you had never left.'

For long after the cab had passed around the corner Paul stood by the archway staring in that direction, but presently he aroused himself and returned to the courtyard. He tried the handle of James's door but learned that the bolt remained fastened, whereupon he determined to proceed to Thessaly's flat.

A definite change had taken place in the relations existing between himself and Flamby. For all her wildness and her reckless behaviour, that day she had appealed to him as something fragrantly innocent and bewilderingly sweet. The memory of the Charleswood photographs had assumed a different form, too, and he suddenly perceived possibilities of an explanation which should exculpate the girl from a graver sin than that of bravado. He had seen something in her eyes which had rendered such an explanation necessary, had found there something stainless as the heart of a wild rose. Devil-may-care was in her blood and he doubted if she knew the meaning of fear, but for evil he now sought in vain and wondered greatly because he had so misjudged her. He experienced a passionate desire to protect her, to enfold her in careful guardianship. He knew that he had not wanted to leave her at the gate of the studios, but he had only recognized this to be the case at the very moment of parting. He had never entertained an interest quite identical in anyone and he sought to assure himself that it was thus that a father thought of his child. He wondered if it had been her hair or her lips which had maddened Orlando James; he wondered why she had been in the studio; and a cold hatred of James took up a permanent place in his heart.

In the narrow thoroughfare connecting Victoria Street with that in which Thessaly's flat was situated were a number of curious shops devoted to the sale of church ornaments, altar candlesticks, lecterns, silk banners, cassocks and birettas, statuettes of the Virgin, crucifixes and rosaries. Paul stood before the window of one, reading the titles of the books which were also displayed there, *Garden of the Soul, The Little Flowers* of St. Francis of Assisi. A phrase arose before him; he did not seem to hear it but to see it dancing in smoky characters which partially obscured a large ivory crucifix: 'To shatter at a blow the structure of the ages.' He recalled that Cardinal Pescara had used those words. His mood was unrestful and his brain was haunted by unaccountable memories, so that when he found himself in the shadow of the lofty campanile of Westminster Cathedral his spirit became translated to an obscure lane in Cairo. Faint organ notes reached his ears.

Thessaly received him in a little room having a balcony which overhung the street. Delicate ivory plaques decorated the walls and the fanciful curtains of Indian muslin hung like smoke of incense in the still air. There were some extraordinary pastels by Degas forming a kind of frieze. The evening was warm and the campanile upstood against a sky blue as a sapphire dome. The Cairo illusion persisted.

'Do you know, Thessaly,' said Paul, 'tonight I cannot help thinking of a scene I once witnessed in El Wasr. I formed one of a party of three and we were wandering aimlessly through those indescribable lanes. Pipes wailed in the darkness to an accompaniment of throbbing—throbbing of the eternal *darâhbukeh* which is still like the pulsing of evil life through the arteries of the secret city. Harsh woman-voices cried out in the night and bizarre figures flitted like bats from the lighted dance halls into the shadows of nameless houses. We came to a long, narrow street entirely devoted to those dungeon like chambers with barred windows whose occupants represent all the classified races of the East and all the unclassified sins of the Marquis de Sade. Another street crossed it at right angles and at the cross roads was a mosque. The minaret stood up blackly against the midnight sky and as we turned the corner we perceived what appeared to be another of the "cages" immediately facing the door of the mosque. Out of the turmoil of the one street we came into this other and leaving discord and evil behind us entered into silence and peace. We looked in at the barred window. Woman-voices reached us faintly from the street we had left and the muted pulse of the *darâhbukeh* pursued us. Upon a raised dais having candles set at his head and feet reposed a venerable *sheikh*, dead. His white beard flowed over his breast. He reclined in majestic sleep where the pipes were wailing the call of El Wasr, and the shadow of the minaret lay upon life and upon death. Is it not strange that this scene should recur to me tonight?'

'Strange and uncomplimentary,' replied Thessaly. 'Whilst I have no objection to your finding an analogy between my perfectly respectable neighbours and the women of the Wasr, the role of a defunct and saintly Arab does not appeal to me.' Some reflection of the setting sun touched him where he stood and bathed him as in fire. The small tight curls of hair and beard became each a tongue of flame and his eyes glittered like molten gold. 'Pardon my apparent rudeness, but I don't think you are listening.'

'I am not,' murmured Paul. 'Your words reach me from a great distance. My spirit is uneasy tonight, and whilst myself I remain in your ivory room and hear you speak another self stands in a vast temple of black gleaming granite before the shrine of a golden bull.'

'You are possibly thinking of Apis. From Cairo you have proceeded to Sakkâra. Or are the gaudy hue of my hair and the yeoman proportions of my shape responsible for the idea?'

'I cannot say, nor was I actually thinking of the Serapeum.'

'You are not yourself. You have been studying the war news or else you have passed a piebald horse without spitting twice and crossing your fingers.'

Paul laughed, but not in the frank boyish way that was so good to hear. 'I am not myself, Thessaly, or if I am I do not recognize myself.'

'You have committed some indiscretion such as presenting your siren-haired protégée, Flamby Duveen, to your wife.'

'I have not,' said Paul sharply.

'I am glad. He who presents one pretty woman to another makes two lifelong enemies.'

'I did not know that you had met Flamby.'

'She has been described to me and she sounds dangerous. I distrust curly-haired girls. They are full of electricity, and electricity is a force of which we know so little. Does the idea of a cocktail appeal to you? I have a man who has invented a new cocktail which he calls "Fra Diavolo." Viewed through the eyes of Fra Diavolo you will find the world a more cheery globe.'

'Thanks, no. But I will smoke.' From his coat pocket Paul took out a briar pipe and the well-worn pouch. 'In a month, Thessaly, *The Key* will be in the printer's hands. I found myself thinking of Pandora this morning. There are few really virtuous women and truth is a draught almost as heady I should imagine as Fra Diavolo.'

'My dear Mario, you must admit that virtue is the least picturesque of the vices. When aggressive it becomes a positive disfigurement. The "on guard" position, though useful in bayonet-fighting, leaves the Fsthete cold. You would not have us treat our women as the Moslems do?'

'Women can rarely distinguish the boundary between freedom and license. Honestly I should like to revise the position of women in Europe and America before I entrusted *The Key* to her keeping. Unmarried, she has quite enough freedom, married she has too much.'

'Therefore she conceals her age and dyes her hair.'

'Showing that she is not invulnerable to flattery.'

'No woman is, and flattery may be likened to the artillery preparation which precedes a serious advance. But, my dear Mario, to deprive a woman of admiration is to deprive a fish of water. In London when a woman ceases to interest other men she ceases to interest her husband, unless he is not as other men. In Stambfl on the contrary the odalisque who bathes in rival glances finally bathes in the Bosphorus with her charming head in a sack. Fortunately we are at war with Turkey.'

'Have you considered, Thessaly, what appalling sins must have been committed by the present generation of women in some past phase of existence?'

'There are instances in which the sins belong to the present phase. But I agree with you that the women are suffering more than the men. Therefore their past errors must have been greater. They are being taught the value of love, Mario. In their next incarnation they will remember. They will be reborn beneath a new star—*your* star. Something perturbs you. You are harassed by doubts and hunted by misgivings. I have secured permission to toil up hundreds of stairs in order that I may emulate the priests of Bel and look out upon the roofs of Babylon. This spectacle will cheer you. Join me, my friend, and I will show you the heart of the world.'

IX

'Look,' said Jules Thessaly, 'below you stretches the Capital of the greatest empire man has ever known.'

They stood in the topmost gallery of the campanile looking down upon a miniature London. The viridescent ribbon of the Thames bound bridge to bridge running thematically through a symphony of grey and green and gold. A consciousness of power leapt high within Paul. Only the sun was above him, the sun and the suave immensity of space. How insignificant an episode was a human life, how futile and inept; a tiny note in a monstrous score. Below in the teeming streets moved a million such points, each one but a single note in this vast orchestration, a bird note, faint, inaudible 'mid the music of the spheres. Yet each to each was the centre of the Universe; all symbolized the triumph to the false Self-centre as opposed to the true God-centre. Men lived for the day because they doubted the morrow. Palaces and hovels, churches and theatres, all were products of this feverish striving of the ants to plumb the well of truth and scale the mountain of wisdom; to drain at a draught the gourd of life which the gods had filled in the world's morning. Thessaly began to speak again, standing at Paul's elbow, and his deep rich voice carried power and authority.

'Look at London and you look at an epitome of humanity. The best that man can do, and the worst, lie there beneath you. In that squat, grey, irregular mound which from earth level we recognize to be the Houses of Parliament, men are making laws. The laws which they are making are the laws of necessity—the necessity of slaying Prussians. Many of the larger buildings in the neighbourhood are occupied by temporary civil servants engaged in promulgating those laws. Thus by the passing of an Act having twenty clauses, twenty thousand clerks are created and five more hotels sequestered for their accommodation. No laws which do not bear directly or indirectly upon the slaying of Prussians have been made in recent years. This is sometimes called government, but used to be known as self-preservation when men dressed in yellow ochre and carried stone clubs.

'Eastward over the Thames hangs a pall of smoke. It is the smoke of Silvertown. Left, right, and all about are other palls. They are created by the furnaces of works which once were making useful things and beautiful things; paints and enamels and varnishes, pottery and metal ware, toys for sport and instruments of science. Today they make instruments of death;

high explosives to shatter flesh and bone to pulp and powder, deadly gases to sear men's eyes, to choke out human life. It is called work of national importance, but Christ would have wept to see it. Squatting in Whitehall—look, the setting sun strikes venomous sparks from its windows—is the War Office. Ponder well the name of this imposing pile—the *War Office*. Nearly two thousand years have elapsed since the last of the Initiates delivered His Sermon on the Mount. See! the city bristles with the spires of His churches; they are as thorns upon a briar-bush. Look north, the spire of a church terminates the prospect; south, it is the same; east and west—spires, spires, spires. And squatting grimly amid a thousand shrines of Jesus Christ is the War Office—the *War* Office, my friend. Watch how the spears of light strike redly into that canopy of foulness hanging above Kynoch's Works. A Ministry of Munitions controls all that poisonous activity. Mario, it is the second Crucifixion. The Jews crucified the Body; all the world has conspired to crucify the Spirit.

'The Word has failed. There lies the reading of your day dream, Mario, your dream of the *Sheikh* of El Wasr. Look how the shadow of the campanile creeps out beneath us, over church and War-Office-Annexe, over life and over death. Religion is a corpse and the world is its morgue. But out of corruption comes forth sweetness. No creature known to man possesses more intense vitality than the *dermestes* beetle which propagates in the skull of a mummy. From the ashes of the Cross you arise. Christ is dead; long live Christianity. Behold the world at your feet. Courage, my friend, open the Gates and lead mankind into the garden of the gods.'

X

That Paul had established a platform strong enough to support the tower of a new gospel became evident. His second book of Revelations, *The Key*, was awaited eagerly by the whole of the civilized world. In determined opposition to the wishes of Bassett, unmoved by an offer from an American newspaper which would have created a record serial price, Paul had declined to print any part of *The Key* in a periodical. With the publication of *The Gates*, which but heralded a wider intent, he had become the central figure of the world. Politically he was regarded as a revolutionary so dangerous that he merited the highest respect, and the tactful attitude of the Roman Church was adopted by those temporal rulers who recognized in Paul Mario one who had almost grasped a power above the power of kings.

'In Galileo's days,' said Thessaly on one occasion, 'a man who proclaimed unpalatable truths was loaded with chains and hurled into a dungeon. Nowadays we load him with honours and raise him to the peerage, an even more effectual method of gagging him. Try to avoid the House of Peers, Mario. Your presence would disturb the orthodox slumbers of the bishops.'

On the eve of the opening of the German offensive Paul received a long letter from Don which disturbed him very much. It was the outcome of Don's last interview with Flamby and represented the result of long deliberation. 'I have had a sort of brainwave,' wrote Don in his whimsical fashion, 'or rush of intellect to the brow. I suppose you recognize that you are now the outstanding figure of the War and consequently of the world? Such a figure always rises out of a great upheaval, as history shows. His presence is necessary to the readjustment of shattered things, I suppose—and he duly arrives. I take you to stand, Paul, for spiritual survival. You are the chosen retort of the White to the challenge of the Black, but I wonder if you have perceived the real inwardness of your own explanation of the War!

'You show it to be an uncrop of that primitive Evil which legend has embodied in the person of Lucifer. Has it occurred to you that the insidious process of corruption which you have followed step by step through the art, the music, the literature, the religion and the sociology of Germany may have been directed by *someone*? If you are the mouthpiece of the White, who is the mouthpiece of the Black? It is difficult to visualize such a personality, of course. We cannot imagine Pythagoras in his bath or even Shakespeare having his hair cut, and if What's-his-name revisited earth tomorrow I don't suppose anybody would know him. I often find it hard to realize that *you*, the old Paul with the foul briar pipe and the threadbare Norfolk, really wrote *The Gates*, not to mention *Francesca*. But you did, and I have been wondering if the Other Fellow—the Field-Marshal of the Powers of Darkness—is equally disappointing to look at—I mean, without halos, or, in his case, blue fire. In short, I have been wondering if, meeting him, one would recognize him? I have tried to imagine a sort of sinister Whisperer standing at the elbows of Germany's philosophers, scientists, artists and men of letters; one who was paving the way for a war that should lay religion in ashes. And now, Paul, forgive me if I seem to rave, but conditions here are not conducive to the production of really good literature—I wonder if you will divine where this line of reflection led me? The Whisperer, upon the ruins of the old creeds, would try to uprear a new creed—his own. *You* would be his obstacle. Would he attack you openly, or would he remain—the Whisperer? To adopt the delightful mediFval language of the Salvation Army, watch for the Devil at your elbow. . . . I wish I could get home, if only for a day, not because I funk the crash which is coming at any moment now but because I should like to see *The Key* before it goes to press. . . .'

Paul read this strange letter many times. 'The Whisperer . . . would try to uprear a new creed—his own.' Paul glanced at a bulky typescript which lay upon the table near his hand. *The Key* was complete and he had intended to deliver it in person to Bassett later the same morning. Strange doubts and wild surmises began to beat upon his brain and he shrank within himself, contemplative and somewhat fearful. A consciousness of great age crept over him like a shadow. He seemed to have known all things and to have wearied of all things, to have experienced everything and to have found everything to be nothing. Long, long ago he had striven as he was striving now to plant an orchard in the desert of life that men might find rest and refreshment on their journey through pathless time. Long, long ago he had doubted and feared—and failed. In some dim grove of the past he had revealed the secret of eternal rebirth to white-robed philosophers; in some vague sorrow that reached out of the ages and touched his heart he seemed to recognize that death had been his reward, and that he had welcomed death as a friend.

So completely did this mood absorb him that he started nervously to find Jules Thessaly standing beside his chair. Thessaly had walked in from the garden and he carried a flat-crowned black felt hat in his hand.

'If I have intruded upon a rich vein of reflection forgive me.'

Paul turned and looked at the strong massive figure outlined against the bright panel of the open window. The influence of that mood of age lingered; he felt lonely and apprehensive. He noticed a number of empty flower vases about the room. Yvonne used to keep them always freshly filled. He wondered when she had ceased to do so and why. 'You have rescued me from a mood that was almost suicidal, Thessaly. A horrible recognition of the futility of striving oppresses me this morning. I seem to be awaiting a blow which I know myself powerless to avert. If we were at your place I should prescribe a double "Fra Diavolo," but, failing this, I think something with a fizz in it must suffice. Will you give the treatment a trial?'

'With pleasure. Let it be a stirrup-cup, or, as our northern friends have it, a *doch-an-dorroch.*'

Paul stood up and stared at Thessaly. 'Do I understand you to mean that you are about to set out upon a journey?'

'I am, Mario. Like Eugene Sue's tedious Jew, I am cursed with a lack of repose. I sail for New York tomorrow or the following day.'

'Shall you be long absent?'

'I cannot say with any certainty. There seems to be nothing further for me to do in England at present. I feel that England has ceased to be the pivot of the world. I am turning my attention to America, not without sparing a side glance for the island kingdom of the Mikado. You know how unobtrusive I am, Mario; I am taking no letter of introduction to President Wilson, nor if I visit Japan shall I trouble official Tokio. Mine is a lazy life, but not an idle one. I am an enthusiastic onlooker.'

Paul gazed at him reproachfully. 'You never even warned me of your projected journey, Thessaly. Do you leave all your friends with equally slight regret?'

Thessaly gazed into the peculiar hat, and something in the pose of his head transported Paul to the hills above Lower Charleswood, where, backed by the curtain of a moving storm, he seemed to see Babylon Hall framed in a rainbow which linked the crescent of the hills. 'You misjudge me,' replied Thessaly. 'What I have said is true, but I go in response to a sudden and unforeseen summons. Death and a frail woman have tricked me, and at one stroke have undone all that I had done. I am compelled to go.'

Paul detected in the deep voice a note of pathos, of defeat. 'I am sorry,' he said simply. 'I value your friendship.'

'Friendship, Mario, is heaven's choicest gift. The love of woman is sometimes wonderful, but it always rests upon a physical basis. The love of a friend is the loftiest sentiment of which man is capable. Its only parallel is the unselfish devotion of a dog to his master.'

A servant came in with the refreshments which Paul had ordered. Directly she had departed Thessaly began speaking again. 'I have lived in Germany, Mario, and in my younger student days—for I am perhaps an older man than you imagine me to be—I have met those philosophers, or some of them, to whom Germany owes a debt of hatred which cannot be repaid even unto the third and fourth generation. I have lived in France, and in many a sunset I have seen the blood that would drench her fairest pastures. I have watched the coming of the storm, and I saw it break upon the rocks of these inviolable islands. I thought that I knew its portent; I thought that I had discerned the inner meaning of the Day. Mario, I was wrong. Humanity has proved too obstinate.'

He spoke with a suppressed vehemence that was startling. 'The point of this escapes me,' said Paul, watching him. 'For what or for whom has humanity proved too obstinate?'

'For *us*, Mario—for *us*. There is many an ancient knot to be untied before man can be free to think unfettered. The myth, Imperialism, alone is an iron barrier to universal brotherhood. Not even in the spectacle of the Germanic peoples pouring out their blood in pursuit of that shadow has the rest of the world perceived a lesson. A colony is like a married son with those domestic arrangements his father persists in interfering. The jewels in an imperial crown mean nothing even to the wearer of that crown, except additional headache. But attack the blood-stained legend of Imperialism and you attack Patriotism, its ferocious parent. Humanity has grown larger since the wolf suckled Romulus, but no wiser, and strong wine is not for weak intellects.'

He laid his hand upon the typed pages of *The Key*. 'Is our friendship staunch enough to sustain the shock of real candour, Mario?'

Paul was deeply and unaccountably moved by something in Thessaly's manner. 'I trust so,' he replied.

'Then—forgive me—burn *The Key*. It is not yet too late.'

'Thessaly! *You* offer me this counsel! Do you realize what it means to me?'

'Some day, Mario, you may comprehend all that it meant to *me*.'

Paul stared at him truly dumfounded. 'What can have happened thus suddenly to divert the current of your life and the tenor of your philosophy?'

'The inevitable, against which we fight in vain.'

'And your advice—that I burn *The Key*—is given sincerely?'

'It is.'

'I cannot realize that you mean it, Thessaly. I cannot realize that you are going.'

'I am sorry, Mario. In these troublous days a cloud of misgiving hangs over every parting, since *au revoir* may mean good-bye. But I must go, following the precept of that wise man who said, "Live unobserved, and if that cannot be, slip unobserved from life."'

An hour later Paul was about to leave the house when a telegram was brought to him. He experienced great difficulty in grasping its purport. He could not make out from whom it came, and it seemed at first to be without meaning . . .

"Regret to inform you Captain Donald H. Courtier,—Coy., Irish Guards, killed in action. . . ."

XI

On the following day a phenomenal storm burst upon London out of a blue sky. Tropical rain beat down into the heated streets and thunder roared in Titan anger. Paul came out of the War Office and stood on the steps for some moments watching a rivulet surging along the edge of the pavement . . . 'I am sorry, Mario, but it was mercifully swift, and his end was glorious. Ireland has disappointed some of us, but fellows like Courtier and those who went with him make one think. . . .'

Paul walked out into the lashing rain, going in the direction of Charing Cross. He was thinking of another storm which had struck swiftly out of a fair sky, of the aisles of the hills, and of one that he had met there. Today Jules Thessaly was leaving England. Don was dead. Some who knew Paul and who saw him driving on through the downpour as if fury-ridden or sped by some great urgency, wondered and later remembered. But to him London was empty, and heedless of the curiosity of men and the tumult of the elements he pressed on. Nothing penetrated to his consciousness save the eternal repetition of his own name and the name of his book. Evidences of his influence seemed to leer at him from window and hoarding. A performance of the French symphony, *Dawn,* was advertised to take place at the Queen's Hall, and he found one bill announcing an exhibition of pictures by an ultra-modern Belgian—pictures which their painter declared to be 'illustrations' of *The Gates.* And in his pocket were the papers deposited with Nevin to be given to Paul only in the event of Don's death. Paul had read them, and whilst he longed with a passionate longing to go to Flamby, he knew that today he dared not trust himself within sight of the clear grey eyes, of the alluring lips, within touch of the red-brown hair. But he recognized that he must go ultimately, and so he drove on through the storm and right and left of him were traces of his mark upon the world.

Tropical heat prevailed throughout the following day and Paul spent the morning pacing up and down his study. Yvonne was in Brighton. Paul long since had realized that the sympathy between them was imperfect, but always he had counted upon re-establishing the old complete comradeship when his great task should be at last concluded. This morning he had learned the truth, that Yvonne was with Orlando James, but his brain was still too numb fully to appreciate it. Towards noon he sat down at his writing-table and began to read with close attention the typed pages of *The Key*. Bassett was becoming anxious, and had rung up more than once during the morning. Arrangements had been made to publish simultaneously in the principal capitals of the world, and the publishers had been busy for several months accumulating paper to meet the unparalleled demand for this vast first edition. . . . Eustace knocked three times at the study door to announce that luncheon was served, but Paul continued his reading. During the afternoon he caused a fire to be lighted in the study grate. It was late evening before he left the house, and he set out with no conscious objective in view, yet subconsciously he was already come to his journey's end. His ideas were chaotic, and he seemed to be spiritually adrift. That his book was indeed the Key he was unable to doubt. He had truly grasped the stupendous truth underlying that manifestation called life, but seeking to discern retrospectively the path whereby he had pierced to the heart of the labyrinth he found confusion and stood dismayed before the dazzling jewel which he had unearthed. The past intruded subtly upon him, and he was all but swept away by sorrowful memories of Don. He saw him coming along the Pilgrim's Way and heard his cheery greeting as he stepped upon the terrace of Hatton Towers.

Where that night's wandering led him he knew not, but there were those who saw him passing along Limehouse Causeway as if in quest of the Chinese den where once he and Thessaly had watched men smoke opium, and others who spoke to him, but without receiving acknowledgment, in the neighbourhood of Westminster Cathedral. He appeared, too, at the Café Royal, standing just within the doorway and looking from table to table as one who seeks a friend, but went out again without addressing a word to anyone. At a late hour he saw a light shining from a casement window and mechanically he pressed the knob of a bell above which appeared the number 23. Flamby opened the door and Paul stood looking at her in the dusk.

XII

'Oh,' said Flamby, 'I had given you up.'

She wore a blue and white kimono and had little embroidered slippers on her feet. Under the light of the silk-shaded lamp her hair gleamed wonderfully. She had matured since that day in Bluebell Hollow, when Paul and Don had first seen her. The world had not hardened her and the curves of her face were almost childlike, yet there was something gone from her eyes and something new come to replace it. Resourcefulness was there, but no hint of boldness and her moods of timidity were exquisite. Now, having naVvely confessed her dreams, her sudden confusion was lovable.

'I scarcely know,' declared Paul. 'I scarcely know why I have come at such an hour. It is not fair to you, and it is not practising what I preach.'

'Please come in. You are welcome at any time, and as nobody will see you there can be no harm done.'

Paul entered and stood looking vaguely at the parcel which he carried. It contained the manuscript of *The Key*. Thus reminded of its presence he found himself wondering why, since he had forgotten that he carried it, he had not absently left it behind somewhere during his aimless wanderings. He laid it with his hat on the open bureau. The little apartment had assumed very marked individuality. Many delightful sketches and water-colour drawings ornamented the walls and a delicate pastel study of Dovelands Cottage hung above the famous clock on the mantelpiece. Paul crossed and examined this picture closely.

'Who is living in Dovelands Cottage now, Flamby?' he asked. 'I believe Nevin told me that it had been sold.'

Flamby turned aside to take up a box of cigarettes. 'Don bought it,' she said slowly. 'I don't know why he didn't want you to know, but he asked me not to tell you.'

Paul continued to stare at the picture, until Flamby spoke again. 'Will you have a cigarette?' she asked, her voice low and monotonous.

'No, thank you very much.'

'I can make coffee in a minute.'

'Please don't think of it.'

Through the little mirror immediately below the pastel Flamby studied Paul covertly. He had aged; all the beauty of his face resided now in his eyes. Two years had changed him from a young and handsome man to one whose youth is left behind, and who from the height of life's pilgrimage looks down sadly but unfalteringly into a valley of shadows. He turned to her.

'Mrs. Chumley?'

'I was with her this morning. She is staying for a while at the cottage. I think she is nearly broken-hearted. From the time that his mother died, when

Don was very little, Mrs. Chumley looked after him until he went away to school. You know, don't you? But she is so brave. I wish,' said Flamby, her voice sunken almost to a whisper, 'I wish I could be as brave . . .' She sat down on the settee, biting her lower lip and striving hard to retain composure.

'You are very brave indeed, and very loyal,' answered Paul, but he did not approach her where she sat. 'You have taught me that there are women as far above pettiness and spitefulness as every man should be, but as every man is not.'

'I wasn't like it before I knew Mrs. Chumley and—Don.'

'You were always true to yourself, and there is no higher creed. Flamby, I have received some papers which Don left with Nevin to be delivered to me. You thought me so mean and lowly so ignorant and so vainglorious that I could judge a girl worthy of Don's love to be unworthy of my friendship. You were right. No! please don't speak—yet. You were right, but you suffered in silence, and you did not hate me. I don't ask you to forgive me, I only thank you very, very sincerely.' Flamby held a handkerchief tightly between her teeth, and stared fixedly at a photograph of one of her propaganda pictures which hung on the wall to the right of the bedroom door.

'There on your bureau,' continued Paul, 'lies my second book. It contains the key to mysteries which have baffled men since the world began. I do not say it with vanity; vanity is dead within me, I say it with fear, for *I* did not unravel those mysteries; I did not write that book.'

'Oh,' whispered Flamby.

'Yes—again you saw clearly, little wonder-girl. Don has told me how you traced the black thread running through the woof of *The Gates*, and that black thread was *truth*. It is truth that slays and truth that damns. Not for a million ages can men be sufficiently advanced to know and to live. Hypocrisy triumphs; for the few is the fruit of knowledge—for the multitude, the husk. I have seen the Light of the World, but I stand in the shadow. Yet from the bottom of my heart I thank God that at the price of happiness I have bought escape from a sin more deadly than that which any man has committed. Only by renouncing the world may we win the world. This is the lesson of Golgotha. Behind the curtain of the War move forces of incalculable evil which first found expression in Germany today as they found expression there in the Middle Ages. It was in a Rhine monastery that the first Black Mass was sung. It was in a Rhine town that Lucifer opened his new campaign against mankind; it was in German soil that he planted his seed. Flamby, I tell you that the Hohenzollerns are a haunted race, ruling a haunted land, doomed and cursed. About them are obscene spirits wearing the semblance of men—of men gross and heavy, and leaden-eyed; and upon each brow is the Mark of the Bull, the sigil of Hell.'

Flamby watched him, listening spellbound to his strange words. He was inspired; anger and sorrow drove him remorselessly on and a chill finger seemed to touch Flamby's heart as she listened; for resignation and finality informed his speech.

'Each human soul must fight its way out of the night of the valley, Flamby, before it can pass the gates of dawn. Each error is a step in the path and there are steps right to the top. To me it was given to see but not to understand until this very hour. What I have done it was ordained that I should do; what I was about to do God forbade.' He paused, glancing at Flamby and quickly away again. 'Don's letter has opened my eyes, which were blinded. I shall not ask you for what purpose you risked so much to visit the studio of Orlando James. I know. Your fire is laid, Flamby; may I light it?'

'Of course, if you wish.'

Paul stooped and held a match to the paper, watching the tongues of flame licking the dry wood; and ere long a small fire was crackling in the grate! He turned to Flamby, pointing to the parcel which lay upon the bureau. 'The purpose with which I set out recurs to me,' he said. 'I have destroyed all the typed copies and every note. It is my wish that *you* shall destroy the manuscript.'

'Of *The Key?*' she whispered.

'Please.'

'But—are you sure?'

'Quite sure.'

Flamby met his set gaze and unwrapping the manuscript she approached the fire. Paul stood aside, resting his elbow upon a corner of the mantelshelf. Flamby's hands were very unsteady.

'Tear out the pages,' said Paul, 'and throw them loosely on the flames. They will burn more readily.'

Flamby obeyed him, and page by page began to destroy the book containing the truths which were known in the sanctuaries of Memphis but which the world was yet too young to understand. Excepting the voice of the flames there was no sound in the room until Flamby had laid the last page upon the pyre, when she sank upon her knees and hid her face in her hands.

Her hair rippled down and veiled her redly. Paul watched her for a while and then, irresistibly, inevitably, he was drawn down beside her; his arm crept round the bowed shoulders and he pressed his cheek against fragrant curls. 'Flamby,' he said, 'dear little wild-haired Flamby. The sorrow of the world has claimed us both. Let us both be brave—and true.' And although he would have bartered many things once accounted of price for the right to crush her in his arms he rose to his feet again and moved away to the corner of the mantelshelf, for the nearness and the touch of her intoxicated him. Flamby did not stir. The mound of ashes settled lower in the grate. Paul took up his hat and walked to the door.

'Good night, Flamby,' he said. 'Wait for me. I shall be waiting for you.'

The door closed and Flamby heard footsteps retreating along the gallery. As the sound became inaudible, a maroon burst dully at no great distance away. Flamby leapt to her feet. Her eyes were wild as she stood there, hands clenched tightly, and listened. A second maroon gave warning of the approaching air raiders. Flamby ran to the door, threw it open and sprang out into the brilliant moonlight as police whistles began to skirl in the distance. The slender chain about her neck parted unaccountably and unperceived by Flamby her locket fell at her feet.

'Paul!' she cried. 'Paul! come back—come back!'

But only an echo which dwelt in the arch of the entrance answered her, saying sadly: 'Paul . . . Paul . . .'

Heedless of those who urged him to take cover, of the flat shrieking of whistles and later of the roar of the barrage, Paul walked on under the stars of a perfect night and above him droned the Gotha engines. He prayed silently.

'Master of Destiny, all-Merciful God, suffer me to die that I may be reborn a wiser and a better man. Of Thine infinite mercy guide the steps of Yvonne who was my wife. Grant her the happiness for which she sought and which I denied her. To those who wait give faith and fortitude: to me, O God, give death. Amen.'

A bomb fell shrieking through the air and burst with a rumbling monstrous peal, digging a pit, a smoking grave, on the spot where Paul had stood. His body was scattered like flock by the wind; his spirit was drawn into the ceaseless Loom.

OM MANI PADME HUM.